Praise for Karen Kincy's
Other

"This who-done-it is an unusual blend of mystery and fantasy, starring original characters not often featured in modern urban fantasy for teens. I really enjoyed it."

—Annette Curtis Klause, author of *Blood and Chocolate*

"*Other* has it all: love, shifters, pookas, and nail-biting action. What's even better, Kincy's characters are vibrant, real, and lovable. This is a debut that leaves you aching for more."

—Carrie Jones, *New York Times* bestselling author
of *Need* and *Captivate*

"Gwen is extremely likable as the impulsive, conflicted heroine . . . [and the] romance is a dynamic counterpoint to the suspenseful mystery."

—*Booklist*

"The emotional turmoil of the characters is evident and will appeal to readers who have felt misunderstood or as if they don't belong."

—*School Library Journal*

Bloodborn

Bloodborn

karen kincy

flux
™
Woodbury, Minnesota

First Edition
First Printing, 2011

Cover design by Lisa Novak
Cover image of couple © 2011 Pixland/PunchStock
        forest moon © 2011 iStockphoto.com/Ryan Howe

Flux, an imprint of Llewellyn Worldwide Ltd.

Library of Congress Cataloging-in-Publication Data
Kincy, Karen, 1986–
  Bloodborn / Karen Kincy. —1st ed.
     p. cm.
  Summary: Brock has always hated werewolves and Others like them, but once he is bitten by one he struggles with his identity, trying to keep from transforming but wondering what it would be like to accept his new reality.
  ISBN 978-0-7387-1920-7
  [1. Werewolves—Fiction. 2. Supernatural—Fiction. 3. Identity—Fiction. 4. Self-acceptance—Fiction. 5. Youths' writings.] I. Title.
  PZ7.K5656Bl 2011
   [Fic]—dc23

                          2011014158

Flux
Llewellyn Worldwide Ltd.
2143 Wooddale Drive
Woodbury, MN 55125-2989
www.fluxnow.com

Printed in the United States of America

To my dad,
though there are no transporter accidents in this book

one

It isn't working. The doctor said it would, but it isn't, even though I keep taking the pills, and I keep seeing Dad sneak into the bathroom and count how many are left. As if I would stop taking them. As if I would let myself become a beast.

God dammit.

I tacked a heavy blanket over the blinds, but an icy pale glow trickles through a crack. I lurch out of bed to yank the blanket straight. My hand slices through the moonlight. The animal inside me leaps to the front of my eyes, and everything becomes bright and sharp until I close my eyes and stagger back into the darkness.

I tighten my abs against the twisting in my gut. No. I'm stronger than that.

For a moment, I can smell the old yellow stink of sweat

and the furry mice in the wall and the sweet night air outside—

Shit. I almost lost it.

I close my eyes and grope for the curtain, then tug
it over the moonlight and the mouth-watering night air
creeping past the window. Sweat drips down my shoulders
and sticks my T-shirt to my skin. I pad barefoot across the
scarred floorboards, my bedroom as stuffy as July though
it's the middle of September. The doctors said something
about a higher body temperature being normal. Yeah, like
I'm normal.

I snatch the bottle of pills from my nightstand, flick
on the light, read the label again.

> Koeman, Brock
> Take 1 capsule by mouth twice daily
> or as needed for management of con-
> dition. Do not exceed 4 doses in 24
> hours.
> Lycanthrox 325 mg Capsules

I've only had three pills today. And I sure as hell need to
manage my condition.

I twist off the cap and shake one of the red pills into
my hand. Right. Water. My sweaty fist clenched around
the pill, I lumber to the bathroom. My shoulder hits the
door frame and I swear quietly, so Dad won't hear.

I'm not sure, but I think I got bigger after it happened.
Taller, stronger.

I hunch over the sink, fill my free hand with water, then down the pill in a gulp. It slides down my parched throat, dissolving in my stomach, seeping through my blood, poisoning the animal inside me. Or at least it should be.

I peel off my clothes and crawl into bed. Lycanthrox always makes me dead tired. My eyelids feel heavy, like granite, like they are thudding shut and trapping me in a tomb. I fight to stay conscious, out of reflex, out of fear, but the darkness wins. It always does. And in this darkness, I'm forced to face my nightmares.

❦

Black trees slash the sky. Rain hisses to the ground. I run naked through the forest while the moon dangles above, a cold white eye, watching me. My feet pound the dirt. I fight my way through brambles, ignoring the thorns and blood, and burst into a clearing. Moonlight gleams on my skin, makes me look shiny and unreal like those oiled-up bodybuilders. And I'm as muscular as them, too. Strong enough to crush trees.

I tear into an alder sapling, my fingers, my claws, shredding the tender bark. I yank whole ferns from the ground and fling them into the air. I'm tough. I'm badass. I'm ready to defeat any fool who stands in my way.

I want something to fight. To kill. My teeth itch into fangs, and I bare them at the moon.

"Brock?" says a soft voice I know.

I close my mouth to hide my fangs, then face her. "Cynthia."

Cyn stands by a tree, hesitant, her slender arm wrapped around its trunk. I try not to stare through her thin white nightgown. Her chestnut hair shines in the moonlight, and she looks as pretty as an angel who lost her way.

"Oh," Cyn says, covering her red lips with her hand. "Brock."

She stares at my naked body, but I'm not ashamed. The way she looks at me makes me feel like a man, not an animal. Heat pools in my stomach. I walk to her, my heart thumping in my ears, and see her smile. She's so, so beautiful.

I know what to do. I'm not clumsy or ignorant at all as I curl my hands around her hips and tug her to me. She flings her arms around my neck and kisses me, and I kiss her harder, devouring the delicious taste of her lips. She moans, urging me on, and I know that she wants me to lower her to the ground. I protect the back of her neck from the cold earth, and she looks into my eyes with such sweet trust and want.

"Brock," she whispers.

I lean in to kiss her again, kiss her neck, her collarbone. Against my lips, I feel her pulse beneath her skin. I bury my face in the hollow of her neck and inhale slowly. I smell her sweat, her blood flowing, her tender flesh—

"Brock?" Cyn's voice sounds higher, birdlike with fear. "What's happening?"

The roots of my teeth itch; the tips press into my lower

lip, sharpening into fangs. I grip her waist with claws. My mouth waters at her scent.

"Brock! Brock, no!"

Her voice, chirping, squeaking like a little animal, drives me wild. I grin at her, my mouth fully fanged, and my drool dribbles onto her face. Then I sink my teeth into her peach-soft shoulder, biting to the bone and drinking the juice of her blood. She screams, and the animal in me lunges to the surface. My skeleton shatters, dissolves, and in that agony, it reshapes and clicks back into place. Reborn, I tear into the girl beneath me, shredding and gnawing and licking while I satisfy the wolf I have become.

"Cynthia!"

I claw aside my blankets and fall out of bed. Panting, I crouch on the floor. Rivers of sweat run down my face and back. I rub my hands over my skin—skin, not fur. I'm still human. I still haven't changed.

Fuck! I hit the bedpost and wince when the screws groan.

I'm always afraid those dreams are real, that I've sleep-walked my way outside and transformed without even knowing it. Jekyll and Hyde.

I fumble on my nightstand and grab a crumpled picture. It has that cheapass photo-booth look, but it's still one of the best photos I own: me and Cyn, with her smiling while she pretends to sneak up behind me and strangle me.

One photo still isn't enough to soothe the ache inside me. I tug open my drawer and carefully unfold the sweater she borrowed. With my eyes closed, I press my nose to the wool and inhale. I know Cyn's scent by heart: a sinfully bittersweet almond-vanilla aroma, lingering on my clothes and the places we slept together.

I sigh, and fold the sweater again.

For an unbelievable eleven and a half months, I was Cyn's boyfriend. She dumped me two weeks before our one-year anniversary. She said I wasn't "the right kind of guy." Bullshit, of course, but her eyes told me what she really meant. She was scared of me and Chris going curhounding, and the murders in Klikamuks—

There's a rap on the door. Dad.

"What's going on, Brock?"

I hide the photo. "Nothing." My voice sounds harsh, and I cough. "Bad dream."

Dad jiggles the locked doorknob. "Brock. Open the door."

I climb to my feet, my legs weak, and do as he says. Dad stands in the shadows, already dressed in dirt-stained jeans and a red flannel shirt. His wiry salt-and-pepper hair looks as tousled as it always does. I glance at the clock. The glowing red numbers read 4:12 AM. Almost time to herd the cows to the milking barn.

"You been taking your medicine?" Dad says.

"Yeah." I clench and unclench my fists. "Of course."

"Good." Dad clears his throat, like he wants to ask something else but doesn't know how.

"Dad, you need some help?"

"No. I've got it under control."

He hasn't let me near the cows since it happened. He doesn't know, but I've tried already. When I get too close to a cow, its nostrils widen, its eyes roll back, and it trots to the opposite end of the pasture. They smell the wolf in me.

"Get some sleep," Dad says. "We've got a long drive to Grandma June's."

"Yes, Dad."

He clomps down the hallway in rubber boots. He never did that when Mom was still here; she was so proud of her peach pebble carpet. I shut the door behind Dad. That carpet…me and Chris slaved over it three years ago.

Mom kept saying she wanted new carpet, but Dad kept complaining about the cost. Finally, he caved in after me and Chris promised to rip out the nasty old shit-brown carpet. We crouched at opposite ends of the hallway, cutting the carpet with razors and peeling it away. Just like skinning a rabbit. Once we got down to the carpet padding, we started yanking out a few billion staples with needle-nose pliers.

Dad would wander by every once and a while, tight-lipped and silent, so we tried to beat each other by ripping out the most staples the fastest. Our clumsy leather work gloves slowed us down. Soon enough, Chris ditched his. Metal and splinters gouged his knuckles, but he was smoking me, so I ditched my gloves, too. Blood streaked our fingers. When Dad came by again, he looked at Chris, then me. I was farther along my section of floorboards and had more staples out, but Chris's hands were rawer and redder.

Guess who he thought worked harder.

Pain means you keep going, no matter what. Pain makes Dad proud.

I grab my headphones and turn on my radio. A driving beat, a surge of electric guitars, then the gravelly voice of a singer: "You left us in the cold hard ground/But we're coming out tonight/Nothing you can do to kill us again/The time has come for fight or flight."

I recognize the song as "Undead and Unwanted" by Bloodless, one of the few all-vampire bands worth listening to. Dad would freak if he knew I was listening to them. He can't stand that "those damn gick bands" made it onto the Top 20. Dad says when he was a kid, no decent person would be caught dead listening to music by Others.

But hey, what the hell. I'm a werewolf. I guess I'm one of them now, whatever you want to call them: gicks, paranormals, Others. Lump me in with those vampires, faeries, and demons. Though for some reason Dad seems to think the medicine I'm taking will do more than slow the unavoidable, that it will actually cure me. I wish.

In the morning—what normal people consider morning, not the insanely early time Dad gets up—I drag my ass out of bed and rub my gritty eyes. I didn't sleep much more, but I did finally nod off around six or so. Dad is hard at work burning food in the kitchen, already back from the first milking of the day.

I lumber to the bathroom and start shaving. I'm hideously stubbly; it grows so much faster than it did before. Something like the higher body temperature, I think. Everything in my body is accelerated. Which is cool, because I heal fast if I hurt myself, but the doctors also say I'll have a shorter lifespan. I don't know how they know. I don't know if I even care. Live a long and fruitful life as a werewolf. Yeah, really top of my list.

I head down the creaky carpeted stairs, sliding my hand along the yellowed roses on the wallpaper. On the bottom step I stop, my nostrils widening. Eggs and onion and bell peppers and cheddar cheese and thyme—smells rush into my nose, overwhelming me for a second, before I piece them together into omelet.

"Hey," Dad says. "You hungry?"

I nod. "Yeah."

Now, more than ever. Now, I can't say I'm ever satisfied. *Then I sink my teeth into her peach-soft shoulder, biting to the bone and drinking the juice of her blood.* I shudder and shove that nightmare to the back of my mind.

Blackjack, our brindled pit bull, lies under the kitchen table, his nose on the tiles, his eyebrows jumping as he glances around. Scars crisscross his neck and shoulders. I remember the day he got those scars, the same day me and Chris got bitten. I remember the silver-furred, yellow-eyed werewolf who did it.

"Brock," Dad says. "Bring your plate."

I grab a chipped plate and bring it to the stove. Dad shovels a giant omelet onto it, then starts cracking eggs for another.

"Looks good," I say. "Thanks."

"Welcome," Dad says.

Neither of us meet each other's eyes. It's always been that way.

When I set the plate down on the kitchen table, Blackjack lifts his head with a rumbling growl. I freeze. Before it happened, me and Chris trained him as a curhounding dog, to hunt the very thing that I have become.

"Down, boy," Dad says sternly.

Blackjack's growl rises into a questioning whine. He glances at Dad, his ears pricked, his stump of a tail twitching with anxiety.

"It's me, boy." I bend down by Blackjack and hold out my hand for him to sniff. "See?"

The dog bares his teeth and growls again.

"Brock," Dad says. "Don't."

"It's okay," I say, "he knows it's—"

Blackjack darts forward as if grabbing a scrap of meat, only his teeth close on my hand. I shout and hit him on the muzzle.

"Blackjack!" Dad bellows.

The dog releases me and skitters back under the table, his claws scraping the tiles. He whimpers, his eyes darting between me and Dad.

"Shit," I hiss. My hand has a crescent of red teeth marks on it; no blood, luckily.

"Told you not to touch him." Dad yanks open the back door and drags Blackjack out by his collar. "Stay out there, dog."

Blackjack whines as the door swings shut in his face.

"It's not his fault," I say.

It's not his fault that I'm a cur now. He tried to protect me from the silver werewolf. He's trying to protect Dad…from the wolf inside me.

"Should put that dog down," Dad says. "Useless animal."

"He didn't break skin," I say, as if that makes any difference. I drag a chair out and wince at the screech of wood on tile. "Can I eat this?"

Dad nods.

We don't talk much more during breakfast, mostly just nods and grunts. Then we head upstairs to get dressed for Grandma June's. All my nice shirts are wrinkled. I don't think the clothes iron has been out of the closet since Mom put it there. A lot of things have stayed the same, like the photos I can't stand to look at and the withering rose garden outside the kitchen. This farmhouse is too big and empty for two.

It's been two years now since Mom passed away. I remember—even while I try not to remember—when she started wearing hats because she'd lost her hair, and how she got so, so thin, like a skeleton, and it scared me but I couldn't cry, I was too old for that. Toward the end, when Mom stayed at the hospital more than at home, I remember

Dad telling me to hold her hand. I was afraid of hurting her. She felt fragile, almost papery.

Now, standing before my mirror, I blink and scowl at myself. Do I even look like Mom? Grandma June says I have my mom's eyes, the same gray-blue. But my square face and my hair, cropped and dishwater-blond, are my dad's.

"You ready?" Speak of the devil.

"Almost!" I holler back to Dad.

I tighten a sloppy knot in my tie and yank my shirt straight. Grandma June insists that we all dress really nice when we visit for dinner. I hurry to polish the scuff marks off my fancy black shoes, then hear a horn honk outside.

"I'm coming, I'm coming," I growl.

I thump downstairs, yank open the door, and nearly trip over Blackjack, who barks and jumps aside. Dad's idling the pickup in the driveway. He waves at me and I sprint to him, yank open the door, and haul myself inside.

As I buckle my seat belt, he glances at me, his face blank. "Klutzy, huh?"

I grit my teeth. Dad's always going on about how clumsy I am. Not like Chris, who was the star quarterback for the Cougars of Klikamuks High. I joined up, too, but I never amounted to much of anything on the team.

Dad shifts to drive and rumbles down the driveway. Blackjack trots hopefully after the pickup, but stops at the fence, his head high. I sigh. Poor dog. He can't help that I fucked up my life in a really spectacular way. If I were smart enough, which I know I'm not, I'd build a time machine and never do what I did.

We drive in silence away from the dairy, our windows rolled down, through cornfields hissing in the wind of the truck. Out by the Rutgers's orchard, apples weight the trees and dot the grass like rubies that fell from a crown.

"Oh, hell," Dad mutters, his foot on the brake.

"Aw, somebody hit a dog," I say.

On the side of the road, a brown animal slumps in its own blood. As the truck crawls forward, I suck in my breath. No…only the hindquarters of a dog, then the naked arms, breasts, and face of a black-haired woman.

"Not a dog." Dad talks through clenched teeth. "A gick."

We slow to a stop, and I can see it clearly now: half-beast, half-woman. My gaze drifts down to where the skin below her bellybutton shades to fur. Her hindquarters look mangled. She must have dragged herself there before she died.

"Werecoyote," Dad says.

"What, really?"

"Haven't seen one in years. Must've strayed from the Indian reservation down south." He snorts. "Road kill was a lucky way to die. Werewolves here would've ripped that bitch apart for trespassing."

All my muscles tighten. I've heard that werewolves and werecoyotes fight over prey and territory, but now it seems more…personal. Like if I sat still enough, I would feel an instinct to hate deep in my gut. Right now, I just feel sick.

"Are we leaving her—it—there?"

"Yeah." Dad lets his foot off the brake. "They'll clean up that bitch eventually, if the scavengers don't get there first."

As we pass the werecoyote, I turn to look at her face. A mistake. She was beautiful, I have to admit, with glossy black hair clinging to full lips, and high cheekbones, and perfect breasts—dangerously deceptive.

I force a laugh. "Must've been a really stupid gick, to get run over like that."

Dad laughs more heartily. "Too bad all of them can't be so stupid."

Yeah, Dad, what about me?

He accelerates, leaving the werecoyote behind. I blow out my breath. I wonder why this werecoyote ventured into dangerous territory, anyway. Was she chased here by werewolves? By the silver werewolf who bit me? I haven't seen him since it happened. I haven't seen any of the pack, but I know they're still here, lurking in the forest and in my nightmares, in the nightmares of everybody in this town.

Dad switches on the radio, and country music replaces conversation and thought.

two

It's just under a hundred miles to Grandma June's. With traffic, we make it to her house in the foothills of the Cascades that afternoon. The sun pours light over the forest. Pretty. As soon as I open my door, the sweetness of pines tingles in my nose. Inside my rib cage, I feel an unclenching. I have an urge to swerve from the door and go into the forest for a good run, but that's got to be the wolf talking.

Grandma June's little wooden house hides behind giant rhododendrons and ivy. When Dad rings the doorbell, I stand behind him like I can possibly hide in his shadow; he's a good six inches shorter than me, and not nearly as bulky.

"Kurt! Brock!"

Grandma June opens the door and bundles us both into a hug. She's a tiny pewter-haired lady, but she still manages to do it. Dad squeezes her back; I pat her on the shoulder, trying to be extra careful, afraid of being too strong. Grandma June always smells like oatmeal soap, and when I close my eyes, I feel like a kid again.

"Let me have a good look at you, Brock," says Grandma June.

I swallow hard. She hasn't seen me since it happened.

She pulls back and studies my face. "Still handsome. Though a little bristly."

I duck my head, my face hot. She always embarrasses me, never fails. When she looks away, I rub my cheek. Stubble already? Wow.

"Come in!" Grandma June sweeps us inside. "Turkey's in the oven, rolls are next."

I can tell. My nose quivers at the delicious aromas floating on the warm air, and my stomach growls even though we stopped at an Arby's on the way here and I had two roast beef sandwiches and an apple turnover shake. Good thing Grandma June likes to serve dinner really early.

Grandma June's house is infested by knickknacks, collectable plates, and other junk. One of these days, I'm going to accidentally break a porcelain kitten or something. Chris smashed a little figurine on purpose once, on a dare. It was this hideous little statue of toddlers kissing, but I still felt horrible not telling Grandma June.

Dad nudges me in the ribs. "Go help Grandma June with the rolls."

"Okay."

"Wash your hands first."

"Okay."

Grandma June bustles around the kitchen, doing a dozen things at the same time. I sidestep past her and start washing my hands in the kitchen sink. She scolds me for getting in her way, but gives me some carrots to chop for salad.

Soon enough, she asks it. "How is Chris?"

"Still in the hospital." I concentrate on the carrots.

Grandma June sighs. "I already know that. How *is* he?"

"Okay, I guess. Not really better." I lower my voice. "He still isn't healing."

"After a month?" Grandma June whispers.

"Yeah. Doctors say he'd be healing better if he was…you know. But Dad told them to give Chris extra Lycanthrox so it doesn't happen."

I don't need to say what "it" is. We both know Chris will become a werewolf, eventually.

"He's still in our prayers," Grandma June says.

I'm not sure who, besides herself, she means by "our." Grandpa passed away six years ago, and I'm not sure anybody else in my family gives a damn about me, or Chris. We're not really family anymore, are we?

The doorbell rings and in comes Aunt Martha and Uncle George and their matching blond-ponytailed junior high girls, Kaitlin and Jordan, followed by Uncle Jeff and his new girlfriend, Carla. All of them greet us with smiles and hellos, but I can tell by their tight jaws and sharp eyes that they don't want to get too close to the beast inside me.

Even Carla; she must be one of the lucky few who was told about my secret.

I shut up and keep staring at the cutting board and the knife in my hand. When I finish the carrots, Grandma June gives me some lettuce to wash. I hunch over the kitchen sink, rubbing the lettuce, trying not to shred it too much.

"Too rough, Brock!" Grandma June says. "You're bruising the lettuce."

"Sorry," I mutter.

I doubt werewolves are built to handle lettuce. It's so stupid, I laugh. Grandma June frowns and gives the rest of the lettuce to Kaitlin. I sidestep out of the kitchen, accidentally elbowing Jordan, who squeaks and leaps back.

"Sorry!"

I head for the door. Outside, it's much more open. I can fit here, in the spaces between the trees and the sky. The mountains are beautiful now, the sun dripping gold syrup onto the vanilla-ice-cream snow. I stride into the forest, and I want to go farther, out away from the houses and the lawns and the fences. In the wilderness, there's no one to point at me and whisper what I should and shouldn't be doing. But I know the wilderness isn't empty. The werewolf pack lives out here, running and hiding and killing.

What would they think of me? What would they do to me?

I fold my arms tight and dig my nails into my biceps. I wish I could tear the flesh from my bones and yank out the wolf inside me. I would chase it into the wilderness and it would never come back and I could get some sleep.

"Brock."

I turn around. Dad stands behind me, looking tired, a glass in his hand.

"Is it time to eat?" I ask.

Dad nods.

I stare at pine needles, my shoulders rigid. "I don't belong in there."

"Why?"

It's fucking awkward. Out loud, I say, "You know I don't like social stuff."

"Me neither. But we have to. For Grandma June."

So I go back inside, even though I hate sitting in my too-small chair with my too-big appetite, listening to them chatter and laugh like nothing's wrong at all, like my brother's not in the hospital and I'm not thinking about splintering the arms of my chair in my hands, claws just waiting to slide out of my fingertips. Grandma June's food tastes amazing—it always does—so I concentrate on wolfing down turkey and potatoes and gravy and green bean casserole. But not so fast that they stare.

Do any of them notice how they gossip and pretend to be human, but underneath their words there are yips, whimpers, and growls? They fight and play dominance games while pretending not to, and Grandma June is the silver alpha watching over her little pack. I blink. I've been reading too much about wolves.

After dinner, Dad switches on the TV, and we all

lounge on couches and chairs, overstuffed except me and Jordan, who's on a diet. Dad flips through the channels rapid-fire, and Aunt Martha complains that's what all men do. Laughter. I lurk in the flickering shadows-and-light, feeling like a gargoyle in some forgotten corner.

A lady with gold hair and nice boobs delivers today's news on the TV.

"...residents on the outskirts of Klikamuks remain concerned, particularly for their children and pets. Sheriff Royle spoke with us earlier today." The shot cuts to a beer-bellied, bald guy with his thumbs hooked in his belt. "In light of recent events, we can understand why the folks of Klikamuks might be a little apprehensive about the continued presence of the werewolf pack in the Boulder River Wilderness Area, but we urge citizens to remain calm and lock their doors at night only as a precautionary measure."

In light of recent events. I remember those events. Hell, I was part of them.

It all started with the werewolf pack. Me and Chris couldn't stand those gick curs in our backyard, pissing on fence posts like they owned the place. We got together with some friends, Josh and Mikey, and decided to do something about it. With Blackjack and a borrowed shot-gun, we went out into the woods to scare some curs. What happened instead? This red-headed gick bitch got in our way, along with her tree-girl friend.

We were pissed, to say the least, but then this guy, Benjamin Arrington, offered to help us out. To make a long story short, it turned out he was killing gicks. He got caught by the police and thrown in jail for murder. Yeah, the law counts gick-hunting as murder now. Josh and Mikey chickened out way earlier than that, so they escaped, but me and Chris had to deal with a load of shit from the police before they let us go.

I realize everybody in the room is staring at me, as if I should make some wise comment.

"Damn gicks," I say.

Grandma June clucks her tongue, disapproving of my language, approving of my attitude.

On the TV, Sheriff Royle is gone. Now they're showing a fuzzy home video of a silver wolf loping alongside a fence. A ball of rage tightens in my gut. Is it him? The wolf who bit me, still running loose out there when he should be dead, bones in the dirt and a pelt on the wall? Someone touches at my arm, and I nearly whirl and snarl.

It's Grandma June. "Are you all right?"

I exhale shakily. "Yeah." I'm not going to let myself become one of them.

"You sure?" she asks, and I don't know how to reply.

The next day, I ride my bike down the back country roads, trying to burn off extra energy. I whiz past sunflowers, fields dotted with dairy cows, bigleaf maples dropping floppy yellow leaves that whirl in the wind I make.

Up a really steep hill, I stand so I can push harder on the pedals, the muscles in my legs burning. On the way down, I coast, picking up speed, wind whistling past my ears. I shut my eyes for a second and imagine what it would be like to run this fast, to be able to rocket through the forest on muscle-power alone. Humans have a top running speed of about twenty miles per hour. Wolves, a bad-ass forty.

A car horn blares. My eyes snap open. I'm swerving into the opposite lane and oncoming traffic. I yank my bike back to the edge of the road. I'm getting close to downtown Klikamuks now. The glittering Stillaguamish River twists through farmland and poplars, crossed by the old bridge that looks like something made out of a kid's building kit. Fog floats from the water and joins the clouds of steam billowing from the sawmill. My nostrils widen at the wet sweetness of wood: cedar and maple, mostly.

I bike over the bridge, pumping my legs, passing the cars that crawl along. There's Christina's Seafood Cave, right on the water, leaking the smell of smoked salmon into the air. My mouth waters. And nearby, there's the BBQ Hut, also smelling delicious. Dammit, why do I have to be so hungry all the time?

Ahead, in the intersection, red and blue lights whirl. Cop car. I brake and scuff my foot on the sidewalk to steady myself. None other than Sheriff Royle himself leans toward the open window of an all-too-familiar silver Toyota sedan that makes my stomach do an all-too-familiar somersault. I've seen it before, driven by her—Cynthia Lopez. Just her name makes me feel unsteady, even after almost six weeks apart.

I glance toward her car's rear window, but the headrest blocks my view.

"Excuse me, miss," Sheriff Royle drawls, as if he were Southern and not a Klikamuks native. "I need to see your license and proof of insurance."

"Certainly," Cyn says, using her chirpy helping-customers voice.

I coast closer, flip out my kickstand, and pretend to check my front tire. Now my stomach feels like it's tying itself into knots. Damn. I haven't seen her since we broke up. Klikamuks is so small, I should have brushed elbows with her at least once in the past six weeks. Unless she's been avoiding me.

"Nice day, isn't it?" Sheriff Royle says to Cyn, with a too-sweet smile. "Where're you headed?"

"Work," she says.

Royle makes a big show of checking his watch. "Aren't you a little late?"

"I will be."

Jesus, Cyn's as reckless as ever. Everybody knows Royle pounces on the tiniest excuse to exercise his power as a sheriff.

"Here's my license," Cyn says, "and my proof of insurance."

She passes them to him. I glimpse her hands, with doll fingers and wrists like the stems of wine glasses. She's tiny. Not anorexic tiny, but petite, barely five feet tall. Before, when I touched her, I was afraid of breaking her by accident.

"Is that all in order?" Cyn says, still chirpy.

Royle squints, then nods. "Appears so, miss."

"Can I ask why you pulled me over?"

"One of your taillights is out."

"Oh!" Fake relief almost masks the annoyance in her voice. "Thanks so much for pointing that out, officer." The car jumps as she shifts to drive. "I'll be sure to have that fixed as soon as possible. Have a good day!"

Without waiting for a reply, Cyn rolls up her window. She glances at her side mirror, and—her hair! What happened to it? In her reflection, for a second, I thought I saw a streak of blazing flamingo pink in her chestnut hair.

Then she pulls into traffic, leaving Sheriff Royle muttering.

He glances back at me. The syrupy smile on his face melts into a frown. "What're you loitering and impeding traffic for, boy?"

"My bike," I say. "Thought I had a flat tire."

Sheriff Royle hooks his fingers in the loops of his belt. "Shouldn't you be back over at the Buttercup Dairy, helping your father?" Meaning, shouldn't infected people like you stay off the streets? Wouldn't want to see any trouble.

"See you," I mumble, and pedal off.

Time to go home. And I am, but the wind changes. Sweetness fills my nose, fruit and sugar. I spot candy apples in the front window of the Klikamuks Candy Company, perfectly red and round. My throat tightens. The smell brings back the day me and Cyn met. It's so vivid, all I have to do is close my eyes and I can see it…

Last year, at the Evergreen State Fair, Dad was showing Max, our champion Holstein bull. Max's a real monster, with rippling muscles beneath his dorky black spots, but he's kind of a wimp at fairgrounds. I was walking the bull around his barn when he got spooked, swinging his big head around and tugging on his halter.

And there was this girl standing there with a candy apple. Cyn, though I didn't know it yet.

Max stopped fighting and flared his nostrils, sniffing in her direction. She walked toward him, slow and quiet, her face calm.

"Hey," I said to her, "don't get too close. He's dangerous."

"Dangerous?" Her eyes sparkled. "Really?"

The bull dipped his head down and looked almost bashful. He nosed her candy apple.

"Can he eat it?" she said.

I shrugged. "Won't hurt him."

Max snorted on her apple, and she wrinkled her nose. "Bull boogers."

I laughed, my face hot. "I'll buy you a new one."

And so we spent the rest of the day together. I told her all about the livestock, the produce in the grange displays, and the best or the shittiest tractors. It wasn't at all embarrassing to be a farm boy around her, because she was actually interested. But not as interested as she looked while staring into the eyes of the bull.

I knew right then she was a girl who liked a little danger, and the rest is history.

Well, I guess we're history now.

I blink the memory away, but the candy apple smell still lingers in my nose. I shove open the door to the Klika-muks Candy Company.

Does she remember that day the way I do?

Cyn works after school at Plant Land, a magnet for gar-deners and landscapers. I can guess where she is. She loves the greenhouse full of exotic flowers; it's always tropical, even in the dead of winter. I creep inside with the candy apple behind my back, trying not to look as awkward as a jock in a ballet class for five-year-olds.

The thick, sweet smell of rotten moss and strange flowers fills my nose. Cyn's almond-vanilla scent blends right in, so I don't find her right away. Then, through the leaves of a banana tree, I see her bending over an orchid the exact same pink as the streak in her hair. It throws me off, and she catches me gawking.

"Brock!" The pot she was holding shatters on the floor.

Maybe she's going to take one look into my eyes and know I'm a beast. Maybe she's going to scream and throw something at me.

"Sorry," I say, sweating. "Didn't mean to scare you."

"Well, you did!" Her face looks as red as mine feels. "What are you doing here?"

"What did you do to your hair?"

Flustered, she pats her bangs. "It's *my* hair. And you still didn't answer my question."

I hold the candy apple out to her. "I got you this."

She stares at it, and for a long moment, says nothing. Finally, she speaks. "Why?" Her voice is low and level.

"Don't you remember? Bull boogers?"

"I remember." Her smile fades after only a second. "Brock, I don't want that."

Cyn strides away, grabs a broom, and begins sweeping up the shattered pot. I crouch and pick up shards one-handed, the candy apple still in my other hand, but she shoos me away. I almost drop the candy apple in the dirt.

"Brock."

"I'm just trying to help."

"Brock! I work here. Let me do my job."

I straighten to my full height, trying not to loom over her. It's hard, since she's so small. "Can we at least talk?"

Her face tightens. "I'm not sure I'm ready to."

As if it was hard only for her, the one who ended things.

"Cynthia," I say, trying to sound gentle. "It's been a month and a half."

She keeps sweeping. "And what makes you think things have changed?"

"Because they have."

Cyn has to know I'm a gick now. The werewolf attack was all over the news.

She grips her broom tight and leans on it, staring straight at me. "You're still the guy who thought it was a great idea to use werewolves for target practice. You're still the guy who worked for Benjamin Arrington."

"So I'm guilty because he was?" I mutter through gritted teeth.

"You helped a murderer, Brock."

I drag my fingers through my hair. "I didn't know he was a murderer. Not at first."

"Not at first?" She narrows her eyes. "So you found out later and kept helping him?"

"No!" My face heats. "I don't know what bullshit you've heard, but that's not true."

Cyn sucks in a slow breath, then blows it out. "Who am I supposed to believe?"

"Me?"

She glares at me. "The week after we broke up, my family went to Mexico to visit my abuela. Now that I'm back, everybody is telling me all sorts of crazy rumors about what happened while I was gone." She stares into my eyes, her own dark and glittering. "What really happened?"

I lower my voice. "Arrington seemed like a guy who was into curhounding, nothing more. That's what me and Chris thought. He was paying us to track the werewolves, and it seemed all noble and shit. To keep Klikamuks safe."

Cyn's face twists. With pity or disgust, I can't tell. "And then?"

Maybe she knows, or has at least guessed. Maybe she just wants to hear me say it myself. The blood drains from my face, leaving my skin feeling cold, distant. I stare at a nearby orchid and count its petals until I'm calm.

"We got bitten."

"You—what?"

"Bitten."

Cyn's eyes widen, and in them I see myself reflected, my own eyes smoldering. The blush in her cheeks fades. I can hear her heart beating hard and fast. She backs away from me, slowly, as if I'm going to bite.

"Oh, God," she whispers. "It's true."

I need to talk faster, to explain this to her.

"It happened at the Evergreen State Fair." Which would have been our one-year anniversary. I can tell it hurts her to think about it, but I keep talking. "We were tracking a werewolf that Arrington said was especially dangerous. Blackjack got wind of the werewolf, and he tore after him before I could stop him. Of course me and Chris had to follow. Blackjack attacked the wolf. Chris caught up and got out his gun. The wolf bit him, and when I tried to help Chris, the wolf bit me."

When I say it that way, it sounds matter-of-fact, boring, like something out of a history textbook. But sweat still soaks my armpits, and I find my fingers on my biceps, clutching the scar there as if to stop it from bleeding.

"Brock," Cyn whispers, her knuckles pressed to her mouth. "Is Chris okay?"

"He's in the hospital." My voice sounds harsh. "We don't know when he can come home."

Cyn touches my arm, just brushes it, and her fingertips draw electricity from my skin. I meet her eyes, remembering how I used to be able to stare in them forever without feeling uncomfortable. Her gaze drops to my clenched fist, and I realize the candy apple's stick has splintered in my hand.

I was an idiot for even thinking of it as a gift.

"I'll let you get back to work," I say. "See you later."

"Have a good day," she says, but it's not chirpy at all.

I throw the candy apple into the trash as I walk out.

I shouldn't go into the forest alone, Dad says. He doesn't say why, but I know.

Werewolves.

Not like I've seen any around here in the last million years or so. Hell, they don't own the forest. I've lived here all my life, and I'm not about to stop taking walks in my own backyard just because some curs are loose.

Blackjack barks and lunges at the end of his chain as I hop the fence. I don't have the heart to yell at him. Besides, I don't think any amount of yelling would untrain what me and Chris taught him about werewolves.

The sun slides down the curve of the sky, an egg yolk leaking runny gold. My breath fogs the air, but my skin feels warm. I trot along the lengthening shadows and leave the dairy behind for the shelter of maples and firs. The whooshing of the highway dies away, replaced by the rat-a-tat of a woodpecker. I breathe deep, filling my lungs with the smell of rain, earth, and softly dying leaves.

Out here, I can start to untangle my thoughts. What

am I doing with myself? Why am I not back in school? Like I have a chance in hell of surviving my senior year of high school. Chris got lucky, graduating before he got bitten.

I spot bright blue through the trees. Hidden between two hills, somebody has pitched a tumbledown tent out of a blue tarp and a framework of sticks. The ashes in the fire pit look pretty fresh. On the branch of a cedar, empty bottles hang from colored yarn tied round their necks. I read the labels. Beer, vodka, and wine.

Fucking hippies.

There have got to be some plastic baggies of pot in the tent, or maybe a pagan shrine. I peek inside. Instead, I see a cooler and a neatly rolled, though dirty, sleeping bag. I peek inside the cooler, expecting booze. No, plastic-wrapped meat on Styrofoam trays, with the orange "DIS-COUNT" stickers still attached.

A sick feeling tightens my stomach. I close the cooler and hurry out of the tent, then hike back up the hill. Near the top, I hear a cough behind me. Shit. A man stands at the top of another hill, watching me. He's strongly built, wearing a raincoat and hiking boots, with a shaggy beard and brown hair streaked with silver above his forehead. Not old, though. Late twenties, early thirties. Even with the beard, I remember him.

three

The man doesn't move. I don't move.

I remember his name. Randall Lowell. The werewolf, fresh out of jail. They arrested him thinking maybe he was the serial killer, but let him go when they caught Benjamin Arrington. Of course, me and Chris never told the police what really happened when we got bitten—we made up some bullshit about walking Blackjack in the forest and getting ambushed. Only Dad knows the absolute truth, and he sure as hell didn't tell anybody.

Randall stares at me, silently. A snake coils in my gut, some poisonous feeling I can't name yet, and I'm not sure why I'm not screaming and charging the bastard who bit me and my brother. I'm not sure, either, why the gick, the cur, isn't attacking me.

You fucking gick. Stop staring at me. Stop standing there and finish the job.

Randall's raincoat rustles slightly as he crosses his arms. I flinch a little, as if expecting him to pull out a gun. He doesn't even need a gun. He could just lunge into the body of a silver wolf and take me down any second, tear out my throat and let me bleed. It's hard to glare at him—his eyes are so dark and empty of emotion.

Why aren't you angry? Why aren't you trying to kill me?

I don't want to deal with this now. I don't want to have anything to do with werewolves or the wolf inside me. *What's the matter?* whispers a little voice, my twisted conscience. *Are you afraid?* Part of me is superstitious, as if Randall holds the key to open the last lock between Brock the Human and Brock the Beast.

I step away slowly, not dumb enough to turn my back on a predator. My heartbeat thuds in my ears. My blood burns through my veins. The scar on my left biceps throbs with freshly dug-up pain, remembering teeth biting to bone.

Randall watches me. He blows out his breath in a stream of white. Then he speaks.

"Bloodborn."

What? What does that mean? I clench my jaw so I won't ask, won't do anything but walk away. I keep my legs tensed and my fists clenched, ready to either run or fight, but the gick lets me go. As soon as I'm out of his sight, I run.

It's the only smart thing to do. Right? Get the hell out of here before things get even more fucked up. After all, the worst that could happen ranges from maiming to death. I'm not stupid. I know I got lucky last time, and Chris didn't.

When I get home, I slam and lock the door to my bedroom, then hoist up my mattress. Hidden underneath, a battered old book. The silver letters on the cover are almost rubbed off: *A History of Lycanthropy* by Edwin Brood. I checked it out from the library—not the one in Klikamuks, because they banned these sort of books there. I had to go all the way to the Seattle library to find it. I bet it's almost overdue now, but I'm such a slow reader that I'm not done with it, and I need to read the rest.

I flip it open to the index. "Bloodborn," I mutter. "Bloodborn..."

Page 281. With a musty smell in my nose, I start to read, mouthing the words.

> *Werewolves who inherited the disease from one or both of their parents are known as natural born. Typically, they do not suffer from the violent initial stages of transformation common to werewolves who acquired the disease later in life via infection. These werewolves, bitten rather than born, are known as bloodborn. Most of the bloodborn do not survive their first few months, and hence their numbers in the wild should seem to be lower than those of the natural born. However, the disease has a propensity to spread through violent attacks by werewolves, particularly in more crime-ridden areas. On the outskirts of certain cities, packs of*

bloodborn roam and terrorize humans. As of this writing, efforts have been successful in reducing their numbers.

I don't understand all the words, like *propensity* or *acquired*, but I get the gist of it. So I'm a bloodborn. What did Randall mean by calling me that? Was he amazed that I survived being bitten? Did he want to taunt me?

I growl and slam the book shut. Enough. I don't want to know all the details about being bloodborn. I just want to smash something and be done with it. I mean, who cares? I'm a gick. End of story. End of my life.

I'm sitting on my ass flipping through TV channels because I'm bored out of my mind and Dad's out working. There's nothing but shit to watch on a Friday afternoon. I glance at the clock; my ex-classmates are getting out soon. Maybe I should go back to high school. Even its hellish halls have to be better than this.

On every channel, I see Others. A commercial shows mermaids swimming in the bow wave of a cruise ship, laughing, their boobs carefully covered by blond hair. Yeah, right. In real life, half-fish skanks aren't going to be family friendly. Another commercial stars nearly naked frost spirits modeling diamond jewelry on their sparkling skin. Sex sells, I guess, especially with supernaturally sexy gick-ladies.

On PBS, there's *Little Red*, a retelling of "Little Red Riding Hood," only the werewolf isn't the bad guy. In this pastel cartoon forest, Mr. Werewolf helps the little pigtailed human girl solve her problems with peace and love. All the gicks in this one are totally politically correct. Never mind that the original fairy tale was meant to scare kids away from the packs of outlaw werewolves that used to roam around Europe.

I flip off the TV in disgust, then lumber to the kitchen. Fridge's empty. Great. My stomach rumbles in complaint. There's an ancient bag of hash browns in the back of the freezer. I pop it into the microwave and eat it despite the sour, old-food taste, but my stomach still feels hollow inside.

I sigh. Time to make a trip to Klikamuks.

I bike my way downtown under the patchy cloud-and-blue sky and stop outside the Safeway. The automatic doors slide open and I'm overwhelmed by the aroma of chickens roasting on rotisseries. Mouth watering, I make a beeline for the chicken, eyes half-closed at the thought of sinking my teeth into juicy, tender meat—

"Whoa!"

I plow into some guy. I don't like the looks of him, all squirrely and skinny, with a too-quick nod and laugh.

"Brock! Hey, man! I haven't seen you in ages."

The skinny guy…I know him. Josh Gunter, one of the people I used to hang out with. He's taller now, an inch more than me, but only half as big, with zero muscles. I realize I'm glaring at his pimply face and force myself to relax.

"Hey," I say, and it comes out rough, growling. I clear my throat. "Long time."

"Yeah! I mean, I haven't seen you since…" Josh laughs nervously. "Like, how are you anyway, man? How you doing these days?"

I shrug. "You know."

He hesitates, scratching the back of his neck. "And Chris?"

"Still in the hospital."

"That's rough." Josh's gaze slides away. "My sympathies."

"Yeah, thanks." I pause. "You heard anything about Cyn?"

"What?"

"Cynthia Lopez."

Josh still won't meet my eyes. "Oh, your ex? Yeah."

"Yeah?"

"Man, you haven't been in school in ages."

My stomach sinks. "Is she, like…dating anybody?"

Josh just shrugs and gives me this look of pity. He must think I'm pathetic, a high school dropout still trailing after the girl who dumped him while the werewolf virus multiplies within his blood, over and over and over.

"But hey!" Josh perks up. "There's this sexy new girl from Hawaii." His voice drops to a whisper. "Rumor is she's not human at all, if you know what I mean. I'll bet she's a succubus. Seriously, though, she's like porn-star hot."

Never mind that I've always thought porn stars were too skanky for my tastes.

Or maybe he thinks I'm only good enough to date gicks, now that I am one.

I grimace. "I've got to go."

"See you around," Josh lies, eager to get away.

I watch him go, then glance back at the chicken. I'm not hungry anymore.

Cyn must have found herself a new boyfriend by now. A girl that smart and sexy wouldn't stay on the sidelines for long. I was a moron for trying to talk to her again. I'm a moron for even thinking about her, but she's like a song that won't stop echoing in my head, or a perfume that won't wash off my skin.

Saturday. It didn't used to be so important, but now it ties my guts into knots. Usually both Dad and I head out, but lately he's been "too busy" to go, so I have to drive myself to the hospital and explain this to Chris.

I take the pickup down the back roads, windshield wipers swishing away the rain. The forest is so green and wet it looks aquatic. I roll down the window a crack so I can breathe the sweet smell of dampening earth. I wish I were driving east, not west, away from the hospital and into the wilderness for a nice hike. But no, I'm taking the highway on-ramp, driving far beyond Klikamuks, all the way into the shining glass skyscrapers and grassless sweeps of pavement that are Seattle. God, I hate cities.

As I pull into the parking garage, the ceiling of the truck scrapes the low concrete. I grit my teeth. I should be driving one of those perky little sedans made for compact parking spaces. I should be one of those street-smart guys who knows the city and knows how to handle visiting his most likely dying brother.

I square my shoulders and tense my jaw. Ready, set, go. Armored behind my best Sunday suit and a blank face, I walk into the hospital. I hate the stink here: industrial cleaners, all fake-lemony-fresh, to cover up the smell of rusty blood and the old, the sick, and the dying. Even the lights look sick here, a greenish-blue fluorescent that makes everybody look ghostly. The receptionist smacks gum loudly, like a cow chewing its cud, and I clench my fists so hard my knuckles crack. I hate gum chewers. So fucking rude.

The receptionist raises her penciled eyebrows, and I wonder if my disgust is so obvious. Or is it a flash of fang, or yellow eyes? Maybe the seams of my sheep's clothing are fraying, the wolf inside peeking out. I hurry past her, into the bathroom. The dim, cheap mirror distorts my pale face, but it looks normal otherwise.

"Okay," I mutter to myself. "Human."

My heart still thumps hard, my skin sweaty like I've run a mile. What's the phase of the moon tonight? I haven't been keeping track, as if not knowing about the full moon will give me some sort of placebo effect.

But still…"It's the middle of the fucking day. You're good. Let's do this."

A toilet flushes, and a guy comes out from one of the stalls. Red-faced, he adjusts his tie and leaves without even washing his hands.

Whatever. He can deal.

I take the elevator up to the fourth floor and linger outside Chris's room. The door opens and a nurse walks out, frowning over something on a clipboard. I don't even want to ask. Chris lifts his head from his pillow and waves.

"Hey," I say, and I can't stay outside any longer. "They been feeding you?"

I wonder if he feels the same gnawing hunger that I do.

"Kind of," Chris croaks.

He looks skinny as hell, bandages mummifying his neck, wrist, and shoulder. I wince, remembering how the silver werewolf gnawed on him like a chew toy. It's been one month to the day since it happened, but he's been too sick to heal. Yeah, he'd heal if he weren't taking mega-doses of Lycanthrox…and he'd also be a werewolf, if the transformation didn't kill him first. When the full moon last came around, it tore him up inside. He's not strong enough to fight the virus, but he's not strong enough to change.

The doctors say my body is handling the infection better, which must mean I'm already more of a beast than my brother. Lycanthrox is supposed to keep the virus from spreading—but it can't kill it. Just keeps the wolf at bay.

Like I said, I don't know why Dad thinks there's a cure.

Chris blinks and swallows hard. "Brock?"

"Yeah."

"Why are you here?"

"To visit you." I twist my mouth into a smile. "You're my brother, remember?"

He frowns, not getting the joke. "Yeah."

Chris has been feverish forever. Nothing the doctors have given him has helped so far, and sometimes his temperature skyrockets.

"How you been?" I ask.

"Tired."

"Dad couldn't make it," I say, even though he didn't ask. "Too busy."

"Oh. How's…" Chris pauses and squints. "Cynthia?"

"We broke up," I say flatly. "A while ago."

Of course, I already told him this. Three times now. He's been having problems remembering what month it is, even what year.

"Shit, man. She was a really great girl."

My throat hurts. "I know."

Chris licks his chapped lips, frowns. "Brock. We should have never done that."

"Done what?" I say, but I know what he means.

"Don't ever do that again, you hear me? Don't ever."

It's too late, I want to say. There's no reset button on life. Instead I just stand there, deaf and dumb, trying to be some kind of comforting.

"That guy…Ben…" Chris coughs. "He was no good."

It hurts to watch him try and talk. His chest heaves as he forces out the words.

"Yeah." My voice sounds raw, and I clear my throat. "He's in jail now."

"Those gicks…they really fucked us over."

"Chris," I say, "don't worry. Don't—"

His eyes roll back, baring white, before his eyelids flutter shut. He convulses, fists clenched, back arched. The hinges of the bed rattle.

"Hey!" I shout. "Somebody get the hell in here!"

A nurse runs to the doorway, then shouts for someone to get a doctor. She tries to jab a syringe into Chris's arm, but he's thrashing too hard.

"Help me hold him down!"

I obey the nurse and pin Chris's shoulders to the mattress. He's so weak compared to me. His skin feels scalding hot beneath my hands. The nurse successfully empties the syringe into the vein on the inside of his elbow, and after thirty seconds of eternity, the earthquake within Chris dies down, leaving him limp and sweaty.

"Chris?" I say. "Chris, are you okay?"

"He's unconscious," says the nurse. "But he should recover."

The doctor strides through the door, all white-coated importance, and starts rattling off medical terms that make no sense to me.

I breathe deep and try not to shout. "Excuse me! What just happened to Chris?"

The doctor stares at me. "I'm sorry, you're going to have to leave."

"He's my brother, for Christ's sake. Tell me what happened."

"Your brother has a history of febrile seizures," the doctor says, her face bland and emotionless, "which may explain this one."

"Why isn't he getting better? Why did I get better, but not Chris?"

"Many factors. You may have a genetic predisposition that allowed you to survive, or his immune system may have been weakened."

I growl under my breath. Enough with the hand waving and medical gibberish.

"You have to go," the doctor says. "Now."

"Is he going to be all right?"

"Yes."

That's all I need to hear. I don't want to keep hanging around. If I stay too long, I might see something horrible. Fists clenched, I stride out of the room and start trying to breathe again. That scared the shit out of me.

Dad's wasting money on these special paranormal-expert doctors. They don't know jack shit about taking care of Others. If all their fancy medical diplomas really mean anything more than the tissue-paper gowns here, why is Chris getting worse? He hates being in a Seattle hospital. He should be home right now.

I shake my head, hard.

The stink of the hospital is starting to mess with my

head. Too much sickness. I've got to get out of here. As the doors to the elevator slide shut, I stare at myself in the polished stainless walls, then punch my reflection and dent the steel.

Damn it. I forget how strong I am now. But why do I feel so useless?

When I get home, I take an icy shower until my skin feels numb, though nothing can numb the ache inside me. I do finally get the hospital stink off of me, thank God. Afterward, I sit at my computer with the window open, letting the cold evening wind take over my bedroom. I wait for the hideously slow Internet to load my email.

Huh. An email from Josh. Maybe running into me yesterday guilt-tripped him into writing.

> hey brock
> just wanted to let u know that im going to a bonfire party tonight. its behind bobs corn maze on the other side of the trees. there will be drinks and girls. hope to see u there.
>
> peace
> josh

A bonfire party? Tonight? I can't believe Josh actually wants me to come along.

Outside the window, the moon hides her silver face behind a scarf of clouds. How full is she now? The wind scrapes the sky clean, and I squint at the pallid moon. About three-quarters full, and growing. An electric shiver skitters down my spine, and I curl my toes into the carpet. Time for another hit of Lycanthrox. After I swallow the magic pill, I tell myself that I feel calmer. That there won't be a problem tonight.

I almost believe myself.

four

I don't even have to creep downstairs. Dad snores like a bulldozer on the couch, the laugh track on the TV too loud. He won't check my room to see if I'm gone. I know. I've snuck out before, and done far worse things.

I bypass the truck and wheel my bike out from behind the garage. My legs itch with unspent energy. I pedal hard, until my muscles burn and the whistling wind stings my eyes. Down in the valley, fog overflows from the river and spills over the sleeping fields. The thick wet air tickles my throat, scented with river mud, wet grass, ripening corn, and the roast beef of a recent dinner trickling from a window.

My stomach growls. I yank an energy bar from my pocket and stuff it, whole, into my mouth. There. Shut up. You're not hungry anymore.

Bob's Corn Maze stands beside a backwater pond in the poplars. The spicy honey smell of the trees mingles with woodsmoke. The fog, thinner here, glows in the flickering yellow of a nearby bonfire. I ditch my bike in the bushes and trot down the muddy side road. Hoots of laughter and shouts rise from the area of the bonfire.

When I come to a circle of people, I stop. A knot tightens in my gut.

"Hey, Brock!" Josh scrambles to his feet, a bottle in his hand. Drunk already?

"Hey," I grunt, like a caveman.

"Have a seat and some beer," Josh says. "Ed got some from his dad, so it's good stuff."

"Thanks."

I pace around the people circling the bonfire, then sit next to strangers. Those who know me vaguely glance at me, curiosity sharpening their eyes. If Josh told them anything, I'm going to cut off his balls.

"Are you *sure?*" says a familiar voice, approaching the bonfire.

"I'm sure," says another.

A sigh. "This better be worth it."

Cyn. Through the swirling flames, she walks toward me, every step making my heart beat faster. She's wearing a red hoodie, but she crosses her arms tight against the cold. I wish I could hold her close and rub her hands warm.

Where's this boyfriend of hers? Or is she hunting for a new one?

Josh cuts through the circle of people. "Want a drink?" His voice cracks, jittery. He presses a cold beer into my hand, and I take it from him.

My eyes on Cyn, I down the beer in one swig. I'm not supposed to be drinking. Alcohol and Lycanthrox don't mix, the doctors say. But the doctors say a lot of bull.

Some new guy follows on the heels of Cyn and her friends. He hefts a plastic Safeway bag high into the air, and a few guys at the bonfire cheer. "Sausage!" bellows one of them, and others join him in a sort of fake manly battle cry.

My nose twitches. Yes. Sausage.

I keep my eyes on Cyn while I hear them ripping open plastic and sliding meat into the air and dangling it in flames so that it sizzles—dammit, hungry again? I lumber over to the guy with the package of sausages.

"Hey," I grunt. "Can I get one of those?"

Shadowed by me, he looks up, his eyes wide. "Sure, man, no problem."

That was quick. Did I intimidate him? He holds out the sausages to me, and I grab two. As I walk back to my spot, I can't help but gulp one down raw. It tastes good. People are staring, so I stab the other sausage onto a twig and hold it over the fire. Delicious. As I eat the sausage, smoke drifts my way, carrying Cyn's voice with it.

"…but is there *really* just one drink? I mean, beer has a pretty low alcohol content. What is it, five percent? Yeah, it says four point five percent on these. But anyway, I'm female and small, both factors that make me more likely to get drunk faster. You have to take genetics into account, too, and I'm not even going to go there."

Sometimes Cyn can be too smart for her own good. I mean, I know she's one of the geniuses at school, all prepped for a full scholarship at college, but seriously. You have to know when to turn your brain off and just have fun.

"Whatever," her friend groans. "Enough with the lecture."

"I'm just saying," Cyn says. "It's better to calculate before you inebriate." She laughs. "Think before you drink."

I've heard enough. I climb to my feet, snag a beer, and head over to Cyn.

"Hey," I say, and wince. Aren't I great at the cave-man-grunt introductions?

"Oh. Hi." Cyn looks disoriented, snapped out of her thoughts. "Brock?"

"What?"

"What are you doing here?"

"I was going to ask you that." I try to smile, and fail.

Cyn just arches her eyebrows and takes a beer from her friend. She pops the top and sips slowly, staring at me over the top of the can. Any other guy would think she was coming on to him, but I recognize the challenging glint in her eyes. She's wearing heavy mascara, which is unusual for her. What girls would call war paint.

I drink from my beer. "This stuff's not too bad."

"I've had better." She studies me. "So I suppose we could awkwardly ignore each other, or we could awkwardly try to talk."

I feel a little leap of hope. "Do you want to talk?"

"Everybody's a little curious about their exes."

Cyn beckons me nearer with a wave of her beer. I hear it sloshing in the bottom, nearly empty. Her eyes look glossy. Firelight and shadows flicker over her face, confusing her expression—I can't tell if she's excited or afraid.

"How do you feel?" she murmurs.

I frown. "Fine."

"No, how do you feel?"

Is she asking if I've changed? If the wolf inside me is awake?

I lower myself into a crouch until I'm eye level with her. I steady myself with my fingers splayed, my nails biting into the earth. She draws back, her lips still wet with beer. I can hear her breathing. And her heart, beating hard.

"Cyn," I say quietly. "I'm still Brock."

"I'm done with the old Brock." She sounds sober now. Or maybe she's talking really carefully because she knows she's getting drunk. "But I don't know the new Brock. Maybe I never knew you, even before you got bitten."

My face heats. "Don't say that here. Please?"

"But I want to talk."

"Not about *that*. Not now."

"Fine." Cyn drains her beer. "Have fun without me."

I nod and walk away before I can say something I'll regret. Cyn pops another beer while her friend complains about calories. The guys, on the other hand, chug beer and crush the empty cans barehanded. A little bit of conversation makes the rounds, but I don't have much to say, so I eat and drink and watch Cyn.

Above us, the moon sails out from a cloud sea. My skin itches, but my body holds steady.

For now, at least.

Cyn whispers something in her friend's ear, who nods. They climb to their feet, soon followed by a few other girls. They link arms and meander into the cornfield, going backward through the maze. I watch their long legs and shining hair disappear into the darkness. Where are they going? To gossip about us? About me?

"I've got to take a leak," I say to no one in particular.

I climb to my feet and make myself walk past the entrance and exit of the corn maze. I turn the corner of the field and stop by the ditch. The moon's reflection wavers in the murky water, and I piss on her face. Then I hear voices, coming from inside the corn maze. I finish and zip up my fly. The voices grow fainter. I jog alongside the corn maze, my ears pricked, my nostrils flared as if I might sniff them out.

"…that guy is sort of creepy," says a girl, not Cyn. "Don't you think?"

My stomach sours. I'm not sure I want to hear this.

"Yeah, he seems like he should be in middle school, not high school. Even though he is kind of tall, he acts totally immature."

"Yeah. And those pimples…yuck."

Oh. They must be talking about Josh. I hope.

"Guys," Cyn sighs. "Can we talk about something else?"

"Like what?"

"I don't know. Anything."

Their voices fade again. They must be moving deeper into the maze.

"Hey, whatever happened to that Koeman guy?"

"You mean my ex?" Cyn says.

"Yeah."

Wind hisses through the corn, rattling stalks and shaking leaves. Shit. I can't hear. I shove through the corn and sidestep into the maze, trying—and failing—not to leave a swath of destruction behind me. I stumble onto a muddy path that branches into three more. Okay. I know that Bob made the maze in the shape of a tractor this year. I've already been through it once, so that should give me an edge.

I inhale through my nose. The mingling perfumes of different girls float my way on the breeze. I'm not very good at picking out individual people's smells yet, but there's no way I could miss Cyn's bittersweet scent.

I trot down the leftmost path. The wind dies down, and I hear them again.

"Yeah," says a girl. "I heard that, too. Do you think it's just rumors?"

"Who knows." Cyn's voice sounds oddly flat.

"But you guys were dating for what, a year?"

"Which is why I went to Mexico. I wanted to get away."

"What, so tonight's the first time you saw him again?"

Cyn pauses. "No."

"Oh, don't tell me he's been stalking you!" The girl sounds thrilled by the idea. "Is he trying to, you know, bite you?"

I can't hear Cyn's reply.

My heart drums in my ears. Sweat beads on my skin, even in the chilly night air. The girls walk away again, and

I run after them, not about to let them get away from me again. My footsteps pound the dirt.

"Who's that?" Cyn says, her voice clear.

"Somebody's following us." A girl giggles. "Probably one of the boys."

"Let's hide!" another girl says, like it's a game.

Laughing, they take flight, their voices darting away. I burst into a crossroads and glance around. No sight of them. I charge after the voices. Ahead, right before a turn, I see Cyn slowing, glancing back. I almost say her name.

Our eyes meet. And then she runs away.

I'm faster than her, I know it. I'm going to catch up with her and that look in her eye. Then she's going to tell me what it meant.

My legs swing and arms pump as I race down the path. I take the corner fast, but Cyn's already gone. There's a long stretch of curving path ahead. I pick up speed as the clouds bare the moon's face above me. A prickling, electric excitement builds inside my gut. My legs feel liquid. I stumble, then stop, breathing hard.

"Fuck," I gasp.

I stare at the moon. She isn't full. She shouldn't have that much power over me.

"Cyn!" calls a girl. "Hurry up!"

I grit my teeth and sprint toward the voice. I'm going to catch them. My blood rushes through my veins, as hot as lava. My eyesight sharpens, focused by adrenaline. I cut the corner, leaves slapping and stinging my skin.

There. Cyn stands at a dead end, a moonbeam upon her like a spotlight. Got you.

The prickling excitement in my gut grows until it's humming through me and I'm triumphant and thrilled by pursuit. Cyn steps back, then stops as if her legs have locked. I'm barreling down toward her.

"This isn't funny!" she says, her voice high and sharp, her face pale in the moonlight.

I jog to a halt, then pace across the path, back and forth before her only escape. I'm breathing hard. I'm shaking.

"Cyn," I say. "Why are you running from me?"

She narrows her eyes. "Wouldn't you run if a werewolf came barreling after you?"

"I'm not." My voice roughens into a growl, betraying me. "I haven't changed yet."

"After a whole month? I'm sure there was at least one full moon in there somewhere."

"Don't you believe me?" I advance on her, resisting the urge to bare my teeth like a caged beast. I'm the beast doing the caging. "I'm not a liar."

"Let it go. Let me go."

"Who do you think I am?" I'm backing her into a corner now, getting closer and closer. "Come on, Cyn, you know me better than that."

She shakes her head, her eyes glassy. "Stop it. You're drunk."

I hate the fear in her words. "I'm not going to hurt you," I say.

I try to reach for her, to touch her shoulder and convince her that everything's all right, but she staggers away from me.

"Brock!"

You think I'm the big bad wolf. You think I'm going to eat you up.

A tightening ache inside my throat makes it hard to breathe. My hands shake, my skull throbs, and I wonder if this is it, my first transformation. Cyn stares at me, then looks over my shoulder and throws up her hands.

"Beth! Hey!"

One of her friends has come to save her? I turn to face this Beth girl, but see only a long stretch of dark path. Then Cyn sprints past, her hair flying behind her like a comet's tail. I'm going to chase her—no, I won't—catch her—let her go. I clench my fists, a burning coal stuck somewhere near my Adam's apple.

And then she's gone.

I turn and plod through the corn, stalks drooping in my wake, the moonlight chilling me until I don't feel anymore. God, I'm such an ass. Why did I even show my face tonight? Back at the bonfire, I snag another beer and try to drink myself into oblivion, so the laughing voices and faces of the girls blur and fade away.

Cyn, why do you have to hate me? Who do I have to be, for you to care?

The night rises around me, drowning me in darkness.

Crows caw hoarsely. An earthy smell fills my nostrils. I fidget and feel cool mud streak my naked chest, then yawn and curl into a ball.

Naked. Fuck.

My eyelids spring open. White clouds blind me. I squint, eyes watering. A headache hammers inside my skull. Each time I move my head, a fresh wave of nausea rises in my throat. I gag, clench my jaw, then give up and vomit. On my hands and knees, I realize I'm still wearing jeans, but my shirt is long gone, and I'm covered with mud all over. From the brightness of the overcast sky, I'm guessing it's early morning.

Last night flickers in my mind like a bad dream. I'll remember pretty soon, I think.

I crawl to the ditch, swill gritty water in my mouth, spit. I taste blood, and my heart thuds to a halt for a second—no, I didn't. I couldn't have. I took my meds…but then I got shitfaced. What does alcohol do with Lycanthrox? Why can't I remember? Those doctors didn't tell me. Or maybe it was on the bottle, in tiny letters.

Jesus Christ. You knew this was going to happen, but you did it anyway.

I stagger to my feet, clenching my leg muscles so I stay upright. Crows flap into the trees. I feel like a herd of rhinoceroses stampeded over me. Maybe this is what it feels like after you transform—but no, I'm still wearing my jeans. Maybe I didn't change all the way: a wolf-man, half-furred, half-naked, stalking his prey.

No. Hell no. Don't even think that.

I'm a little bit lucky when I find my bike in the bushes, not stolen, and manage to get on and start pedaling home. A pickup passes me, and the driver's head swivels in my direction. I know I must look like shit. I keep my face stony.

Got to go faster. Got to leave last night behind.

Back at the dairy, Dad's pickup is gone. I know— I hope—he's out milking the cows. I ditch my bike and let myself inside, quietly. The kitchen floorboards creak beneath my feet. I kick off my shoes and tiptoe upstairs, even though I'm way too big and bulky to be sneaking around. In the bathroom, I stare at myself in the mirror. Blood crusts my chin. I wash it off, then see I've bitten my lip. Okay. Maybe I didn't bite anything else last night. I get in the shower and try to scrape the sweat and mud and memories from my skin.

Somebody pounds on the bathroom door.

"Just a minute!" I call.

An icy fist clenches my heart. I gag again, then hunch, my hands on my thighs, my hair dripping into my eyes. Bile rises in my throat. My mouth waters, my stomach clenches, and I hope I'm not going to throw up again.

The pounding on the door gets louder. "Brock!" Dad bellows.

I kill the water, grab a towel, and yank open the door a crack. "What?"

Dad's glaring at me. "Where were you last night?"

Shit. He checked. But he never checks.

"Uh…what do you mean?"

"Your room was empty. You left your phone behind."

So he cares where I go at night, now that I'm a gick? Does he think I'm going to prowl around and eat bunnies and little girls?

"What are you smiling for?" Dad pushes the door open. "Get out."

"Let me get dressed."

He tilts his head away, his arms crossed, a vein in his forehead bulging as he clenches his jaw. I yank on my jeans and shoulder past him. Dad beats me to my bedroom door and stands in my way, his stance wide.

"Answer my question," he says in a soft voice.

"I went out for a ride," I say. "On my bike. I got tired of being cooped up inside."

Dad's eyes glitter, dark in the shadows of the hallway. "The mud?"

"I, uh, kind of crashed into the ditch. I'm fine."

"Liar." Dad's voice is even softer. He's going to start yelling soon, I know.

I have nothing to say, so I stare him in the eyes with no hope of staring him down. Even though I'm taller than him, I feel smaller.

"What's your excuse for the beer on your breath, huh?"

I narrow my eyes. I won't blink.

"What's your excuse for drinking?" Dad's voice rumbles from a whisper to a shout. "You haven't got one, have you? You know goddamn well you're not supposed to touch alcohol, you idiot. How could you be so stupid?"

My eyelids flinch, and I look away.

"You know what Lycanthrox does when you drink?" He waits for me to reply, but I won't. "It stops working."

Vomit rises in my throat. I press my lips together.

"You're hopeless," Dad says. "You're going to throw your life away. You're going to fucking get yourself killed."

I turn my back on him and run for the bathroom, my throat burning with acid. I don't make it to the toilet in time, and my puke splatters on the floor. I stare at it, my face flaming with shame, Dad's voice following me.

"Clean it up," he says.

Mute, I grab a towel and start to mop up the vomit.

"How much did you drink?" Dad says.

I rub the towel over the floor, soaking up the puddle, then drop it into the shower to rinse.

"How much?"

His voice sounds far away; my ears are buzzing. I turn on the water. Dad hits the back of my head, and I stumble forward into the chilly spray.

"Answer me, dammit."

"I don't know!" My voice sounds like a rusty screech. "A few beers, maybe."

Dad exhales in a hiss. "Where at?"

"Behind the corn maze at Bob's. I got drunk with some friends, okay? That's all."

But I can't remember, and so anything I say is no better than a lie.

"Friends?" Dad pounces on the word. "Who?"

I shrug. "Josh, and some guys from school."

"You're not allowed to drink with them again. Period. Is that clear?"

I nod. It's not like I haven't already learned my lesson. Dad hesitates, as if he expected me to fight back. He stalks away, his elbow knocking a glass onto the floor. It shatters into glittering shards. Dad glances at it, then slams the door, done being a father for now. A bitter taste on my tongue, I sit on the cold tile floor and stare at nothing. Dad's shouts echo in my ears, louder and louder, until I clutch my head and growl.

I try to remember how I used to live, but the old Brock is all in pieces.

I can't stand staying inside the cocoon of my bedroom, so I slip out the back door and stand outside the kitchen, in Mom's old garden. Wilting leaves hang from the thorny black skeletons of roses. A miniature rose, the toughest of the lot, raises a rosebud high like a signal flare. I stare down at it, my fists tight.

If Mom were here, she would know how to step between Dad and me. She was always the cool water on ground scorched by anger. If Mom were here, she would know how to help me, how to save me from becoming a beast.

She lies stone-still, her face as beautiful as a statue, and just as dead.

I blink, memories of the funeral still too raw to touch.

A green-and-gold hummingbird whirs into my vision. It hovers in front of the rosebud, dips its head, and tries to drink from the clenched petals. Failing, it flies away.

Stupid bird. There's no nectar here. Hasn't been for two years.

I fall to my knees and tear a hunk of weeds out of the earth, toss them over my head, grab another bunch. I break the spines of dead rosebushes and throw them onto the growing pile of useless plants. Thorns snag my skin, stinging, drawing beads of blood. I dig my nails into the pelt of grass and rip it away, baring the cool soft flesh of earth. Sweat trickles down my face; it feels good. I breathe deep, tasting green in the air.

I work until twilight purples the sky. The garden looks naked, but clean.

"Hey." Dad's voice makes my back stiffen. "You hungry?"

I face him, streaked with dirt and sweat, and nod.

We walk into the kitchen in silence, both too stubborn to say anything. There's a stack of frozen Hungry-Man TV dinners melting on the counter. Dad throws one into the microwave and punches some buttons, then heads for the TV. A loud commercial blares to life, filling the space where our conversation should be. I don't care.

The microwave beeps, and I hesitate until Dad hands me the steaming tray. I tear off the plastic wrapper covering the food. Barbeque pork, chicken, mashed potato. Supposed to be one of those XXL-size dinners, but I know we're going to go through at least two apiece. They taste kind of shitty, but I sit on the couch and eat. Dad joins me soon after, and we slurp and smack together. The commercials end.

"And now, back to the evening news," says a too-tan guy with brilliantly white teeth. "Earlier this week in Tacoma, Washington, police raided a warehouse suspected of housing illegal drugs and discovered faerie wine. The total value of the drugs recovered is estimated at just under one point three million dollars. No suspects have been arrested yet in connection with this drug bust, but police are continuing investigations." While he's talking, they show a short clip of police unloading crates of wine bottles.

"Well, they're fucked," Dad says.

I gnaw on a chicken wing. "Who? The cops?"

"Yeah. Faerie wine? That's got to be Zlatrovik property."

Zlatroviks. The werewolves everybody talks about on TV, but nobody even thinks about badmouthing in public. They've got faerie connections, and give "protection" to those smart enough to take it. The dumb ones end up dead.

I grunt. "Don't even know why the cops bother."

The camera moves from too-tan guy to the blond news lady. "Closer to home, residents of Klikamuks continue to be alarmed and disturbed by the close proximity of the werewolf pack in the Boulder River Wilderness Area."

A shot of a fat guy with a pasty-scared face. "…It's really scary to think that these werewolves, these Others, live so close to our homes and children. And after the recent murders here, anything could happen. It's really scary."

Back to the blond news lady. "Canadian officials have informed local police that many members of the werewolf pack are fugitives, wanted for multiple counts of attempted murder, aggravated battery, mauling, firearms violations, carjacking, felony resist and obstruct, failure to appear, and flight to avoid prosecution."

Damn. I'm not even sure what some of those crimes are.

"Snohomish County police are working to apprehend the fugitives and extradite them to Canada. Officials warn that these suspects are considered armed and dangerous. Do not attempt to apprehend them. If you have any information regarding these suspects, contact your local police station immediately."

Dad grunts and switches to another channel. I unclench my muscles. For a second, I thought he was going to start yelling about how me and Chris attempted to apprehend the werewolves earlier and failed so bad. I glance away from the TV, my gaze snagged by movement outside the living room window.

Holy shit.

In the shadows of the trees, hiding in the twilight, stands a silver wolf.

five

The wolf swings his head low, staring directly at me with intelligent yellow eyes. A wind ruffles the thick fur around his neck. He's long-legged, rangy, with powerful jaws and a granite-gray pelt tipped with black.

"Dad," I say in a strangled voice.

He glances at me, then follows my gaze out the window. His eyes spring into surprised circles. He bolts from the couch and into the garage, the door slamming behind him. I'm halfway onto my feet by the time he's back inside, carrying his favorite shotgun, slipping rounds into the magazine with a silky clicking noise.

"Damn gick," Dad mutters, as if he's talking about nothing more than a pesky dog.

He racks the shotgun, and my heartbeat jumps at the cha-chink.

"Dad," I say, but before I can say *be careful*, he's out the door.

I glance out the living room window. The silver wolf pricks his ears. Our eyes meet, and then he turns tail and melts into the trees. I run outside right as a shotgun blast shatters the evening. Birds cry out and flutter skyward.

I stand beside Dad, breathing a lot harder than I should be. We stare into the forest.

Finally, Dad says, "Go back inside." He racks the shotgun again.

I stare at the spent shell on the ground. "Where are you going?"

"The barn. Check on the cows."

"Dad."

"Inside. Now."

I grab his elbow. "Don't go out there alone. That's the wolf who bit me."

He stares at me, his blue eyes as sharp as ice.

"I'm going with you," I say.

I don't flinch under the chill of his gaze, and at last he nods. We walk together as the sky darkens, our shoulders bumping. I grit my teeth and keep scanning the shadows, but I see no sign of werewolves. When we reach the old red barn, Dad unlocks the door and peeks inside. The cows shuffle and moo, their hooves kicking up sawdust.

"Hmm," he says softly, lowering his shotgun.

I retreat from the open door, knowing my scent will scare the cows. I turn my back on Dad, facing the darkness. The moon rises like a rotten silver fruit, oozing juice onto the land. A shiver scuttles down my arms. A wind blows my way, filling my nose with the scent of arriving rain, lichen, leaves…and the faint, wild, musky smell of wolf. I clench my toes inside my shoes, tense but unsure where to go or what to do.

A hoarse whisper, close to my ear. "You know you don't belong here."

My head snaps to the right, and I'm staring into the dark eyes of him, Randall, the werewolf. A fist clenches my guts. Words choke my throat. You want to fight? You here to kill me? Get off my land, gick. Get out of my life.

Randall jerks his head in the direction of the moon. "It's almost time for you to go."

I glance up and the cold light stabs me, shivers me. Randall stands and watches.

"Brock? I think the cows are all right." Dad's voice, close behind me. "Brock?"

I look over my shoulder, at Dad stepping out of the barn, and look back at Randall. He's gone, vanished like smoke in the wind.

"Yeah." I cough. "Good."

Dad squints and scans the moonlit forest. "See anything?"

I open my mouth, shut it, shake my head.

Dad holds his shotgun at his hip and ruffles his hair with his free hand. "Inside."

I wait until he starts walking before I head toward the house. Randall's whisper echoes harshly in my ears. *You know you don't belong here. It's almost time for you to go.* I slam the door as if I can shut my fears outside.

Monday afternoon, I shovel rotten leaves from the clogged ditch beside our driveway. Wind rattles the trees, sprinkling new leaves onto me. I grimace and keep digging, but I'm liking the sweat and hard work.

Footsteps slap the pavement. I glance down the road.

Oh, Jesus.

Cyn jogs nearer, her hair bouncing in a high ponytail, the white wires of earbuds snaking into her pocket. I quickly glance over her skin, looking for any scratches or bruises, and find a thin slash on her cheek. Oh, shit. Did I do that to her at the bonfire? I look away so she doesn't think I'm checking her out like a creep.

Okay. She's not going to stop. She's going to jog right past…

Cyn sees me and slows, tugging the earbuds out. "Brock."

I raise my hand in a feeble wave. "Hey."

"What the hell did you think you were doing?"

"Me?" I stand like a criminal in the glare of a cop car's lights. "When?"

Cyn gives me a ferocious glare. "You've got to be shitting me." She usually doesn't swear, so I know she's really going to rip into me now. "Bonfire, Saturday night. You, smashed out of your mind. Me, followed into the corn maze."

"I didn't do anything," I say, even though I don't know that for sure.

"Oh, really." Cyn throws back her head and laughs. "I should have called the cops on your ass. Any other girl would have."

I clutch the shovel in both hands and stare at the ground. "Is that…? The scratch…?"

"What?"

"On your cheek."

"From a tree." Cyn narrows her eyes. "Can you really not remember?"

I shake my head. My stomach curdles like I'm going to puke.

"We ran into each other later." She speaks in an intense murmur. "You were even more smashed at that point. You kept saying, 'I'm sorry, I'm sorry,' over and over. I couldn't get away from you, and then you got even more stupid."

I don't even want to know.

"You tried to kiss me."

A jolt of surprise yanks my gaze back to her face. She's staring straight at me, her face blazing, her eyes glittering.

"I was drunk," I say, keeping my voice flat. "So were you."

She jabs her finger into my chest. "Has it occurred to you that even when I'm totally smashed—which I wasn't—I might not be interested in kissing a disgustingly drunk ex-boyfriend?" She says this all in one breath.

"Cyn, I wasn't thinking straight. I've been taking this drug—"

"You're doing drugs now?"

"No. It's a prescription." I heave a growling sigh. "Lycanthrox. Keeps me human, but I'm not supposed to mix it with booze."

Her fingers tighten around a fistful of my shirt. "Don't fuck around with shit like that."

I crack a smile. "You must be pissed. That's a lot of swearing for you."

"Don't think it means I care."

"Bullshit."

Cyn says nothing, her eyes sharp, her nails pinching me through my shirt. We lock gazes; I can't look away. Only then do I realize she's shaking, holding on to me to hold herself upright, and the sharpness in her eyes must be fear.

I close my hand around hers and gently pry open her grip. "Cynthia."

She curls her fingers around mine—involuntarily, it seems—then yanks away with a glare, as if to prove she doesn't want to touch me. I step back from her like I don't care, but I know we're both only pretending.

"Saturday night…" I hesitate. "You said you wanted to talk."

"About?"

"Me."

Cyn flashes me a burning look, then tucks her earbuds back in. "Maybe later." With that, she jogs away, her arms swinging, legs pumping.

It's all I can do not to run after her. But I don't know if that's me, or the wolf.

I dutifully take my Lycanthrox and avoid looking at the phases of the moon. It works until Wednesday, when the merest glimmer of moonlight sends me crazy with the desire to tear my clothes and leap outside and bite something.

I lie in bed, sweating, the curtains shut tight. An owl hoot-hoots outside my window, followed by the yip of a fox. I remember a yellow-eyed owl hanging around the werewolves. It always seemed to foretell the arrival of some sort of gick.

The owl hoots again. It must be in the tree outside my bedroom window.

"Damn bird," I mutter.

I haul myself off the mattress and trudge to the bathroom. It's darker there. I fill a glass with icy water and swig it down with two more pills of Lycanthrox. What happens if you OD on this stuff? Hell, I don't even care.

A spasm in my gut doubles me over. I gasp and clutch the sides of the counter. The pain fades, and I blow out my breath. The bathroom doesn't seem so dark anymore. I can see myself in the mirror. I tilt my head and my eyes flash orange.

Shit. Got to get out of here.

I pace in the bathroom, my bare feet slapping the tiles. Maybe the cellar? No, that would mean walking through moonlight. The roots of my teeth itch, ready to become fangs. Bones in my fingers and toes have been aching for a while now.

Two full moons. I can do this. I can totally beat this transformation.

I stride into my bedroom and yank open my curtain. The full moon sails high, ruling her queendom of sky. I lock my legs to keep them from shivering. I slide open my window, and the sweet, sweet perfume of the night nearly undoes me.

The owl sits in the maple outside my window. Gray-feathered, with big yellow eyes.

I bare my teeth. "Get off my property, gick."

The owl floats from the maple on wide wings and perches on a low cedar branch, its talons crunching bark. It swivels its head toward me.

"You here to spy on me?" I say. "You work for the werewolves?"

A red fox trots from the bushes and glances at the owl. The owl looks at me and shakes its head. I knew it. Definitely a gick.

"What do you want?" I growl.

The moon presses on my bones, bending them out of shape. I clench my abs and grab the windowsill, keeping myself together. The owl blinks slowly. The fox sniffs the air, one paw raised, then snarls and paces beneath the owl.

I lunge and clap my hands. "Scat!"

The fox narrows its eyes, giving me a very human look of contempt. Also a gick.

"Leave me alone," I say.

The owl screeches, then pumps its wings and scoops higher into the sky. The fox trots after the owl's shadow, leaving me standing by the window, my hands limp and useless by my sides. What does everyone want from me? Are they here to deliver the killing blow? Or welcome me to my new life as a gick?

Moonlight burns my skin like cold fire. I'm panting now, breathing shallowly.

I glare at the moon. "You think you can win, bitch?" I snarl. "I'm too strong."

Clouds drift across her facelessness as she stares down at me. I climb through my window and lower myself to the roof. I stand, shaking, my eyes on the moon. She can't stab me in the back if I'm watching her. I'm as rigid as a figurehead, withstanding the waves of moonlight and shudders that crash over me.

I laugh, and it sounds harsh, a barking cough. "I was a good boy. I took my medicine."

The moon burns brighter. She is determined to pierce my flesh and make me hurt. She whistles softly to the wolf inside me, urging it to claw free from my rib cage. The owl is back now, perched in the maple, watching me.

"I'm not a gick," I tell the owl as I gasp for air. "I…am…a human."

The owl fidgets its feet, inching farther along the branch.

I yank off my shirt just to let the moonlight pour over my shoulders and trickle down my back, just to prove that it can't touch me. This silver glow, the opposite of sun-light, bathes me in coolness I never felt before, when I was human.

A cramp rips through me and brings me to my knees. I stumble down the slope of the roof and grip shingles to keep from falling. My vision swims, sharpens, the night snapping into focus, clearer than it ever should be.

"No." I spit the word.

I grit my teeth and squint. Moonlight sweeps over me, leaving cool tingling in its wake. I steal a glance at the sky and see clouds advancing across the face of the moon. She vanishes into the darkness, veiling herself from my eyes.

I straighten, witnessing my salvation, then stagger inside. I fought the wolf and won.

Two moons down, forever to go.

In the morning, I ache like I got tackled by every player on the football team, but I feel fucking awesome. Of course, that doesn't mean it won't happen again. I'm a walking time bomb, and there's no way to defuse this disease.

I'm in my bed, reading the book on werewolves, when someone knocks on my door. I clap the book shut and dump it into the crack between my bed and the wall, like I was caught reading some really bad porn.

"Yeah?" I call.

Dad opens the door, his head bowed. "Brock."

Shit. My gut tightens. What did I do now? Dad's got that granite look to his face and a dangerous softness to his voice.

"Dad?" I keep my face blank.

He grabs my bedpost and leans forward. "Last night was the full moon."

What did he see? I didn't lose it. I stayed human.

"Well, last night…your…" Dad clenches his jaw, the muscles in his temples moving. "Your brother didn't make it."

"What?" I feel like I've jumped into a cold pond, only I'm not sure whether it's relief or fear. "You mean the Lycanthrox didn't work?"

Dad nods.

"And he turned into a wolf? Holy shit, that must have scared the nurses and—"

"Chris didn't make it."

"You already said that."

Dad just stares down, his gaze moving over the pattern of the floorboards.

Chris. Didn't make it.

"I don't get it," I whisper.

Dad swallows hard. "Chris passed away last night. His body couldn't take it anymore."

Chris, convulsing on the bed. Fur bristling from his skin. A tail wriggling from his spine, claws curving from his fingertips, teeth erupting into fangs, yellow eyes rolling back. His body tearing apart from the inside out. Blood. Silence.

"Brock?" Dad's kneeling in front of me, his eyes on mine.

"How did it happen?" I hear myself asking, sounding normal.

"He didn't turn into a wolf. Not all the way. His heart just gave out."

"Just gave out."

"Yes."

Chris's heart, beating fast, faster, then stuttering to a halt.

I realize I'm clutching my shirt over my own heart, my nails digging into my skin. I pry my hand away and flex my fingers.

"So he's gone."

"Yes." Dad's voice sounds croaky. "He's gone."

He leaves. I'm staring at my fingers, wondering what just happened, wondering what I should be feeling right now.

Chris is gone. He passed away. He. Is. Dead.

I run the words through my head, testing the newness of them. I'm never going to see him open his eyes again. Never going to talk to him. Never going to have a brother. My family is almost gone. It's just me and Dad now.

I want to quit and start over, but yeah, life doesn't have a reset button.

I slam the door so hard it rattles on the hinges, then

claw at the wall, my nails shredding curls of wallpaper. A high, keening whine escapes between my clenched teeth. I'm going to kill Randall. I'm going to fucking tear his throat out.

The werewolves howl that night, taunting me in a triumphant chorus. Dad doesn't hear them—he's passed out drunk on the couch after a day talking to the hospital and the funeral home. I'm not going to any funeral, period.

I go downstairs like a walking statue, unfeeling, unthinking. In the garage, the musty, mousy smell twinges my supersensitive nose. I can hear a rodent scratching in the wall, even the high squeaks it makes to its mate. I grab my coat, two boxes of rounds, and Dad's favorite shotgun. I'm more than a match for the werewolves.

I slip outside, shadow-quiet, and lock the door behind me. Darkness shaved a sliver from the moon, but she still has power over me. I grit my teeth and stride straight through her light. My skeleton creaks and stays human.

The silver glow erases all of the deadness from Mom's garden. Grounded leaves shine like a windfall of faerie coins. The single bud of the miniature rose blossomed into a tiny, perfect, blood-red flower. I twist its stem from the branch and bring the flower to my nose, the perfume tied to memories of Mom. I'm glad she never had to know what happened to her sons. I tuck the rose into my breast pocket, trying not to bruise its petals.

I'm sorry I'm such a disappointment, Mom. I'm going to fix things now.

The werewolves are howling again, their ghostly voices drifting over the sea of trees. I stop at the edge of the lawn, my head tilted in their direction. They can't be more than a mile or two away. I enter the forest, passing through puddles of moonlight and a shimmering rustling of ferns, all shadow and glow.

I'm coming for you. No one will have to hear your howls again.

The farther into the wilderness I go, the faster I walk, until I'm running, my arms swinging, boots pounding the dirt. I clutch the shotgun so it won't slip out of my sweaty hands. I can't hear the werewolves anymore, but I'm going to find them. My calf muscles burn from the effort of sprinting. My breath comes in quick gasps.

The moon sweeps across the sky, dressed in a ragged ball gown of clouds. Electric-shock excitement worms its way deeper into my chest. I charge up a hill and sprint down, feet skimming the ground. I feel fast enough to outrun any werewolves, tough enough to fight the whole pack, even if I have to take them down with me. A log juts from the ferns and sends me flying. I tumble into a ravine, the shotgun spinning from my hands.

I spit the dirt and leaves from my mouth. "Fuck."

Lightning crashes in the mountains, followed by the

pattering of rain. Rounds flew from my pockets and now lie, glinting in the moonlight, scattered all over the forest floor. I scramble to pick them up and return them to their boxes.

A growl rumbles from the darkness.

My breath sticks in my throat. I ditch the rounds and grab—no wait, where is it? What happened to the shotgun?

Ferns rustle. Two eyes flash yellow. Randall. I know it's him.

"Hey, gick," I say, bravado steeling my voice, even though my knees feel like water. "Stop cowering in the shadows."

A black nose pokes through the ferns, followed by the massively muscled head and body of the silver wolf. He's got to weigh between a hundred-fifty and two hundred pounds. Real wolves don't get that big. He bares wicked fangs.

Where the hell is the shotgun?

"I was looking for you," I say, stalling for time. "You following me?"

The silver wolf cocks his head.

"Can't talk, huh?" I sweep the leaves with my gaze. Every stick and log looks like the barrel of the shotgun. "Guess it's just barking."

A louder growl rumbles from the wolf's throat. He stalks toward me, bristling. Then I see it, wedged between a fern and a boulder. The shotgun. I dive for it just as the wolf lunges, quicker than me but farther away, and I—

Jesus fucking Christ.

I'm staring right into the green-gold eyes of a soot black wolf. It lifts its lip and snarls. I freeze in a crouch, my hand halfway toward the shotgun, but also very close to the black wolf's jaws. Behind me, I hear the silver wolf pad closer. Movement flickers in the corner of my eye, and I glimpse yet another wolf circling me.

I withdraw from the black wolf guarding the shotgun. I stand.

I am surrounded by wolves.

six

Twining between the trees and shadows, the wolves circle me like a tightening knot. Suddenly there's no air in my lungs and no spit in my mouth. I've walked right into the middle of the werewolf pack.

Well, this was what I was going for. Right? But I can't say I'm not scared shitless.

The silver wolf, Randall, breaks free from the swirling pack and stands before me. He bares his teeth in what may be a snarl, or a smile.

You killed my brother. You took my life away from me.

I lunge at the silver wolf. Surprise in his eyes, he leaps aside, but my boot connects with his ribs. He yelps. I laugh. Randall flattens his ears and snaps at me, his teeth clicking. I grab a stout stick off the ground and raise it high.

A woman's voice cuts through the night. "Enough!"

Randall lowers his head and retreats from me. The

swirling wolves halt, their ears pricked, paws raised questioningly. A tawny-skinned woman with a long mane of black hair strides into the circle of wolves. She's wearing ragged jeans and a loose shirt that doesn't conceal that she's pregnant. Silver bracelets glint on her arms.

"You found the bloodborn," says the black-haired woman. It isn't a question.

Randall dips his shaggy head in a nod.

"I want to talk with you," says the woman, her gaze still on Randall.

He closes his eyes for a moment, with the slightest of sighs. Then the fur melts from him like candle wax, baring naked skin. His skeleton grinds and clicks as it reshuffles into the shape of a man. The yellow fire in his eyes dies to dark coals. Randall shudders with the final stages of transformation, then stands.

"Winema," he says, avoiding her stare. "Forgive me. I didn't plan to—"

"I can see this wasn't your plan," says the woman, Winema. She eyes the shotgun rounds scattered at my feet. "What was the bloodborn doing?"

"Me?" My voice sounds hoarse, and I cough. "You gicks killed my brother."

"You will not use that word here," Winema says.

Under the force of her stare, my eyes start to sting until I blink and look away. *Bitch.* Only I can't bring myself to say it out loud.

Randall glances at me. "He didn't survive the full moon?"

"Of course not, you goddamn cur," I say.

Winema snaps her fingers, and the soot-black wolf soars and knocks me to the ground. Air swooshes from my lungs. Huge paws pin my shoulders. I smell blood and meat on the wolf's breath, and see its teeth glinting very close.

Winema looks down at me. "Show some respect, bloodborn, or you will be punished."

"My—name—is—Brock."

She stares at me until I flinch away. The black wolf pants in my face.

"He's rather…aggressive," Randall says, his voice soft and level, "though I don't think he's made his first transformation yet."

The black wolf inhales my breath, then snorts. Wolf-snot speckles my face. I wonder if it can smell the fear in my sweat.

"Interesting." Winema crosses her arms. "It must be that experimental drug."

The black wolf shifts its weight, squeezing my lungs, and I try to breathe shallowly. I twist my head to the side. A rank of wolves stands silhouetted against the trees, watching me. Same on the other side. A caged jittering builds inside my chest.

"How are we going to take care of him?" Randall asks.

They're going to kill me. Maybe torture me first.

Winema tilts her head, her face stony. "I haven't decided yet."

I'd rather die running.

A bellow roars from my throat, and I fling the wolf off of me. Caught off guard, it twists in midair and thuds on the ground. I lunge to my feet and barrel through the line of wolves as they leap aside and rough fur brushes my ankle but I'm still running I'm going to make it maybe I can outrun them and maybe—

A shotgun blast deafens me. I'm too pumped full of adrenaline to know whether I've been hit, and I'm still running, my feet weightless. Paws thunder behind me, thumping closer and closer. An image of Blackjack furiously pursuing a school bus pops into my mind, and I want to laugh a crazy laugh. Wolves like to chase things.

Something slams into me from behind. I'm tumbling, rolling, sprawling on the ground. Teeth sink deep into my calf. I'm shaken, a growl vibrating through my leg bones. I'm still not feeling pain, but I am feeling hot blood soak my socks.

I'm going to be eaten alive. They're going to rip open my belly and drape my glistening guts across the dirt, chew my bones and crunch my skull and eat my eyes like grapes…oh, man, oh, God, I don't want to die like this.

I scream, no words, just terror as sound. The black wolf is gnawing my left leg. I claw at its pale eyes with my weak human fingernails, but it squints and squeezes its jaws tighter, its fangs scraping grooves in my bone. I grope frantically and grab a stone and smash it on the wolf's muzzle. It whines but won't let go.

If you're going to kill me, I'm going to take you down with me.

I gouge my thumbs past the black wolf's eyelids. It yelps and releases my leg. I stand, crumple to one knee. Blood puddles in my shoe, slick between my toes. I tackle the wolf and wrap my arms around its neck, choking it as hard as I can. The wolf whines and scrabbles beneath me, trying to shake me loose, but I'm not going to let go.

"Bloodborn!" Winema's voice snags my attention.

She's standing right in front of me, the shotgun in her hands. I bare my teeth at her.

She growls, then raises the shotgun and smashes the butt on the back of my head. My vision flickers—and then I plummet into blackness.

Pain throbs in my head with every heartbeat. I pry open my eyelids and squint at white overcast sky, then haul myself upright. The movement sends fresh, sickening pain rippling out from the back of my head. When I can see again, I climb to my feet. My left leg aches. I glance down at it, at my shredded jeans, stiff with blood.

Where did the werewolves go?

I limp in a slow circle, swinging my head from side to side. What the fuck? *You know you don't belong here*, Randall said. *It's almost time for you to go.* I thought he was going to take me out. But the pack left me here to bleed.

My leg, and my head, are killing me. Dad must be awake now. He's definitely going to kill me. Or maybe he thinks I'm already dead. Gritting my teeth, I limp along the trail of scuffed leaves and dried blood—my blood—from the night before. I can't find Dad's shotgun. They must have taken it.

Armed with nothing, bearing no excuses, I stagger toward home.

Of all people, guess who I see on the doorstep, small and bright in her red hoodie.

"Brock!" Cyn's fists ball by her sides. "What *happened* to you?"

"I don't even know why you're here," I say, not looking at her, walking straight past. When I try the door, it's locked. "Nobody's home?"

She gapes at me. "No. When I called, your dad sounded …really weird."

Dad must have been drunk, or crying, or both.

"I thought something happened," she says, "so I drove here."

I rummage behind a rock, find the spare key, and let myself in. I need to find some painkillers and get this blood off of me, fast.

"You need to go," I say. "Now."

Cyn gives me a look. "Brock. You need help. You're covered in blood and you're limping…did something bite you?"

I give her a look right back.

"Oh. God! Was it the werewolves?"

"What do you think?" I say.

When I hobble upstairs, Cyn follows me. It's dark and quiet in the house. Where did Dad go? Shit. I'm getting blood on Mom's carpet. I hurry to the bathroom and yank open the medicine cabinet. My hands shake as I screw open a bottle of aspirin. I pour five into my palm, but Cyn grabs my wrist and shakes her head.

"Too many. You'll overdose."

"It really hurts," I say through clenched teeth.

"You should call 911."

"Yeah. Right." I pop two aspirins into my mouth and swallow them with water. "Cynthia. Why are you still here?"

She folds her arms. "Because I'm not going to let you do something stupid."

"I need to take a shower." I peel off my shirt and turn on the water. "Go."

"It's not like I haven't seen you naked already," Cyn mutters, but she leaves the room.

I shut the door and gingerly strip off my jeans, hissing at the pain. The bloody, ragged denim clings to the gashes in my skin.

"Where's your dad?" Cyn calls from behind the door.

I step into the shower and yank the curtain shut. "I don't know," I shout back.

With the water near-scalding, I scrub myself hard, as if I can wash away all traces of the werewolves. The pounding in my head slowly numbs. When I crouch and inspect my leg, the torn flesh looks less ragged than it did an hour ago.

Clean, I shut off the water and yank open the curtain. I breathe in the steam.

"Brock? Are you—" Cyn opens the door.

I grab a towel, but she's still staring. I bend my leg gingerly, even though the pain feels older and more distant now.

"Your leg," she says. "Is it…already healing?"

"Yeah. One of the perks." I wrap the towel around my waist and sidestep past her, to my bedroom. "I'll see you later, Cyn. Goodbye."

"I'm not going."

I shut the door of my bedroom, but she opens it again right as I'm pulling on a new pair of jeans. Is she *asking* for trouble?

"What do you want?" I say. It sounds harsher than I intended.

She crosses the gap between us and stares up at me. Frowning, her fingers shaking a little, she takes my face in her hands, then slides her fingers into my hair. I wince when she touches the wound on the back of my head. Deeper than that, her touch feels like a key in a rusty lock, twisting my insides with a sweet ache.

"Brock," she says. "You're hurt. What happened?"

"Chris," I say. "He…"

Her eyes glimmer as she stares at me, waiting.

"Chris is dead."

Her face tightens with lovely sadness. "I'm sorry."

I try to pull her closer, but she flinches away. I let my hands fall to my sides. She withdraws from me, her face blank.

"I heard the werewolves howling last night," I say, "so

I went out to meet them. I found the whole pack. One of them bit my leg, and then this woman cracked me over the head with a shotgun. When I woke up, they were gone."

"And Chris…?"

"The full moon." I force out the words. "His body couldn't take it anymore."

"I'm sorry," Cyn says again.

"You don't have to keep saying that. It's not going to make any difference. I'm the one who has to fix things. He was my brother."

"What do you mean, fix things?"

"Kill the werewolf who bit us both." I clench my jaw and grab a shirt, a jacket, my shoes. "He can't keep hiding in the forest forever."

"Brock. You can't go out there now—"

"I have to."

"Are you crazy? They kicked your ass last night. You got knocked out by a shotgun. You're not thinking straight."

"I'm thinking straighter than I ever was before." I head for the door.

"Brock!" She laughs an I-can't-believe-this laugh. "You're not even dressed."

I sit on the floor and start pulling on my shoes.

Cyn stands in the doorway, blocking my path out. "I can't let you go."

Finished dressing, I advance on her. "Move. Please."

"No." She braces herself in the doorway, her arms on the frame. "I don't want to be the one who could have stopped you and didn't. I wasn't there when you were bit-ten, and I can't stop thinking about it."

We stare at each other, only a hairsbreadth away. I'm holding my breath, and I think she is, too. Neither of us blinks. Her eyes glitter with fire. She slides her foot toward me and closes the last fraction of distance between us.

I'm distracted by the warmth of her body so close to mine. "You can't do this."

"Why not? We can work this out together."

"There is no *we*." I bare my teeth, since it's easiest to feel angry. "You dumped me. You don't get to come back whenever you feel like it and pick up your discarded boy-friend."

Cyn sucks in her breath. "Do you have any idea how hard it was for me to break up with you? How hard it's been to stay away from you? I'm trying to help you. I can't believe you're throwing this back in my face."

She's saying what I've wanted to hear for so long, but she's saying it too late.

I look away. "You can't help me." I sidestep past her and stride into the hallway.

Smack in the middle of Mom's carpet, I see a small bloodstain. Frowning, I crouch over the spot. No, it's the miniature rose I picked from the garden, before I went after the werewolves. I can't believe it survived the night, and fell here.

"Brock," Cyn says, right behind me. "Stop."

I straighten quickly, the rose in my hand. Her eyes

snap onto the brilliant red, and her fingers drift to it as if she can't help herself.

"What's this?" she says.

"A rose," I say, "from my mom's garden." I hold it out to her.

She lifts it from my fingers, twirling it between her own. A few petals have opened since I plucked it. "Why is it here?"

"Doesn't matter. You can have it; I won't need it where I'm going."

If I stay any longer, I might change my mind.

I jog downstairs and open the kitchen door. I stride outside, letting the door swing shut behind me, but Cyn still slips through.

"I'm going to call the cops," she says.

"On me? You *are* crazy."

She jogs alongside me. "I think you've got things backwards."

"Cyn!" I growl. "If you're going to follow me, at least be quiet."

She makes an impatient noise.

I break into a run, half-hoping she won't keep up, half-wishing I could just turn back and work things out with her, but it's far too late for that now. That, more than anything, really twists the knife of regret deeper into my heart.

Of course I can't stay. Of course I wish I could.

I shake my head to fling these thoughts away and concentrate on following my own blood back through the forest. Where could the werewolves be now? Surely, when

Cyn sees them, she'll run away. She should be running from me.

Behind me, I can hear her quick footsteps. At least she stopped shouting at me.

"Brock!" Cyn hisses, surprisingly close. "Get down!"

Startled, I duck behind a tree. She crouches beside me.

"Look," she whispers, pointing.

Ahead, squatting in the leaves, I see the unmistakable figure of Sheriff Royle.

seven

Royle crouches beside a streak of blood in the leaves. Next to him stands a ginger-haired guy with a pinched, hungry look on his face. He looks young, not much older than Chris was, with a uniform too big for his skinny frame.

The sheriff snaps his fingers. "Deputy Collins."

The young guy's head snaps up like a bird dog's. "Yes sir?"

"Have a look at this blood."

Collins bends over Royle's shoulder. "What do you think it is, sir?"

Mine, probably. I hope they don't do any forensics.

Royle dips his pinkie into the blood and sniffs it. "Were-wolf." He squints into the trees. "There must have been a fight."

"This is good," Cyn whispers. "Let the police handle the pack."

"Shhh!"

Royle straightens. "Collins. Follow me."

Together, the two of them saunter through the trees as if they aren't afraid of anything, though their hands stay close to their holsters.

"Can you smell anything?" Cyn whispers.

I shiver at her hot breath in my ear. "No. I already told you. I'm not a werewolf yet."

"Oh, they're getting away." She scrambles to her feet. "Come on!"

"Hey," I mutter, "whatever happened to not doing anything stupid?"

She either doesn't hear or doesn't want to, which is more likely, and tiptoes after them. Typical reckless Cyn. I follow her, though not nearly as gracefully. It must be nice to be so tiny that your feet glide over the leaves in silence—

"Brock!" she hisses.

"Sorry."

Luckily, Royle and his deputy don't seem to be paying too much attention to our whispers.

"Collins," the sheriff says, "are you aware that I have made this my personal mission?"

"Your mission, sir?"

"To rid Klikamuks—and the whole of Washington State—of this menace. It was a grievous oversight on our part, allowing that werewolf and his pack to escape prosecution. I intend to rectify that mistake."

Collins sounds puzzled. "You mean the Arrington case? The Other murders?"

"What else?"

"But we didn't have any evidence that the werewolves actually—"

"Evidence? We have overwhelming evidence that the werewolves have committed an obscene number of crimes in the US and Canada."

"Yes, sir."

"Eyewitness testimonies, for Christ's sake."

"Yes, sir. My apologies, sir."

Royle claps his deputy on the back. "Keep your eye on the big picture, Collins."

Cyn drags me into a crouch behind a fern. Ahead, peeking through a blackberry bramble, shine two green-gold eyes. Holy shit, it's that wolf who tore up my leg. Sheriff Royle and Deputy Collins don't seem to have a clue.

A growl builds in my throat, and I realize I'm baring my teeth.

Cyn glances at me, her eyes wide, and shakes her head. "Don't."

"Sir," Collins says. "What—"

Royle shushes him. Then, speaking louder, he says, "We know you're watching us. Come out slowly, and don't try anything funny."

The wolf stalks out from behind the blackberries. Collins draws his gun.

"Steady," Royle mutters. To the wolf, he says, "Turn into a human."

The wolf lifts its lip. It could be snarling, or grinning.

Then, behind the sheriff and his deputy, a silver wolf creeps closer. And a gray wolf, and another silver wolf. I clench my fists, ready for Randall to leap out and tear into Royle's neck—or maybe mine.

Collins whirls around, fear plain on his face. Royle, however, surveys the situation with a thin smile, his fingers on his holster.

"Brock," Cyn whispers. "They're behind us, too."

Great.

Surrounded by bristling fur and bared fangs, Royle remains amazingly calm. "Collins," he says, "would you like to call for backup?"

The deputy fumbles for his radio while still pointing his gun at the wolves.

"That won't do you any good." Winema strides from the trees with wolves at her heels.

Royle doesn't even try to hide his sneer. "This one's their Alpha," he says to Collins. "The ringleader of this particular pack."

"I know, sir," Collins mumbles.

Cyn has a look I've seen before: too much curiosity and too little fear. "Wow," she whispers. "I didn't know they had a female Alpha."

"Shhh," I say.

Winema looks at Royle as if he's a pile of dog shit she

just stepped in. "By the time your backup arrives, Sheriff, it will be too late."

"I'm well aware of your tendency to scurry deeper into the forest at the threat of danger."

"You don't seem to know what I'm talking about," Winema says, her eyes burning. "You're familiar with our long criminal records. The death of one more backwoods county sheriff wouldn't be much more than a footnote."

Collins looks about as pale as a sheet of paper, the radio halfway to his mouth.

"What are they going to do?" Cyn whispers, so quiet I can barely hear her. "What—" Her words turn into a gasp.

I lunge up just as Randall's fingers close around her arm. He yanks her to her feet.

"Cyn!" I shout.

Randall clutches her to his chest. She lifts her feet off the ground and kicks backward, then bites his arm. It doesn't do any good through his thick jacket, but he does seem amused to be bitten by a human.

Spurred into action, Collins radios in. "This is Collins and Royle. We have a hostage situation here. The werewolves are—"

"That's enough!" Winema silences him with a slice of her hand. "Turn that off."

Collins does as she says.

The Alpha stares Royle down. "Unless you want this girl's blood on your hands, I would advise leaving immediately."

My heartbeat pounding in my ears, I step between them. "Let her go."

Winema bares her teeth at me. "Bloodborn. You really are an idiot. You've brought this upon your own girlfriend, leading the police to us."

"No." I can't make myself meet her fiery eyes. "That's not what—"

"Brock," Cyn says, "why don't you just shut up and let me do the talking?"

"You're hardly in a position to," Randall says, smirking.

Cyn kicks him again. "First, Brock is not my boyfriend. Second, I was trying to stop him from coming out here at all. Do you think we don't already know that this is your pack's territory? We don't want to—"

Winema listens with an expression of mild interest, then shakes her head. Randall jams a rag between Cyn's teeth, muffling her outraged yelp. Royle clenches and unclenches his jaw as he watches, his fingers hovering over his gun.

"All it takes is one bite," Winema says, "and then this girl—or maybe that squirrely deputy of yours—is infected forever."

Collins swallows. Cyn looks furious, so I know she must be terrified.

"Deputy Collins." The sheriff snaps his fingers. "Let's go."

"Sir?"

"You heard me."

Together, they back away from the pack, their guns

still drawn. The werewolves drive them onward with ferocious snarls. At the last minute, Collins turns and breaks
into a run. Royle swears and sprints after him.

"Deputy Collins!" he bellows. "You run, you're prey!"

But the werewolves let them go. When I glance back,
another man is holding Cyn: an old guy with a tangled
gray beard and long ratty hair beneath a trucker's cap. He
looks like he should be sleeping in a cardboard box. No, he
looks like Gandalf after Vietnam. The sight of his disgusting hands on her makes me snarl.

"Bloodborn." Randall advances on me. "What in
Christ's name were you trying to pull?"

"Let Cyn go," I say, my voice hoarse. "You don't need
her."

"Actually," he says, "she's a lot more useful to us than
you."

I bare my teeth. "You're fucking dead, you piece of
gick shit."

Winema gives me a weary look, her eyes like embers.
"We don't have time for this. Randall, secure the bloodborn. He's obviously more dangerous as a lone wolf than
he is with us. We can't afford any more mistakes like him."

I'm a mistake? Yeah, I'm the biggest one these gicks
will ever make. And the last.

Randall advances on me, his face unreadable, his stare
fixed on my face. A snarl rumbles from my throat, but he
remains silent. Behind him, I can see the disgusting homeless-guy werewolf dragging Cyn farther away. She isn't

struggling now, her face small and ashy, her body limp like a doll. What did they do to her?

"You're all dead," I say. "The police will hunt you down and rip you to pieces."

Winema, walking away with wolves at her heels, glances back at me. "Including you."

"Fuck no. I'm not a gick like you."

Winema laughs.

You think this is funny, bitch? I lunge at her. Randall tackles me and I hit the ground hard. Before I can throw him off, he's twisting my arms behind my back. Cold metal slides over my wrists with a raspy clink. Handcuffs. I growl, my muscles straining in sheer frustration. Randall pins me to the ground with his knees, even while I twist and fight and brace myself against the dirt. Holy shit, he's strong.

"Get off of me, gick." My words sound less human, more growl.

"Gick, gick, gick." Randall growls. "You're going to be difficult, aren't you."

"I'll—show—you—difficult."

I'm having trouble breathing now because of his weight on my back, and because he's tightening a leather dog collar around my neck. He's going to strangle me. Panic electrocutes me with new energy. With a roar, I surge to my feet, sending Randall sprawling. I teeter, unbalanced with my hands behind my back, then fall.

"Fuck!"

"Shut up or I'll gag you." Randall nudges me with his

boot, a grimace twisting his face. "Move your ass. You're coming with me."

"No."

He sighs, then plants his foot between my shoulders and clasps a leash to my collar.

My chin in the dirt, I lift my head. The rest of the pack—and Cyn—are already gone. I have to get her out of here. Images flicker through my head: the homeless-guy werewolf strikes her down with a clawed hand, his sleazy smile warping into fangs, as he tears her clothes off and pins her down and—I squeeze my eyes shut.

I told you not to come, Cyn. I told you to leave me alone.

"Up." Randall yanks on my leash. "Come." As if I'm a dog.

But I know that fighting all the way isn't going to get me any closer to Cyn right now, not with these fucking handcuffs and collar.

I'll have to kill him, then get the key.

Randall and I sit on the bench seat of a baby-blue pickup truck. He's driving. I'm staring out the window, gnawing on the inside of my cheek, being rattled to bits by the washboard road. Pine trees crowd the way, their needles brushing the windows. Rain hisses from the sky, speckling the windshield, and Randall turns on the wipers.

On the radio, buzzing with static, we listen to the local news station.

"…breaking news. Earlier this afternoon, Snohomish County police reported the alleged kidnapping of a Klikamuks resident by the pack of werewolves currently residing in the Mount Baker-Snoqualmie National Forest. A teenaged male, also a resident of Klikamuks, allegedly aided the werewolves in the kidnapping."

"What the—" I sputter.

"Quiet." Randall turns up the radio.

"These werewolves are convicted fugitives, and police consider them armed and dangerous. Do not approach or attempt to confront them. The alleged kidnapping victim is described as a girl in her late teens, about 5'1", petite, brunette, with a streak of pink dyed in her hair. If you have any information about this case, or know of the pack's whereabouts, please call the Snohomish County Sheriff's Office at…"

"Bullshit!" I say. "I haven't allegedly aided anyone."

Randall glances at me. "Guilty until proven innocent. Get used to it."

"Believe me," I mutter, "I'm going to let the cops know who's really guilty."

He just rolls his eyes.

I haven't seen Cyn since the rest of the pack left us behind. All of them must be far ahead by now, fleeing the police. How the hell did I end up in this situation? I mean, first I'm hunting the werewolves, ready to kill them, and then they're kicking my ass, and then they're being all calculating and shit. It's fucking disorienting.

"What's her name?" Randall says.

"Who?"

"Your girlfriend."

"Ex-girlfriend. Cyn."

I bite the inside of my cheek. Why am I even talking to him?

He arches an eyebrow. "As in, sinful?"

"No," I mutter. "Short for Cynthia."

Silence for another few swishes of the windshield wipers.

"Your brother," Randall says.

"What?" My throat constricts. "What about him?"

"How did he die?"

"What do you mean, how? The change killed him. Why do you care?"

He glances at me, his eyes smoldering. "Because I bit him."

"You bit me too, gick, and I don't care if you get your head blown off. Actually, I'd love to see you get your head blown off."

Randall makes a noise between a growl and a sigh. "Raging at me won't help."

"How about you unlock these handcuffs. That'll help."

He snorts. "You can't go back, you know."

"I have to. My dad doesn't know I'm gone, and when he finds out, he's going to flip. And I left something important behind."

"What?"

"Lycanthrox. The only thing that's keeping me from changing."

Randall glances at me. "You know that stuff doesn't always work, right?"

"It's been working for two full moons."

"A lot of bloodborn don't transform for the first few moons. The lycanthropy virus incubates for at least a month. That's why I wanted to know what happened to your brother, since you got bitten at the same time."

Heat drains from my face, leaving my skin icy. "You saying because Chris died, I'm going to die soon, too?"

"No. He was in the hospital, wasn't he? You recovered."

The silver wolf flings himself on Chris, clamping his jaws around his arm. He shakes Chris like he's killing a rabbit. Chris screams and fights back, but the wolf's jaws crunch his wrist, then close around his neck, pressing his windpipe.

"You didn't bite me like you bit him." My voice sounds small.

Randall nods, his face masklike. "Either way, you're my fault."

"That make you feel any better?"

He looks at me, his eyes the color of tarnished gold. Weariness creases his face. "No."

"You killed my brother. You deserve to die."

Randall hits the brakes and the truck skids off the road, gravel spraying behind the tires. He yanks the parking brake savagely, then leans into my face, so close his breath dries my eyes. "Listen," he says in a velvety growl.

"You know damn well that you and your brother were asking for what you got."

"So Chris deserved to d—"

"Shut up. I didn't want to kill him. I just wanted to scare the shit out of you two, but no, you kept coming back. I didn't want to bite you. I had to."

I'm shaking in my seat, the chain on my handcuffs jingling. "Liar."

Randall's eyes flame. "You're a fucking moron, aren't you?"

"Get away from me, gick."

"Sorry. But we're stuck with each other now. And guess what, you're a gick, too."

"I'm not a gick!"

"You were bitten." Randall speaks in a deliberate rhythm, his words dropping like spent shells. "You are bloodborn."

I clench my fists, my nails digging crescents into my palms. "I am who I want to be."

He laughs. "That's a nice thought." He lets the parking brake go and accelerates back onto the road. "I wised up a long time ago."

How was he bitten? I want to ask, but I don't want to hear his goddamn voice.

Rain rattles harder on the roof of the truck. We're driving along a ridge now, and all around us, a dark pelt of forest ripples over the hills. I have no idea where we're running. I hope the police find us soon and shoot every last one of the werewolves.

I'm not sure whether that would include a bullet in my head.

We drive for hours in silence. Every milepost on the shoulder ticks off just how far away from home I am now. Randall navigates one-way dirt roads and hairpin switchbacks though Mount Baker-Snoqualmie National Forest. There's around 50,000 acres of trees out here. I've explored the edges of the forest before, while out hunting deer with Dad and Chris, but we were all too chicken to go much deeper.

A memory of Chris cracking a joke drifts into my mind, but his face is blurry, pale, and sickly. I can't seem to see him anymore. I fall into a daze listening to the endless rumble of the engine and the hiss of passing trees. A rhythm of *Chris is dead, Chris is dead* drums inside my head. I glance at Randall, still very much alive and breathing even though he deserves a horrible fate. He's the one who did this…

Where are the police? Why aren't they right on our tail?

Then again, I know how useless they can be. That Benjamin Arrington guy killed at least five gicks in Klikamuks before his next target tipped off the police. But of course, those were all gicks getting murdered. Surely the kidnapping of a human girl like Cyn would make the police get off their fat asses. Come on, Sheriff.

I sink lower and lower in my seat, rattling through my cluttered thoughts as if I'll find answers there, some magic

Houdini escape for all the trouble I've gotten myself into. But I just feel too exhausted to think of anything...

My gaze drifts to Randall's hands on the wheel, and the fuel gauge. Nearly empty. He's going to have to stop for gas sooner or later. But around us, I see nothing more than trees, mountains, and more trees. We're deep in the wilderness.

"Where are we going, anyway?" I say.

"Guess," he says.

"You're high-tailing it so far into the trees that the police will never find you. But eventually you're going to have to go back into town for food and supplies. No, probably not food, because you're hunters. But you'll go back one day, and the police will be waiting. If they don't send bloodhounds up here first."

Randall snorts. "You've put a lot of thought into the life of a fugitive."

"I just want to know how you've stayed alive for so long."

He grunts and turns onto another gravel road. We're jostled and bounced all the way to a mercifully paved highway. We pick up speed and pass a few cars. I crane my neck as we overtake them, wondering if they're from the pack. Through the trees, I glimpse milky green flashes of the North Fork of the Stillaguamish River. This must be the Mountain Loop Highway. It curves southeast around the Boulder River Wilderness Area, then backtracks west, which means it's going to spit us back out into civilization eventually. Unless the werewolves plan on taking some forest service road to God-knows-where.

I keep my eyes on the fuel gauge as the needle droops lower and lower.

My salvation appears in the form of a Texaco gas station so old that it can't possibly be pay-at-the-pump. That means Randall will have to get out of the truck and go inside. That means I will be alone for long enough to fight back.

eight

Randall exits the highway and pulls into the Texaco. We're not really in a town, just near a few tumble-down cabins hiding in the trees. Beneath the gas station's rusty roof, a cherry-red '70s convertible sits parked outside.

"Looks like they beat us to it," Randall says.

"They?"

Then I see a dark-skinned woman in a flowery dress that clings to every curve. Her wavy black hair snakes past her high cheekbones. She lights a cigarette, and her eyes—light apple-green, shot with yellow—lock with mine.

Shit, I've seen those eyes before.

"That's Jessie," Randall says. "But you've already met."

So this is the black wolf who chased me and bit my leg so savagely. Pretty, if I didn't know that those red lips of hers were once a bloody muzzle. She doesn't blink. I don't blink. She curls her lip, then gives me the finger.

"Bitch," I growl.

"Well, yes," Randall says. He drives up to one of the pumps, kills the engine, and looks me in the eye. "Stay."

I bare my teeth at him.

Randall hops out of the truck, slams the door, locks it, and saunters to the werewolf woman. "Jessie! Where's Isabella?"

"Inside," Jessie drawls, with a Southern accent that oozes molasses-sweet.

Another woman clicks out of the Texaco in ridiculously spiky heels. She looks a lot like Jessie, only she has sleek, short black hair and dark eyes. Sisters, for sure. "Jessie, honey, I told you they wouldn't have any mentholated cigarettes here."

Jessie sighs a puff of smoke. "Damn."

Randall's eyebrows arch skyward. "You stopped for *cigarettes?*"

"You wouldn't understand," Jessie says.

He mutters something under his breath that I can't hear through the window, then strides into the gas station. I hunch lower in my seat and yank my wrists against the handcuffs. Shit. I need to get them off, but I have no idea how.

I glance at my door, which has one of those push-button locks. Jessie and Isabella still aren't looking my way—too busy talking to each other—so I twist in my seat, bite the push button, then yank it upright and unlocked. Yes! I twist the other way, so my handcuffed hands can reach the door handle, and grope to get it open. With a loud clunk and rusty squeal of hinges, the door swings open. I tumble onto the ground.

Adrenaline floods my bloodstream. Time to get the hell out of here.

Before those two werebitches can even glance over at me, I'm lurching to my feet and sprinting for the trees, head down, breathing hard. I'm halfway across the highway when I hear a laugh. I don't look back. Only when my feet hit the pine needles do I risk a glance over my shoulder, ready to fight that black wolf who—

Jessie and Isabella stand by the Texaco. Smoke ribbons drift from their cigarettes.

What the fuck? I keep running, but can't stop looking at them. A root catches my foot. I stumble and hit the dirt. Air knocked from my lungs, I cough, spitting pine needles. I try to get up but fall again, bruising my ribs. When I look back at the Texaco, both of the werebitches are gone. Shit. They were waiting for me to fall.

"Pity Winema won't let us kill him," Jessie says, her voice much closer now.

Isabella laughs. "You're going to scare that poor blood-born shitless."

I roll onto my side and stare at the trees. Pine branches wave gently in the breeze, masking the monsters behind them. Cigarette smoke prickles my nose. I wriggle on the dirt, trying to haul my ass up, as helpless as a worm.

Jessie runs between the trees, her eyes glowing. She

sighs a cloud of smoke, then flicks her cigarette butt onto the ground and grinds it beneath her sandaled foot. Her toenails have sharpened into black claws.

"Bloodborn," she says, "you were safer with your sire."

"What the fuck are you talking about?" I growl.

Isabella appears from the shadows, her hair less sleek and more like a pelt now. "Randall. He's your sire. You have a lot to learn, honey."

Jessie curls her lip. "Learn? We sure as hell need to teach him a thing or two."

"You're going to regret that, bitch," I say, still trying to get on my feet.

Isabella laughs. "Silly thing. Play nice, bloodborn, and we might help you."

"My name is Brock."

Jessie paces around me, her eyes burning, her fingers tipped with claws. "Brock." She spits the word. "You shouldn't even be alive."

"Fuck you," I say.

"We don't have to help him," Jessie says, flashing a glance at the other woman. "We can just tell Winema he got lost, and—"

"And?" Isabella narrows her eyes. "We were all bloodborn, in the beginning."

Jessie growls, her arms and legs shadowed by the start of a pelt. "But not this stupid."

My heartbeat thuds inside my ears. This is going to be two werewolves against one human who was never very badass to begin with. Oh yeah, and I still have no fucking clue how to get these handcuffs off.

"Really, honey," drawls Isabella. "We all remember the time you tore up that trucker. Lord, that was a lot of blood."

"That was different," Jessie says. "He was—"

"Isabella! Jessie!" Randall jogs into the clearing. "What the—"

"Your dog got lost." Jessie's lips thin into a smile.

Now that Randall's back, at least I don't have to face the werebitches alone. Even if he is giving me the kind of glare that can melt steel.

"Get the hell out of here," he says. "The cops are right on our tail."

Jessie rolls her yellow eyes. "They're always right on our tail."

"Grady reported a patrol car less than ten minutes away."

That wilts the smirk on Jessie's face. "Shit," she whispers.

The two women sprint toward the Texaco, amazingly fast in their high heels. Randall grabs my leash and yanks me to my knees. The collar tightens, choking me, and I gasp, staggering to my feet to stop the pressure.

"Where's Cyn?" I rasp.

"Safer than we are right now. Move!"

By the time we make it back to the truck, it's too late. A state patrol cruiser idles outside the Texaco, and I can see someone talking to the clerk inside. Randall swears under his breath and shoves me into the truck, shutting the door so that it doesn't slam. He glances at Isabella and Jessie. Both women stand taut and ready to run.

"We'll take care of him," Isabella murmurs.

Jessie rummages in a tiny purse and flips open a compact mirror to check her makeup. She slides a fresh stain of blood-red lipstick over her lips. Isabella smoothes her hair, and I can see her face hardening into a calm mask.

"You sure…?" Randall says.

Isabella nods. "Take the bloodborn and get out of here."

Randall walks back to the truck and opens the door, just as the cop exits the Texaco. It isn't Sheriff Royle or Deputy Collins—it isn't even a him. Isabella and Jessie share a glance, and I can see the *oh, shit* pass between them.

I almost laugh. No way in hell are they going to flirt their way out of this one.

The state patrol officer—a middle-aged, iron-haired lady—zeros in on Randall. I'll bet he's got the longest criminal record of all three werewolves. She starts advancing on him, but Isabella flutters into her path like a butterfly.

"Excuse me, ma'am!" Isabella says. "You're just the person I was looking for."

Jessie smiles shyly. "We're a little bit lost, officer."

Distracted, the officer's stare moves away from Randall. "I'm sorry?"

Now's my chance. "Hey!" I shout. "Police lady!"

The officer glances at me. Can't she see the dog collar around my neck? Or does she think it's some sort of punk thing?

"Don't mind him," Isabella says. "He's a little ... disabled. Mentally."

Hands cuffed behind my back, I lurch against the window. "Fuck!"

"Tourette's," Jessie says.

Randall strolls around to the driver's side of the truck, his steps carefully casual. He climbs in, shuts the door, and buckles up.

Barely moving his lips, he murmurs, "If you fuck this up, you're as good as dead."

The officer glances at me again, flips out a notepad, and scribbles something. "All right. You said you were lost?"

Isabella purses her lips. "We're trying to find our way to—what was it called, again?"

"Wallace Falls?" Jessie says.

"Wallace Falls." The officer's forehead creases. She flips out a notepad from her shirt pocket. "Your names, please?"

"My name's June," Isabella says, "and this is my sister, Eve."

"Last names?"

"Montgomery. With two O's. Officer...what was your name?"

Randall twists the key in the ignition. The truck sputters but doesn't start. He keeps glancing at the officer without moving his head. I hunker in my seat, my armpits wet with sweat. Think. There has to be some way to escape.

"I'm Officer Downing," says the cop. "Have you seen anything unusual in the area?"

"Unusual?" Jessie's eyes round, oh so innocent. "What do you mean?"

Randall twists the key again. The engine hiccups, then rumbles to life. He shifts into drive and pulls away from the pump. Officer Downing takes a step toward us, looking right between Isabella and Jessie, but they block her way. Randall pulls onto the highway and revs up to cruising speed.

No shouts. No flashing lights. The patrol officer lets us go.

Aren't the werewolves fugitives wanted for attempted murder, mauling, firearms violations, and a shitload of other crimes?

"Jesus," I mutter. "I don't fucking believe it."

Randall grins at me, his teeth too sharp. "This answer your question about how we've been able to stay alive for so long?"

"What about our plates?"

"Plates?"

"Our license plates. Don't they have them on record?"

"We change them every few states or so. Isn't easy, but Winema knows some faeries who can glamour them to look different."

I shake my head. "Haven't the police caught on?"

"Faeries won't talk."

I heave a growling sigh, my body trembling as the tightness in my muscles relaxes.

"For future reference," Randall says, "if you try to pull another stunt like you did back there, I'm not going to save your ass from Jessie."

"I don't need it."

His eyes go cold. "She would've killed you weeks ago if you weren't my bloodborn."

"*Your* bloodborn?" I grimace. "That makes it sound like we're related."

He laughs, a humorless bark. "We are."

We drive a good ten to twenty miles per hour over the speed limit, depending on how deserted the road is, and cruise out of the Mountain Loop Highway within an hour or so. Spiky pines give way to flat, muddy farmland carpeted with the stubble of old corn. Puddles in the furrows flash silver as we pass, mirroring the clouds above. A string of trumpeter swans hunts for leftover grains, just like in Klikamuks.

Chris is dead.

Randomly, the thought rides in on an unwanted wave of sadness. I take a deep breath and shove it away, but my throat still aches.

"We're making good time," Randall says.

"For what?" I mutter.

Randall doesn't say any more, and I don't bother asking again. Clouds smother the sun, and then darkness smothers the last bit of light. We zoom through towns: Sultan, Goldbar, Index. Highway signs blur together. I start to wonder whether we're driving in an endless loop on the same damn roads past the same damn trees. Unless you count being knocked out last night, I haven't slept in forever. I feel like cement is being pumped into my veins, starting at my fingertips, oozing into my arms and legs, dragging my eyelids down. I bite the inside of my cheek and dig my fingernails into my hands, but it's so hard to stay awake.

I want to sleep…but I can't…sleep, can't…sleep…

My eyelids jerk open when the truck rolls to a stop. Randall yanks the parking break, then hops out. I squint at the glare of the headlights. Is that a picnic table? What the hell? Randall opens my door and I'm dunked in icy air.

"Awake?" he says.

Teeth chattering, I nod. "Yeah. Definitely."

"Get out."

I step onto numb legs and fall to my knees. "Where the fuck are we?"

"Where we're sleeping for the night."

I scrape together the energy to glare at him, then stagger to my feet. It looks like we're at a campground, if it can even be called that. Just a picnic table on some packed dirt, a fire pit full of leaves, and the sound of rushing water in the distance. No lights anywhere. No sign of life. We're alone in the black forest.

I frown, my thoughts still slow. "Why didn't we just pull off on some logging road?"

Randall's eyes flash gold as he looks at me, and I can't help flinching. "Not everyone in the pack is tough enough for that."

What kind of pack is this? Criminals who need the comfort of a picnic table?

I snort, and he yanks the leash on my collar.

"I can tie you to a tree for the night," he says, "or you can cooperate."

I swallow, my throat bruised. "Like how?"

He grabs a sack from the back of the truck and tosses it down. "Help me set up this tent before it's too close to dawn for us to get any sleep."

"Right…" I lift my wrists so the handcuffs jingle. "I can't."

Randall stares straight at me, his eyes glowing in this really fucking creepy way. Then he grabs my arms and unlocks the handcuffs.

I turn on him, my fists raised. "Seriously?"

He just keeps staring at me.

"You're seriously going to do something that stupid?" I say.

"What's stupid," he says, "would be you trying to run away when you don't have a goddamn clue where you are."

"Who says I'm going to run?"

He smiles a thin smile. "What's really stupid would be you trying to pick a fight when you're collared and tired, bloodborn."

I rub the raw skin at my wrists. "Not afraid I'm going to kill you in your sleep?"

Randall turns his back on me and starts unpacking the tent. He tugs out a crumple of fabric, then carries it to the packed dirt. I stamp my feet, trying to get my blood pumping, trying to wake up the anger inside me.

"You going to help?" Randall says, an edge of irritation in his voice.

"Like hell I'm going to help you."

"Suit yourself. It's only going to get colder."

I gnash my teeth. "Stop it."

"Stop what?"

"Pretending like we're not going to kill each other eventually."

"Yeah, right."

I advance on him, my boots thudding on the ground. He doesn't even look back. I take a deep breath and cock back my fist.

"You know I'm right." My voice trembles with rage.

"It's too late for this kind of shit." Randall fiddles with one of the poles for the tent. "Quit making an ass of yourself, bloodborn."

I swing my fist. Then—right before my knuckles hit his head—Randall twists, grabs, and sends me flying. I'm flat on my back before I can even react. He grips my shoulders—

the claws on his fingers cut through my shirt and prick into my skin—his eyes burning maybe two inches from my own, his breath hot in my face.

He growls, a low rumble that vibrates in my rib cage. "Enough."

Looking into his eyes fills me with an urge *not* to look, to stare to the side and whimper. I know that's the wolf in me. Submissive. But I'm not going to give in. Randall's claws pierce my skin; hot trickles of blood wet my shirt. He bares his fangs, and my eyelids flinch shut. Finally, he lets go of me and climbs to his feet.

"I've changed my mind," he says. "You can freeze."

And so he handcuffs me again and collars me to a tree like a disobedient dog.

I thought I knew why Blackjack howled when we locked him outside in his kennel on a cold night, but I didn't have a goddamn clue. Yeah, I guess he had a fur coat, which made things better, and I'm tied to a tree in the mountains wearing nothing but the clothes I came in. I'm starting to wish I was sharing that tent. Hunched against bark, I shiver violently. My teeth chatter so hard my jaw starts to hurt. I'm long past not being able to feel my fingers or toes. Pretty soon I feel like the rest of my body is carved from a block of ice.

Then, thank God, I drift into sleep.

"...said he was a tough one, didn't they?"

"Yeah. But he could definitely benefit from being neutered."

A raspy laugh, which becomes a cough. "Well, he is bloodborn!"

I crack open my eyelids. Randall and the homeless-looking guy are standing nearby. Gandalf after Vietnam. It's not quite registering in my sluggish brain that this guy is a werewolf, that inside the grizzled old hobo is a wolf ready to come out.

He's the one who took Cyn. What did he do to her?

"Winema wants to see you," the old guy says.

"Sure." Randall glances at me. "With or without the bloodborn?"

"With."

Randall sighs.

The old guy laughs again and claps him on the back. "I know how you feel."

"Thanks, Grady."

They both advance on me, Grady smoking a cigarette. I set my jaw and stare them down. Grady nudges my shin with the toe of his boot.

Randall looks me over, his face blank. "All right. Get up."

Yeah, right. I'm hunched with my back against the tree, my muscles cramped and cold, my hands still cuffed behind me.

"Probably a little frostbitten," Grady says.

"Wasn't cold enough for that." To me, Randall says again, "Get up."

I glare at him. "I can't."

He sighs, unties my leash from its knot on the tree, and hauls me upright. "Quit your whining. We're going to see Winema."

Grady laughs again, then hawks some spit on the ground. "Have fun with that."

nine

Me and Randall follow Grady away from our campsite and up the road. Through the gray willows, a stream rushes with snowmelt. No wonder it was so cold last night. Farther along the road, I see one of those bright yellow gates meant to keep people out when campgrounds close for the season, lying in pieces in the grass.

I wonder if the police even have a clue where we're at.

We cross the road and start down a steep slope, crunching dead wildflowers beneath our boots. Head hanging, I stumble on numb feet, then look up.

Holy shit, I don't think I've ever seen so many werewolves in my life.

We're in a meadow beneath a bowl of milky white sky. Jagged pines encircle us, and a hawk wheels low overhead. I see trucks, campers, and tents scattered in the tall tufted grass, and plumes of smoke. All around, men and women mix with wolves. The beasts stand guard, sniff the air, or just lie on the ground, panting lazily like dogs on a lawn. Ordinary at first glance, but completely unreal. A girl walks toward the stream carrying canteens, followed by two trotting wolf-pups with stubby legs and gray lambs-wool fur. The scent of mountain air, sweet pines, and woodsmoke sharpens a craving inside me.

"The Bitterroot Pack," Randall says.

"Pretty, isn't it?" Grady's cigarette smoke unfurls in my face, and I cough.

Isabella saunters toward us, barefoot. One of the straps on her dress has fallen off her shoulder. There's blood streaked across her cheekbone.

"You two missed a glorious hunt," she purrs. "Took down a deer right before dawn."

Randall gives her sad eyebrows. "You know I was busy."

"Aw, honey, I'm just teasing." Isabella smiles. "We're going to start eating soon."

Grady steps closer to her and lowers his voice. "I hear that you and Jessie had a run-in with a policewoman you thought was a policeman."

"At first," Isabella says. "But we knew how to handle her."

Randall looks less than amused. "Did you make a clean getaway?"

"Of course." She touches him on the shoulder. "Come eat."

Isabella leads us to a campfire on the bank of the stream. A deer roasts over hot coals on a spit that looks like it came out of medieval times. My stomach pinches at the tantalizing, savory aroma. Winema sits on a nearby cedar stump, gnawing on a haunch of venison, and a hawk-nosed man with long silver hair eats at her feet.

As I watch, the rest of the pack approaches in turn: first the youngest, then the strongest. There must be at least twenty werewolves in this pack. A man with a long knife carves meat straight from the deer. The best parts go first. Finally, Randall drags me toward the deer. I lean in to inhale the smell—Randall cuffs me away.

"You eat last," he growls.

Of course. I'm on the bottom of the totem pole. Top of the shit list, too.

Randall carves a juicy chunk of meat from the deer's flank, then sits on a stump to eat it, closing his eyes as he savors the taste. My mouth waters so bad it aches. I swallow hard and stare at the ground, my hands useless behind my back. The strong smoky smell of venison fills my nose, and the crunching noises of eating fill my ears. Jessie strolls toward Randall, her hips swaying. She nuzzles his ear, and he cuts her a sliver of his meat and hands it to her. She licks his cheek and walks away, gnawing on the meat. Disgusting.

Finally, Randall thinks to unlock my handcuffs and toss me some scraps.

I get the gristly bottom of a leg, hoof still attached, but I'm drooling over it anyway; I haven't eaten in forever. I rip strips of tough-as-jerky meat away with my blunt teeth. Around me, the werewolves in human form have grown fangs. A scrawny werepuppy trots up to me and whimpers, its blue eyes fixed on my meat. I growl at the little cur. It flattens its ears and paws at my ankle, then licks my shoelaces. I snarl, but the werepuppy jumps on me, whining, and tries to snatch my meat. I knock the vermin away.

A swift blow to the head sends me sprawling. Ears ringing, I look up.

Winema stands over me, staring me down. Again I try to meet her gaze, and again I fail. Power steels her eyes. "You will not hurt the children of this pack." Her voice rumbles like a distant storm. "Is that clear?"

My fingernails bite into the deer leg. "But it tried—"

"Give your food to the child."

The werepuppy stands between Winema's ankles and wags its tail hopefully.

Child? You've got to be shitting me. It's just a gick that hasn't grown up yet.

What I was going to say sticks in my throat. "Didn't want it anyway," I mutter, and I toss the deer leg to the werepuppy.

The vermin, the blue-eyed rat, grabs the bone and drags it away in triumph. My stomach growls in complaint, betraying me. I want that meat so bad. And my face burns to realize it. God, I've been fighting over scraps like a beast.

Winema lowers her voice. "It will be hard, bloodborn, for you to learn your place."

I grit my teeth. Learning my place is the furthest thing from my mind.

"It's a shame your brother wasn't strong enough."

Now I look into her dark eyes, trying to figure out where the hell she's coming from, but I don't see anything taunting or spiteful. I can't think about Chris for too long; the longer I do, the stronger the sadness rises inside me.

"Why do you care?" I say, looking away.

"Because all of us—nearly all of us—used to be you. Bloodborn."

I swallow hard. "I'm not bloodborn. I haven't turned into a wolf yet, not even after two full moons. I've been taking medicine."

"Delaying the inevitable."

"Well, fuck it. I'm going to find a cure."

Winema laughs softly, and I want to strangle her.

"You think this is funny?" My voice sounds tight. "You think I want to be what *you* are?"

"Do you think all of us wanted to be bitten?"

"How the hell am I supposed to know?"

"You should be grateful," Winema says, "for the second chance we're giving you."

Before I can reply, she walks away.

I get off the dirt, my ears scalding. I can feel the pack's stares prodding the back of my head. The werepuppy lies on the ground, so close I could touch it, slobbering on the deer leg that was supposed to be mine. I'm such a dumbass.

A laugh flies across the meadow. My throat tightens. Cyn?

I jog through the pines, fight through a tangle of brambles, and stumble into the open—and there she is, sitting on the stunted grass, three wolf pups prancing around her. She glances up, laughing, her hair shading her face.

Just like nothing ever happened, and this is a walk in Wilding Park.

When she sees me, her laughter dies in her throat. "Brock!"

"Cynthia." My heart's thumping so fast. "Are you okay? Did that werewolf—did he…?"

"What?" She brushes her bangs from her eyes. "I'm fine. They haven't done anything."

A werepuppy spreads its front legs on the ground, wiggling its butt in the air, and yips, just like Blackjack when he wants to play. I stare down at them, my face stony. Another werepuppy marches up to me, a twig in its jaws, and growls at me. I nudge the werepuppy with my boot, and it shakes the twig as if proving its strength. Cyn grabs a battered hedgehog chew toy and tosses it for the werepuppies to maul.

"Don't let them bite you," I say. "They can still infect you."

Her jaw tightens. "Yes, I know. Are you okay, Brock? You look horrible."

I realize I'm shaking, from sheer nerves and starvation. "What do you think?"

She strides across the distance between us and looks up at me, frowning. Her fingers linger on my neck. "They collared you?"

"Yes. I got tied to a tree last night. By Randall, that piece of—"

"Randall?"

"He's the one who killed my brother," I say hoarsely. "He's the one who bit us."

Cyn grimaces. "Oh."

A werepuppy trots up, the stick clamped in his jaws, and whines, his ears quivering. Cyn bites her lip, trying not to laugh.

"I can't believe you're playing with them," I mutter.

She arches her eyebrows. "Honestly, Brock, they're just babies."

The werepuppies do move kind of like little kids do, all floppy feet, their big heads bobbing as they run.

"They don't know any better," Cyn says. "Besides, you have to admit they're cute."

"Cute?" I curl my lip. "That's like calling baby spiders cute."

"Baby spiders *are* cute."

A werepuppy lifts its leg on my boot and pisses a tiny stream of urine.

"Hey!" I yank my foot away. "You little bastard!"

This time, Cyn does laugh, and I can't help laughing in return. It fades fast, though, and coldness seeps back into my bones.

"Brock," she says, serious again, "I'm worried about you."

"Thanks," I say flatly.

"I'm worried that you want revenge so bad you're going to do something crazy."

I meet her eyes. "I don't have anything to lose."

Except you. But I can't make myself say it out loud.

Cyn glares at me. "You think life is a movie? A video game? That acting cocky is going to get you anywhere except dead?"

Dead. Like Chris.

The muscles in my shoulders and back tighten. I speak through gritted teeth. "Not if I kill them all first."

"That's ridiculous."

I shake my head, hunger making the world spin. I fall to my knees and grind my knuckles against my closed eyelids. Got to keep it together.

She kneels before me. "Are you going to kill the werepuppies, too?" she says.

I ignore the sniffling by my ankle, one of the pups checking out my boots. "Why?"

"Why not?" Her voice is icy. "They're going to grow up. They're already gicks."

The pup yanks on my bootlaces. I open my eyes and grab the brat by the scruff of his neck. He squirms and whimpers until I put him down. His gray fur shrinks away to reveal pink skin, his stubby limbs reform, and his tail worms away to nothingness. A fat baby sits in the dirt, staring at me with big blue eyes.

My mouth drops. "They can change already?"

"When I said they were babies," Cyn says, "I wasn't joking."

The werepuppy-baby drools and keeps staring at me. He seems confused.

"Fine." I glare at Cyn. "You win. Now stop playing devil's advocate."

She studies my face like she can read answers there, like I'm some sort of multiple-choice test she can ace. I want to grab her shoulders and tell her to stop being so damn cocky—she can't outthink everyone.

A shrill whistle makes me flinch. I look back and see Randall with his fingers in his mouth. I growl. Do I look like a dog?

"You'd better go," Cyn says.

And so I do.

❦

"I can't let you starve." Randall shoves an opened can into my hands. "Unfortunately."

I crouch in the grass and sniff the contents of the can. Beef stew. I pour it into my mouth, guzzling the chunks of meat, licking the leftover juices. Randall watches me, his nose wrinkled, his mouth curved in a half-smirk.

"Stuff tastes like shit," I say. "Only a little bit better than dog food."

"Hey," Randall says, "I don't see any four-course meals lying around. And you're not going on any hunts until you prove we can trust you."

Hunts? My eyes glaze over at the thought of wolfing down blood-hot venison…

I blink. Don't think that way.

Near the campfire, Winema stands on a stump and cups her hands to her mouth. She looses a keening howl that sends lightning down my backbone. All the other werewolves throw their heads skyward and howl in reply—deep baying from the men, high singing from the women, shrill squeaks from the werepuppies.

My heart drums against my rib cage. Human fear? Wolfish excitement?

Winema silences everyone with a slice of her hand. "I have called this pack meeting to discuss our current situation. We all know how serious it is."

Mutters and nods.

"We are being hounded even more closely by the police, especially Sheriff Royle. He blundered upon our guards at Klikamuks exactly when the bloodborn and his girlfriend went looking for us. This resulted in a standoff."

Grady marches forward with Cyn, who's smiling a lot less than she was with the werepuppies. He trots her around like a dog in a show, displaying her to the pack. They look at her with narrowed eyes.

"Unfortunately," Winema says, "we had to take this girl hostage."

Jessie strides closer and crosses her arms. "Alpha, if I may speak?"

Winema nods.

"I think," Jessie says, "that we should use the advantage the bloodborn has given us."

"Advantage?"

"The girl." Jessie studies Cyn as if she's a piece on a chessboard. "I know we didn't plan on taking any hostages in Klikamuks, but this may prove to be useful. If we make it very clear to the police that she will be harmed if they continue pursuing us, it may buy us some time and a chance to escape. Then we let her go."

Cyn raises her hand in this classroom-perky way.

"Yes?" Winema says.

"Excuse me," Cyn says, "but I'm really not the best hostage."

"Really." Jessie's smile doesn't touch her eyes. "I'm sure it's important to your family whether you come back alive or dead."

Cyn thins her lips. "Yes, but how is this going to make you look very good? The media is going eat up this story. 'Outlaw werewolf pack kidnaps innocent girl from Klikamuks.' They're never going to let you go."

The hawk-nosed man with long silver hair speaks now. "She has a point."

Winema looks down at him. "What do you suggest instead, Charles?"

"We're already the villains," he says. "We're already going to be running for our lives. Rather than publicizing what we've done, we should keep a low profile and try to get rid of the girl as quickly as possible."

Get rid of? I clench and unclench my fists. I've got to get her out of here.

"And then what?" Jessie says. "Sheriff Royle is hell-bent

on catching us. If we're getting rid of anyone, it should be him."

"We're not killing anyone," Winema says, her voice steely. "Not unless we have to."

Jessie lowers her gaze, but I can see the glint in her eyes.

Isabella touches her sister's arm, then steps forward. "There is another option." She speaks quietly, but everyone listens. "We would have to keep the girl for now, so she doesn't tell the police anything about our plans."

"Yes?" Winema says.

"There is Cliff Sterling."

"Cliff?" Jessie says. "But isn't he the Alpha of the—?"

"I know," Isabella says. "He may be able to offer us protection."

Winema doesn't say anything for a long moment. She stares at the trees and rubs the crease between her eyebrows. "I've met Cliff."

Charles glances at her sharply, like she's kept this from him. "When?"

"Before he was the Alpha of the Zlatroviks. He may be our only hope."

Yeah, sure, that's a great idea. Let's hunt for the Alpha of the most powerful werewolf pack in America. Zlatroviks don't fuck around. From what I've heard, they make this Bitterroot pack look like little girls playing at a tea party.

"Winema," Charles says.

"I understand the moral implications," she says. "And that it may be a long journey."

He looks like he wants to say more, but he nods.

"And the girl?" Jessie looks at Cyn. "Do we use her to get the police off our tails?"

Winema heaves a sigh. "Much as I'd like not to add kidnapping to our record, I'm afraid it's already too late. We might as well."

Cyn frowns, and I can tell she's biting back a question, or an argument.

"All right." Winema looks around the Bitterroot Pack. "Let's go!"

The pack scatters, hurrying to break camp.

Winema and Charles walk past me. I jog after them. "Hey!"

Winema keeps walking, though Charles glances back.

"Hey, Alpha! I'm talking to you."

Winema waits for me to catch up with her before she speaks. "Yes?"

"What about me?" My face heats, I'm not sure why. "Am I a hostage?"

"No. You are bloodborn."

"What's that supposed to mean?" Stop with the cryptic mystical trash.

She walks faster. "You are one of us."

"Fuck no," I mutter under my breath.

This earns me a nasty blue-eyed look from Charles. Damn. Good hearing.

"I'm not part of your pack," I say. Even you know that, you stupid-ass gicks.

Winema swivels and stares at me as if I'm a yipping puppy. "You've been bitten. You haven't changed yet. You're a danger to this pack, yourself, and your family. We can't turn you loose on Klikamuks. Is that clear?"

"That's the stupidest—"

She silences me with a molten glare. "Randall? Get your bloodborn out of here."

ten

Randall hauls me to the baby-blue pickup. Around us, the pack collapses tents and tosses their stuff into trucks and cars. Isabella and Jessie shut Cyn into their cherry-red convertible, then speed away and leave us coughing in their dust.

"Why the fuck are we going to the Zlatroviks?" I ask.

"Don't swear," Randall says. "It's getting annoying."

"Who's Cliff Sterling?"

He gives me a sidelong look. "Their Alpha."

"Well, yeah. But who *is* he?"

"Badass. One time, in Chicago, he took down about a dozen werewolves in broad daylight and the police just let him walk away. He's got them all by the balls."

I narrow my eyes. "So he's going to pull some strings for you guys?"

Randall snorts. "If only it were that easy."

"Meaning?"

"Cliff's favors aren't free."

The way he says it sends invisible spiders down my back.

We get into the pickup and pull out of the campground. The rest of the pack trickles from the trees and follows us down a washboard road. Our caravan of fugitives hits the highway, led by a silver sedan driven by Winema. Within twenty minutes, the pack thins along the highway, until me and Randall seem to be alone.

My heartbeat slows to a dull thumping. Maybe today will be less crazy than yesterday.

Fog floats through bristle-brush pines, mixing with sluggish gray clouds. Along the highway, a river winds like a silver snake. I can see bright leaves reflected in the water, all sorts of colors swirled together: pumpkin, butternut squash, rhubarb-cobbler red. My stomach groans. When am I ever going to be *not* hungry?

"I remember when I was first bloodborn," Randall says. "Had a fierce appetite."

I try to sound only kind of interested. "Oh?"

He glances at me, his eyebrows raised, then laughs. "You curious?"

"A little," I mutter, since it's easier to be gruff.

"Hmmm." Randall rakes his fingers through his wild, thick hair. He glances out his window, rolls it down, and rests his arm there. "Well, I was sixteen when it happened. It was Reagan Moore who did it."

I'm silent for a moment. "He's your sire or whatever?"

"She'd be your granddam."

"She?"

"Yeah. Her parents gave her one of those ambiguous names." His eyes look shadowy. "You can usually track bloodlines pretty far back. Especially if they're pack wolves. Not so easy, though, if a lone wolf bites people."

"So what happened with Reagan?"

"We met in high school. She screwed me over. I got into deep shit and left home."

"Wait, wait, that's it? No details?"

Randall sighs. "Reagan was one of those naturally gorgeous girls, you know? She knew it, too, and always dressed sexy. But that actually turned me off at first. I thought she was just a one-night-stand kind of girl."

I nod, thinking of some of the girls at Klikamuks High.

"She was way smarter than that, though." Randall laughs bleakly. "Really knew how to wrap people around her little finger. I started lusting after her, even though my mom called her trouble. Eventually, she started calling her *mardagayl*."

"Huh?"

"*Mardagayl*. Armenian for werewolf."

"You're Armenian?"

"Half. My mom was. My never-present dad wasn't. My sister really got the looks, though. Olive skin, black hair."

"Sister?"

His face tightens. "I had a sister. She hasn't talked to me in years. Neither has my mom."

"Why?"

"They knew Reagan was going to ruin me, even though I didn't believe them. There are some old Armenian stories about women whose deadly sins doom them to live as a werewolf for seven years. My mom really isn't all that superstitious, but after a certain point, even she started looking for Reagan's wolfskin."

"So…you hooked up with Reagan, and…"

"What?" Randall scrunches his nose.

My face flames. "Sex ed. They talked about all sorts of disgusting shit, like herpes and chlamydia. And the werewolf disease."

"Oh? Werewolves are like chlamydia, now? You sure do know how to be offensive." He says this like he doesn't give a damn.

And you sure do know how to be a royal asshole.

Out loud, I say, "You know what I meant. I'm not good with words."

"Clearly." Randall snorts. "And no, she bit me first."

"How?"

Randall's eyes focus on some distant place. "I asked her."

"You asked her? But *why*?"

"She showed me what it was like to be a werewolf. And I was fascinated by how strong and beautiful it could be. I wanted to join her, wanted to know what it was like to be able to run faster and fight harder than any human."

I'm staring at him, my heart thumping.

"You have to understand," he says, "that I grew up in L.A. The gangs were awful. Humans versus Others a lot of the time. So when I asked Reagan to bite me, she understood why I wanted to become a werewolf."

"What happened when you first changed?"

"They hadn't invented Lycanthrox then. Without it, the virus multiplied to a critical level in a matter of weeks. The first transformations were brutal on me, but I didn't dare go to any doctors. Reagan tried to help me, for a while, but she got sick of my unpredictability. She didn't think I'd be so wild. Pretty soon, we were arguing more often than not, and she dumped me for a guy from another pack."

"Wow. That blows."

"That's an understatement."

Silence passes for several miles. We're winding along switchbacks now, climbing higher into the mountains. I steal glances at Randall, trying to imagine what he was like as a human, and as a new bloodborn. Reagan must have really been something, to be able to make werewolves look beautiful to him.

"I need to teach you," Randall says, "how to be a werewolf."

"What does that mean?"

He gives me a piercing stare. "First, how to change."

An invisible fist tightens around my ribs. "It's not the full moon anymore."

"Oh, come on. You already know we don't need that to change. Besides, it's better to do it now, rather than have the full moon forcing you."

I swallow hard and say nothing.

"I know you're scared. I don't think I've ever known a bloodborn who wasn't."

A dozen comebacks spring to my tongue, but I grimace instead. "When?"

He meets my eyes. "When do you want to?"

Spiders of fear skittle down my spine, because yeah, I'm scared. I've spent all my time as a bloodborn trying not to change, and now he's asking me to willingly shove aside Brock the Human and unleash Brock the Beast.

At last, I say, "I don't."

Randall just sighs.

We stop in Skykomish, a tiny town that's mostly a few stores strung along the weed-choked tracks of an old railroad line. Cloudy mountains and tree-furred foothills slumber in the background. Logging trucks brake at the one and only intersection before rumbling on. The buildings look old, two centuries old, with peeling paint, boarded-up windows, and dead grass drying beneath the autumn leaves.

"Why are we stopping?" I say. "Aren't we supposed to be hightailing it out of here?"

Randall says nothing.

Outside a gas station, there's Winema's silver sedan. Guarded by Charles, she drops quarters into a rusty blue pay phone. And there, just round the back, the cherry-red convertible. Jessie and Isabella sit watching Cyn.

Randall gets out and opens my door. "Winema might need you."

I frown at him. What are they going to do?

"Hello?" Winema says. "Is this the Snohomish County Sheriff's Office?"

Oh, shit.

"Yes, I'd like to report something." Winema leans against the wall, her eyes heavy-lidded. "About the kidnapping of Cynthia Lopez. I have information." She beckons for Jessie and Isabella to bring Cyn closer. "If the police continue to pursue the Bitterroot Pack, they will only endanger the girl." She pauses. "What do I mean by that?"

Jessie smiles a cruel smile, enjoying this little act.

"The Bitterroot Pack is tired of being hounded by the police." Winema's voice is soft and dangerous, like steel hidden in velvet. "They want to be left alone. If the police leave the pack alone, then the girl will be safe."

Cyn stares straight ahead, her lips thin, her eyes glittering.

"How do I know this?" Winema laughs quietly. "How do you think?" Her face sobers. "She's here right now. Cynthia."

I step toward them, handcuffed, useless.

"I can prove it." Winema shoves the phone into Cyn's face. "Take it. Tell them."

Cyn's cheeks flush, and she dares to glare at Winema, if only for a second. Her fingers shake as they curl around the phone. "Hello?"

You don't have to help them, Cyn. Don't make this easy for them.

"Yes, this is Cynthia Lopez." She has the nerve to use her singsongy telephone voice. "Yes, I'm all right. The pack hasn't harmed me, but you should do what they say. I—" She frowns, her face even redder now. "Can you do that?"

"Careful," Winema murmurs.

"Mom?" Cyn's voice wobbles. "Yes, it's me." Her eyes glitter. "No, they haven't hurt me. No, Mom. Mom!"

Winema rests her hand on Cyn's shoulder with gentle menace.

"Mom." Cyn's voice catches. "Please, let me talk. You can't send the police after me, okay? I'm safe so long as the werewolves are safe. They just want to be left alone. As soon as they get away, they're going to send me home, but there can't be any police. Mom, listen to me. There *can't* be any police. I have to go. Goodbye." She says this last part very quickly, then hangs up, the glittering in her eyes nearly tears.

"Good," Winema says.

Cyn brushes the werewolf's hand from her shoulder, then gives me a stare that twists my guts. Why me? I'm not the bad guy here.

But I don't manage to get any of the words out.

After making the call to the police, we vanish from Sky-komish and hurry east.

We cross the mountains and drive through endless fields beneath a sky so blue it doesn't look real. I stare at the mashed-potato clouds, and despite knowing who I am and where I'm going, I feel a sort of calm settle in my stomach. I keep thinking of Cyn, and wishing we could walk together. I would point to the crops and tell her the name of each, and how my mom knew how to cook delicious food from every vegetable.

If I ever get out of this, that's what I'm going to do.

It's late when we stop at a pitiful excuse for a town, just a few buildings at the crossroads and wheat fields whispering around us. Crickets chirp beneath the darkening purple sky. A cantaloupe moon glows orange above, about as bright as the old streetlights with moths swirling around them—waning, but still three-quarters full. A shiver trickles down my shoulders, nothing more. When will the Lycanthrox finally wear off?

Randall parks outside a café and checks his watch. "Time for dinner."

I nod, and my stomach rumbles in agreement.

We walk into the café. Inside, it looks kind of like an old diner, kind of like a rustic restaurant. On one of the tables, there's a half-finished, thousand-piece puzzle of a train. The place seems abandoned.

"Hello?" Randall calls.

A white-bearded guy who looks as rundown as the town shuffles out of the back room, drying his hands on his pants. "Evening! My name's Ford."

What, like the car? I glance at Randall, but he doesn't offer our names.

"What'll it be?" Ford says.

"What do you have?" Randall asks, settling in a chair.

"Well…" Ford squints as if remembering. "We have the bacon and cheese sandwich, the grilled cheese, the eggs and ham…" He rambles on for another minute or two while Randall gazes out the window.

Outside, Isabella and Jessie's red convertible cruises up, top down, Cyn in the back.

I clear my throat. "I'll have the bacon and cheese, the Reuben, and some curly fries. Oh, and a slice of blackberry pie with vanilla ice cream, please."

Randall glances at me, his eyebrows raised. "You got money?"

"Uh…" I reach into the pockets of my jeans, but of course I don't have my wallet.

Randall grins, his teeth bright. "It's on me."

"All right, then," Ford says. "And you, sir?"

"Biscuits, gravy, sausage. Thanks."

Ford nods and shuffles off again. I joggle my leg while we wait, and Randall reads a yellowed brochure on tractors. The bell on the door jingles and in walk Jessie and Isabella, followed by Cyn. They stop when they see us.

"Oh," Cyn says, "they beat us to it." Her cheeks look flushed from the convertible ride.

My stomach tightens when I see her looking so wind-swept-beautiful like that. There's a wild glint in her eyes, what she likes to call *adventurous*.

"That's all right," Isabella says. "Not enough of us here for Winema to worry."

Cyn drifts toward the opposite side of the café, sitting in a corner booth. Isabella glances at us, her eyes slightly narrowed.

"Hey," Randall says, waving.

Isabella approaches him. "We've got about an hour, and then we're moving out. Winema doesn't want us staying still for too long."

"Makes sense."

Ford reappears. "It'll be a minute," he says to us. "Got to wake the cook."

Isabella clears her throat, and he looks at her as if he just noticed.

"Evening! My, we don't get this many visitors usually! What you would like?"

"A menu, please."

Ford rummages behind a counter. "Those are a little...outdated..."

"Well, then," Isabella says with a smile, "we'll have your special of the day."

"Sounds good." Ford glances between Isabella and Jessie—I'll bet their dark skin looks foreign to him—and then his eyes settle on the fading streak of flamingo pink in Cyn's hair. "Where are you folks from? Down south?"

"Why, yes." Isabella gives Ford a sweet smile. "And we're all very famished."

Nodding to himself, Ford disappears into the back

again. He shouts something, though I can't make out the words.

"Wow," Cyn murmurs. "I didn't think towns like this still existed."

Isabella chuckles. "This one is only barely existing."

From the kitchen, I hear bacon sizzling, followed by the aroma of crispy-smoky deliciousness. My stomach rumbles like thunder. I start dreaming about how my sandwiches are going to crunch between my teeth.

After a couple of minutes, Randall clears his throat and shuffles his feet. "This is going to take a while, isn't it?"

I shrug.

"I'm going to make a call, all right?" He stands. "Stay out of trouble."

I shrug again. Randall strides out the door. I pick up the tractor brochure he left and pretend to be interested while I eavesdrop on Jessie and Isabella. They aren't talking very loudly, but my hearing is sharper than it used to be.

"Have you ever met Cliff Sterling?" Isabella says.

"No," Jessie says. "Why?"

"They say he never goes anywhere without a gold-and-blue lily pinned to his lapel. It's a gift from the Faerie Queen. His lover."

Jessie rolls her eyes. "Why would she fool around with a werewolf?"

"Think about it." Isabella arches her eyebrows. "His pack has a monopoly on bootleg faerie wine. And he looks a whole lot younger than his age, thanks to being one of the Faerie Queen's favorites. Her magic rubs off on him."

Jessie laughs. "Oh really? I should find myself a faerie, if it's better than Botox."

"I'm pretty sure it's got to be the Faerie Queen."

Jessie grimaces. "Never mind." She pauses. "What about sleeping with Cliff? Would that work? I hear he's real handsome."

"I'm not even going to dignify that with a reply," Isabella says.

Cyn's gaze flicks between the two women as they talk. She's obviously curious. Hopefully not about meeting Cliff herself.

Jessie grabs a menu from another table. "Lord, nothing is cheap anymore. We can't afford all this."

"I'm not that hungry," Cyn says.

Jessie smiles wickedly. "Oh, but we're going to fatten you up, little girl."

Cyn returns her smile. "I think that's Hansel and Gretel, not Little Red Riding Hood."

"Fairy tales." Jessie snorts, but she can't help looking amused. She leans back and crosses her legs. "Maybe you can help us."

"Help?" Cyn says. "What sort of help?"

"You'll see," Jessie says.

Isabella gives her sister a look. "We're talking financial help?"

"Mmm-hmm," Jessie says, and she stands.

Shit. This doesn't sound good.

"Excuse me, sir!" Jessie calls through the back door. "Could I ask a question?"

In a muffled voice, Ford calls, "Yes?"

"Do you have any gluten-free foods? My cousin is allergic."

He pokes his head through the doorway, a puzzled scowl on his face. "Gluten?"

"Wheat products." Jessie waves at the fields outside with a sigh. "No?" She glances at Cyn. "I guess we'll just have to go back to that gas station and try to make a dinner out of snacks. Sorry, hon."

Cyn frowns, but she has no allergies that I know about.

"Just a minute," Ford says to Jessie, and he turns to Cyn. "What *can* you eat?"

"Um…" Face red, Cyn glances at Isabella, then shrugs.

"Let me see," Jessie says, "what you've got round back."

She's already walking behind the counter, hips swaying in an I'm-in-charge-here way. Ford runs his hand over his thin white hair, waves his arm as if it were his idea to let Jessie into the back, and then follows at her heels.

As soon as they're out of sight, Isabella stands. "Wait there, Cynthia."

And Cyn doesn't say anything, just nods.

Isabella ducks behind the counter next, but she doesn't follow Jessie into the back room. Instead, she slides over to the cash register and smiles. She hits a few buttons with expert speed, and the till clanks open with a ring.

Cyn sucks in her breath, her eyes bright.

Isabella scoops all of the money out of the register, unzips her purse, and drops the bills in. Then, she shuts the cash register and steps away just as Jessie and Ford walk out of the back room. The smallest of nods passes between the sisters.

"Find anything?" Isabella says, her hand on her hip like she was waiting there.

"No." Jessie shakes her head. "Don't want to risk it."

Cyn's sitting bolt upright, her fingers gripping the edge of her seat. But she still isn't saying anything. Dammit, do I have to talk?

Just then, Randall walks back in, sliding his cell phone into his pocket.

Isabella taps him on the shoulder. "You might want to get yours to go."

"To go?" A shadow of understanding passes over his face. "Now?"

"Yes," she says. "Unless you just want to come with us."

Randall's hand closes around the door handle. "We're coming with you."

"But…" Ford looks between them, confusion in his watery eyes. "I can make you something special, without any of that gluten stuff…"

This is ridiculous. Fucking ridiculous.

I shove my chair away from the table and lumber to my feet. "Excuse me," I say. "But could I have a word, sir?"

Ford frowns and rubs his nose. "Sorry?"

Randall's hand clamps on my biceps so hard it bruises. "It's not worth the trouble."

"But—"

"Have a nice night," Randall says to Ford, as he steers me outside.

Isabella and Jessie stroll out after us with Cyn. Isabella squeezes her plump purse, then vaults over the closed door of the red convertible and lands in the driver's seat, laughing. Jessie shushes her, but she can't help smiling too. Cyn looks somewhat dazed, a pink flush in her cheeks—what's she thinking right now?

"I can't believe you two," Randall says, shaking his head. "We'd better get out of here."

Jessie leans against the hood of the convertible and grins. "And visit a decent restaurant!"

"That was unbelievable," Cyn says in a quiet voice.

I give her a look. "You didn't have to let them do that."

"What's that supposed to mean?" She glares at me as she climbs into the convertible.

"They robbed an old man!"

Randall shushes me and drags me into the blue pickup. "Shut the hell up before you get us all arrested, bloodborn."

"I'd love to see you get arrested."

He growls under his breath and slams the door behind me.

As we drive away, I see Ford in the doorway, frowning, his hand raised in goodbye.

"Makes me sick," I say. "How can you do shit like that?"

Randall keeps his eyes on the nighttime road. "Where else are we going to get money?"

"You're all criminals."

"Yeah. Exactly."

He rolls down the window, and the wind of our passing hisses through the wheat.

"Maybe if you tried earning some money for once, instead of making things worse—"

"Oh, so you have a job?"

"No, but—"

"That's what I thought." Randall shakes his head. "Good luck putting that on your resume. 'Werewolf seeking position as nanny.'"

I laugh, then swallow. Don't want to sound like I actually think he's funny.

"Your girlfriend didn't seem all that bothered," he says.

"She's not my girlfriend anymore."

Randall smiles, kind of smugly. He turns on the radio and fiddles with the dial. A new hit by Bloodless fills the truck. "Too late to understand/Too late to go back now/I've crossed the turning point/By turning you."

"You like?" he says.

I realize I'm nodding my head, and stop myself. "Yeah," I grunt.

"It's about being bloodborn, you know," he says. "Vampires, of course."

"Well, yeah," I say. "Everybody knows all vampires are bloodborn. No baby vampires." I think for a minute. "Not like werepuppies."

Randall just snorts.

"You guys hate each other, right? Leeches versus curs?"

"That's a stereotype. We get in fights occasionally, but the bloodborn have to stick together."

"Do *not* use this as an opportunity to try and convince me we should be best buds."

Randall laughs, and startlingly enough, it sounds genuine. "You know, I really only care about you not getting killed on my watch or going on a murderous rampage. Other than that, I don't care if we're barely on speaking terms."

"Fantastic," I mutter.

"But if you try hard enough," Randall says, "you might be good enough for the pack."

"Like I'd want that."

"Well, you don't really have many other options." His forehead furrows. "I mean, I've tried living as a lone wolf. It sucks."

I hide a shiver. "So this is it? My life from now on?"

"This is only the beginning," Randall says, and he turns up the music.

eleven

Whatever Isabella and Jessie do with their stolen money, I don't know. Me and Randall stop at the next drive-through along the highway—Bigfoot's Big Burgers, with a giant smiling Sasquatch on the sign, looking about as dumb as a trained bear. Wow, this sure is a backwoods town; back around Seattle, those political correctness people would be all over that sign in less than a heartbeat. "Blatant racism," they'd say, which is a little stupid. As far as I know, Sasquatches don't even come in different colors.

Randall lets me order two Bigfoot burgers and a Cactus Cat shake without even a nasty comment. Fatigue creases his eyes.

"Tired?" I say, as we start driving again.

Randall steers one-handed, a half-eaten Bigfoot burger

in his grip. "I was wrong. You aren't a moron. You're a genius."

"You must be tired. Even your sarcasm sucks."

He gives me a sideways glare, but doesn't say anything more.

"This is a damn good shake," I say, smug now that he's not talking. "Cactus Cat shake." I stare at the cartoon on the side of the cup, a yowling bobcat with spikes for fur. "I've never seen a real Cactus Cat, come to think of it."

"Cause they've been extinct for about a hundred years. Just like unicorns."

"Oh."

You know, I don't even know how many Others got hunted to zero.

Once we cross the state line into Idaho, we make camp in a meadow ringed by ponderosa pines. Thank God I don't have to sleep in the same tent as Randall. Instead, I get a blanket and a spot under the stars. Most in the pack have shapeshifted for sleeping, cozy in their wolf pelts.

The thinning moon, almost a perfect oval, peeks over the mountains in the west. Her power feels stronger, now that I'm closer to the sky. I clench fistfuls of the blanket, my muscles taut, and warily watch the moon. Her glow crests over the peaks, then pours into the meadow, filling it slowly with moonlight.

I glance at the wolves. One of them flicks an ear. Another stretches and yawns, tongue curling, then goes back to sleep.

A shiver skitters down my spine. The night grows brighter and brighter, like someone's turning up the dimmer for a light. Icy tingles cross my exposed skin. I roll over and tug the blanket tight over my head, like I'm a little kid hiding from a monster—if I can't see it, it can't see me.

Only I'm the monster.

A pang shoots through my gut. I curl and hug myself. My nails—claws?—dig into my arms. God dammit. No Lycanthrox here to help me; now I'm really fucked. *You know that stuff doesn't work, right?* If Randall can be believed.

Got to get out of the light. I crawl into the shadows of the trees, wrapping the blanket around me like a cloak. The tug of the moon wanes, and I can breathe a little easier. I realize I'm shaking, cold sweat dotting my skin.

Ahead, I hear whispers.

"Yes, but I didn't expect this would be such a burden."

Randall. And then, Winema.

"You should have considered the consequences before you bit anyone. You have already caused the death of one boy, and the birth of a bloodborn."

"I know." Randall's voice rises. "But I—"

"Shhh," Winema says. "Mind the pups."

I inch nearer in a crouch. My breathing sounds too loud, but I manage to get close enough to see them, standing beneath a tree.

Randall lowers his voice. "But I don't know if I'm ready for this. I don't know if I can handle being a sire. I mean, I'm only twenty-seven."

Winema sighs and her hand drifts to her belly. "I'm not sure any of us ever feel ready."

"If only he weren't so damn *rebellious*," Randall mutters. "Then I could handle it."

She laughs gently. "Remember when you first came to this pack?"

"Hey, I wasn't that bad."

"Oh, yes you were. I'm amazed Jessie even convinced you to come up north. You were a real troublemaker. Had the cops on your tail."

"My dam abandoned me. I didn't know what to do."

"Which is why you can't abandon Brock."

Randall sighs and swings his head toward the moon. "He hasn't changed yet."

"You will need to show him," Winema says.

He nods. "Eventually."

"Soon," she says. "Before it's too late."

"All right." Randall retreats from his Alpha. "Good night."

Winema kneels in a cluster of ferns. I peer harder and make out the shapes of the three werepuppies sleeping in a lump. Winema stokes one between the eyes, and it licks its nose happily. She smiles to herself.

Charles pads closer, his long silver hair bright in the moonlight, and crouches beside her. "How are you feeling?"

"The moon is waning," Winema whispers. "The baby is fine."

"Are you sure?" he says,

"Yes." Her voice sounds tight.

"Winema…maybe we should go to the doctor. Just this once."

"No."

"But you haven't—"

"I said no." Winema sighs. "It's your turn as watch."

Charles straightens. "Be careful." He walks away.

The baby. Go to a doctor. The moon. What does being pregnant do to a werewolf? Or maybe…what does being a werewolf do to a pregnant woman? My ears hot, I start to stand, trying to be as quiet as possible.

"Brock," she says, "I know you're there."

I flinch, grabbing fistfuls of leaves. She must've smelled me.

"Come here," she says.

I climb to my feet, shivery and shaky-legged like a newborn calf. "Yeah?"

Winema meets my gaze, her eyes catching the moonlight. "Do you understand what position you are in right now?"

"Yeah." I look away. "I got bitten, so you guys won't let me go."

"Do you understand what it means to be bloodborn?"

A sweet, fresh wind scented with rain and forest slips across my face. I shudder with longing. I don't want to be here, standing still, not knowing where I want to go, just wanting to run far away and forget it all.

"Brock?"

I close my eyes. "It means I'm going to become a werewolf."

"You *are* a werewolf. You need to understand that."

"Yeah, yeah, I know." I tighten my calves, my muscles itching to move. "I've got to embrace my inner wolf, whatever. What if I don't want to?"

She stares unblinkingly at me. "You can control the wolf, or let it control you."

I frown. "How is the second different from the first?"

"When the full moon comes, the change will tear apart your mind and body. You might die. You might go insane, consumed by the desire to bite and infect. If that doesn't kill you, we will—and it will be the merciful thing to do."

My mouth goes dry, but I shrug and shuffle away. It's only when I'm sure she can't see me anymore that I let myself tremble. I clench my hands to still them. I stare at the moon to prove that I can control myself.

I don't want this. I don't want to have no choice.

You made this choice already, when you decided to hunt the werewolves. You didn't have to follow Randall. You didn't have to fight him.

I growl at my powerlessness and punch a tree, the bark bloodying my knuckles.

Someone coughs nearby, and my head snaps toward the sound. "Cyn?"

She stands in the shadows, leaning against the red convertible, her hoodie shadowing her face. "What happened?"

I fold my arms to hide my scraped fingers. "Nothing."

"Brock," she says, in her I-don't-believe-you-for-a-second voice.

"Winema said they're going to kill me if I can't control the change."

Cyn steps toward me and throws back her hood, her face white in the moonlight. "What are you going to do?"

"Escape? That sound like a good idea to you?"

"But…you can't escape who you are now."

"Thanks for reminding me, Cyn."

She purses her lips, then shudders so hard her eyelids flutter.

"What's wrong?" I say.

She hugs herself and rubs her arms. "It's cold out here."

"Really? I'm actually sweating." I can feel the heat radiating off my skin.

Squinting in the darkness, Cyn comes close enough to touch my forehead with the back of her hand. Her skin's like ice. "Oh, wow, you are."

"You're freezing!" I press her hand between mine. "That hoodie isn't warm enough."

"But you're burning up. Feverish. Are you okay?"

I shrug. "It's normal, I think. For a werewolf."

Cyn looks at me in this strange, soft way. "When we broke up, you hated werewolves so much it scared me. And now that you are one…how do you feel?"

"Like shit."

"And?"

"And what?" I let go of her hand. "What else is there?"

She sighs, and looks so sad that I wish I'd said something different. "I don't know," she says. "Maybe I'm an idiot. Maybe I'm totally wrong about you."

I wish I knew what she thought of me.

She's standing completely away from me now, not touching me anymore, even though she's still shivering in the cold night air.

"Ugh," she says. "I feel kind of lightheaded."

"Why?"

She wrinkles her nose. "Jessie and Isabella ended up spending all their money on meat. I mean raw meat. I wasn't about to eat nasty uncooked beef."

I remember stopping at Bigfoot's Big Burgers. "I should have bought you something for dinner. I didn't think of that."

She shrugs. "I can figure something out."

"Cyn, we're in the middle of the mountains in the middle of the night. There are no towns or anything for miles. The werewolves are watching us, so we can't really borrow a car and drive down to the nearest Safeway."

She sighs a long sigh, and I realize how tired she is.

"Cynthia…come here."

"What?" She just stares at me, her eyes wary.

"Come here. I won't hurt you."

Before she can step away, I rest my hand behind the small of her back and draw her closer. She stiffens at my touch.

"You need to warm up," I say quietly.

Cyn makes a small noise of protest, then sighs again and rests her head against my chest. "Okay. But just because you're hot."

"What?" I laugh, surprised.

"Oh, you know I didn't mean it like that," she grumbles against my shirt.

We stand like that, not quite holding each other, breathing to the same rhythm. A sweetness, warmed by my body, rises to my nose. I glance down and see the miniature rose blossom tucked in her pocket. The scent uncorks a flood of calm throughout my body, the same I felt whenever Mom talked me out of my fear or pain.

"You kept the rose," I say.

"Yeah," she says.

I smile a little. "That thing's indestructible."

"I've missed seeing you smile," she whispers.

I blush, and I don't know what to say.

"Here," I say. "I'm going to get you a blanket so you stop shivering."

"Brock, you don't—"

"And some food," I say. "I can hear your stomach growling from here." That's not really true, but I'm sure she's got to be starving.

Before she can act all tough and too-smart-for-this, I walk round to the blue pickup and yank off the tarp covering everything. Sure enough, in an old duffel bag there are some flannel blankets, worn but clean. I toss one to Cyn, who catches it and gives me a sigh, but I can tell she's trying not to smile.

"Now, food," I say.

I open one of the coolers in the truck, and its hinges make this horrible death-squeal. I cringe and glance around.

A few glowing eyes stare at me, their annoyance as plain as day, but soon enough the werewolves go back to sleep.

"Better be quiet." Cyn hops up beside me on the truck bed. "Let me see what's in there."

We find some sliced American cheese and a couple of cans of baked beans and franks. She wrinkles her nose, but peels plastic from the cheese slices, one by one, and eats them all. I pop open the cans and hold them out to her.

"What a romantic moonlit dinner," she says, with a roll of her eyes.

Startled, I glance at the moon hanging above the pines. She hasn't been tormenting me, even though my skin is drenched in her light. Cyn has more power over me? But no...now that I'm looking at the moon, and thinking about the wolf curled inside me, the familiar sick twisting feeling wakes up in my stomach.

"These are disgusting," Cyn says, as she eats the beans and franks with her fingers.

"Yeah." My voice sounds too hoarse, and I cough. "But you have to eat."

She isn't even noticing how I clench my jaw and ball my hands into fists, how the moon sinks a hook between my ribs and reels me in. A shudder ripples through me, and I bend double for a second. This time, Cyn notices.

"Now *you're* shivering," she says. "Are you sure you're okay?"

I shake my head. "The moon is out."

"Well, get out of the moonlight! You're standing right

in it." Cyn jumps down from the truck and grabs my arm to steer me away.

Her fingers scald my skin. My heartbeat thuds rapid-fire in my chest; my lips are pressed together to hide the fact that my teeth are itching, maybe sharpening into fangs. When I look at her, I feel a longing so sharp it hurts.

What longing? I don't know, and that scares me more than anything.

"Brock, what's going on?"

"You should go," I say. A churning in my stomach sickens me. "I don't...I don't want you seeing me like this."

Cyn furrows her forehead. "You look normal to me. Just sick. Are you...?"

"No. I don't know. Please." My spine crack, crack, cracks and I hunch over. "Cynthia!"

"I'm not leaving." Her face looks hard. "Not unless I know you're going to be okay."

I let her tug me out of the moonlight and into the deepest shadows. I huddle with my back against the bark of a tree, panting, staring at the dizzying pattern of the pine-needle shadows. The Lycanthrox must be wearing off at last. I imagine the virus copying itself over and over in my veins until my blood swarms with squirming disease.

"Better?" Cyn asks, crouching in front of me.

I blow out my breath and nod. "Don't know how that happened. Caught me off guard."

"You still haven't changed yet?"

"Never."

She inspects my face. "You okay now?"

"Yes."

I wipe the sweat from my forehead and climb to my feet. "I'm going to sleep now." I grab another blanket from the pickup truck.

I still don't trust myself. She needs to go, as much as I wish she would stay.

"All right," she says. "Good night, then."

"Good night."

I watch her disappear in the trees, then lie back on the blanket and exhale hard. I'm sure I disappointed the wolf inside me. Tough luck. Around me, the pack sleeps in their fur. I don't see a human among them. I roll away from them and shut my eyes, trying to ignore the silent desperation that swells inside me, filling my chest to bursting.

Sleep, Brock. Sleep.

twelve

I wake up in my bedroom, back home at the dairy. Outside, I hear the buzz of a weed whacker. I jump out of bed, kicking blankets aside, and go to the window. Dad and Chris are trimming the thicket of blackberries out back. I must've overslept; I promised I would help them. Not bothering with breakfast, I go outside.

"Hey!" I shout, waving to get their attention. "Need some help?"

Chris kills his weed whacker and walks to me, tugging off his ear muffs. His skin glistens; his hair stands in sweaty spikes. "About time you dragged your lazy ass out of bed," he says. "Bring the wheelbarrow over, okay?"

I nod. The pungent smell of gasoline and chopped vegetation fills my nose. I jog to the wheelbarrow by the kitchen garden and yank it out of the overgrown weeds. I'm already starting to sweat in the summer sun, so I peel off my shirt.

As I turn back to Dad and Chris, I see them shimmer in the heat. They look tiny against the giant tangle of blackberries. Vines arch high overhead, reaching down, snaking around to dig spikes into flesh. Dad and Chris fight back the blackberries with their weed whackers, but the blackberries keep growing, twisting around their arms and legs, impaling them on thorns. I ditch the wheelbarrow and grab a fallen weed whacker.

"Brock!" Chris shouts. "A little help over here!"

I attack a python-thick blackberry vine, butchering its sinewy stem, and another hisses through the grass toward me. I chop it in half. Above me, Dad and Chris twist helplessly in the grip of the brambles. Their blood drips onto the grass.

I've got to hurry. The werewolves will smell the blood and come for them.

I hack at the vines, killing as many as I can, sweat soaking my armpits, until my arms are slick with red—red? I turn off the weed whacker. The dry grass guzzles the blood that drips from above. Slowly, I lift my gaze.

No. No! I toss aside the weed whacker. My dad and my brother dangle from thorny nooses, their skin slashed to ribbons, their guts bared, their limbs hacked away. I killed them. I killed them both. But I don't know why.

I wake up, really wake up, on my blanket in the meadow. I'm lying on my stomach, sweat pooling in the hollow of my back. Watery light seeps from the gray sky and trickles through the ponderosas. It isn't quite dawn yet.

Okay. That was just a really messed-up dream. Your hands aren't bloody, see?

I press my fist into my mouth, my throat tight, my eyes burning. God dammit. I suck in a ragged breath and bite my knuckles.

How could I forget what it felt like when Mom died? How could I forget what came after the days of feeling numb? But I was only eleven then, and I thought the world was ending. I can't remember how I made the nightmares go away. I mean, I knew my mind was a little screwy, but this is nearing bat-shit insane.

I don't have much time to think. At sunrise, we break camp.

Randall drives with the window down, one arm out, like we're on a road trip instead of on the run. Pine forest gives way to rolling lion-colored hills, pungent with sagebrush, then valleys of golden grain. All around us, tooth-sharp mountains reach for the blue, blue sky. My heart swells against my ribs like it's trying to grow bigger.

"Where are we?" I ask Randall.

"We just left Idaho. We're nearing Paradise Valley, Montana."

"Huh. I've never been to Montana before."

I pretend not to be so excited at the sight of so much wilderness. That's the wolf talking.

Aspens grow here, brilliant against the blue sky, their leaves glittering like golden coins—no, brighter, like yellow dragon scales. I read somewhere that dragons used to be real, but now all you can see are some bones that look like dinosaurs, only different. Humans did that—hunted every last dragon to death. I wonder if werewolves will be extinct one day, just a footnote in some textbook about terrible diseases.

I doubt it. Terrible diseases die hard.

Around noon, we stop at a hole-in-the-wall shack that calls itself a restaurant—Chuck's Chinese. While Randall orders some chow mein to go, I stare at the peeling piss-colored wallpaper and fat bottle flies humming around the ceiling fan. Then this enormous flame-feathered bird catches my eye. It's mounted above the door to the kitchen, its glass eyes dull, its dusty red wings spread like it might still fly.

"Whoa," I say. "What is that?"

"Dead," Randall says, counting change. He must be almost broke.

The Chinese guy at the cash register—Chuck, I guess—shakes his balding head. "*Fenghuang* are immortal. Firebird, in English. Like a…a…" He snaps his fingers as he remembers. "A phoenix."

"Phoenix?" I arch my eyebrows. "I thought they couldn't die."

"Apparently not," Randall says, his eyes on the taxidermied bird.

Chuck shakes his head again. "That's made out of rooster

and pheasant feathers, with whole lot of red dye. A fake feng-huang, for good luck."

Randall squints at him. "So pretending you killed an immortal bird is good luck?"

Chuck shrugs. "Works on the locals."

"I'm amazed you get any business at all," Randall mutters. "Have a nice day."

We exit Chuck's Chinese and share a look.

"People believe some pretty weird shit about Others," I say.

"That's an understatement."

"I wish people thought I was lucky. Kiss my ass and all your wishes will be granted."

Randall snorts, and I can tell he's trying not to laugh.

We gobble the chow mein in the parking lot, then hit the road.

Someone honks at us and the cherry-red convertible cruises up alongside, Isabella at the wheel. Cyn sits shotgun, her feet on the dashboard, her hair flying wild. Behind her, Jessie paints her nails black.

Randall rolls down his window. "Hello, ladies."

Cyn looks languidly at us. Thick eyeliner rings her brown eyes, and I blink at the startling contrast. What did those werewolves do to her?

Isabella looks over her sunglasses. "Excuse me?"

"Kind of chilly day for a convertible, don't you think?" Randall shouts.

Jessie laughs. "You just can't take it, boy."

"Drive faster," Isabella says. "You're holding up the rest of the pack."

She revs the engine and roars past us. Their laughter trails on the wind. Randall doesn't even try to chase them in our old truck.

"Damn," I say. "Are they always like that?"

Randall glances at me. "Isabella and Jessie? Yeah. They're pretty outrageous."

I grimace. "I don't know what's gotten into Cyn. Just last night she was cold and hungry, since Isabella and Jessie totally forgot about her."

He glances at me again, this time with a sharp look in his eyes. "Did they?"

"Yeah. You should tell Winema."

"Cyn is a hostage."

I stare straight out the windshield. "Doesn't mean you have to treat her like shit."

Randall makes a neutral noise that could mean anything.

I hope Cyn isn't up to no good. Sometimes she believes she can think her way out of any sort of trouble, which I know for a fact isn't true.

We keep driving for maybe an hour or two, while darkening clouds boil like devil's soup above the mountains. Ice scents the wind, and I can feel it in my bones—winter's coming. Even the river alongside the highway looks sluggish. Randall keeps his window all the way down, his face blank, the breeze scattering his hair.

Suddenly, he eases up on the gas. "What happened here?"

Not too far ahead, the red convertible rests in the grass, way off the road. Isabella and Jessie stand arguing beside it, jabbing their hands in the air. I spot Cyn standing by herself near the riverbank, her back to the road.

Randall pulls up alongside them and hops out. "Let me check this out."

He leaves his window open, and I can hear everything.

"To hell with these backwoods highways." Jessie drags on a cigarette.

"Flat?" Randall asks.

Jessie narrows her eyes. "What does it look like, sweetie?"

"Honey," Isabella says, "we have the spare. It'll last us the rest of the way."

"What rest of the way?" Jessie's laugh turns into a cough, and she flicks her cigarette onto the pavement. "This sharp gravel is only the start of it. Haven't you noticed the stink of asphalt? Road construction, could last for hours."

She points with a sharp-nailed finger. In the distance, steam rises from freshly repaved road, and the faint beeps of machinery echo off the hills.

Randall swears and pulls out his cell phone. "Winema? We're going to be here awhile."

I open my door and slip outside. My legs feel numb, so I walk toward Cyn, my blood warming as it stirs again.

I walk up behind her, then gently touch her shoulder. "Cyn."

She swings her head toward me like a frightened deer. "You startled me!"

"Sorry."

We stand looking at each other for a moment, and unspoken words drift between us, as thick as the clouds above us. She looks rosy-faced and wild, her hair spiked by the wind.

"Last night," she says, "did you…?"

"Change? No." I clear my throat. "Thanks for asking."

"I appreciate you helping me," she says.

"Me, too."

Her gaze drops to my fingers on her shoulder. I withdraw, my fingers curling into a fist. I wish we weren't so damn awkward. There are a million things I'd tell her if I knew how.

"I wonder how long we're going to be here," Cyn says.

I lower my voice. "Now's our chance to get out of here."

She shakes her head. "They're still watching us. Besides, it's not like we can really escape. We would be totally lost."

"I think we could make it."

Cyn looks past me and shakes her head. "Too late now."

I glance back. Grady climbs out of a falling-apart brown car. He walks over to Randall, Jessie, and Isabella. Pretty quickly, they tell him what's going on, but instead of getting pissed, Grady grins and throws his arms into the air.

"Winter's coming!" he says. "They've got to fix these roads. And we've got enough time to fix ourselves something to eat. Sausages?"

Yeah, I'll admit the thought of sausages makes my mouth water.

"Are you nuts?" Randall says. "Wait, I already know the answer to that."

Hands jittery, Jessie lights another cigarette, but Isabella folds her arms and sighs. "Grady, this is a temporary delay."

"Good enough for me," Grady says. "Now, if I recall, you have a grill in your truck—"

"Shit," Randall sighs.

Cyn's hand closes on my arm. Her touch wakes up tingles in the pit of my stomach. I look at her, then follow her pointing finger.

"A girl!" she says.

And sure enough, there's a tiny little girl, only six years old at most. Buck naked. Wind blows her white-blond hair behind her like a flag. She's crouching downriver from us, a twig in her hand, drawing spirals in the gravelly sand.

"Isn't she cold?" I say.

"Brock, this is totally bizarre." Cyn tugs me forward. "Come on."

I follow her until we're only a few feet from the naked little girl, who glances at us with pale, watery eyes. She barely has any eyebrows, she's so blond.

"You do the talking," I mutter to Cyn, since I don't know what to say.

"Hello," Cyn says in her chirpy voice. "What's your name?"

"Lupine," the little girl says, and she glowers at us. "You don't belong here."

"My name's Cynthia. Where's your mommy?"

A flame flickers in Lupine's eyes. "Mommy's dead."

In the distance, thunder rumbles over the mountains.

"I'm sorry," Cyn says.

I crouch down to her level. "Where's your dad?"

"He doesn't like strangers."

"It must be cold out here." I hold out my hand. "We've got blankets."

Lupine bares her teeth, only they're not pearly little kid teeth—they're fangs. Her watery eyes glow silvery blue.

"Jesus Christ!" I scramble back before she can bite my fingers off.

A growl rumbles from Lupine's skinny chest and she lunges at me. Midair, her body ripples into the shape of a pure white wolf.

I can't fucking believe it. And she actually knocks me flat on my back.

"Brock!"

Cyn grabs the stick Lupine dropped and whacks the little werewolf like she's hitting a golf ball with a club. Lupine yelps and leaps off of me.

"No!" Cyn snaps at Lupine, as if she's a dog. "Off!"

Footsteps thud the ground. I climb to my feet in time to see everybody else jogging nearer. Randall has the same look of disbelief that I'm sure is on my face. Grady's squinting, and Jessie and Isabella are laughing.

Lupine transforms back into a girl, her hands and

knees streaked with mud, her hair a mess, and climbs to her feet. "Leave us alone!" she shouts, with all the rage of a little kid who doesn't know what she's really up against.

Cyn's face darkens. "Us?"

Randall bares his teeth. "We're in another pack's territory."

"Which pack?" Jessie says.

"Fuck if I know," Grady says.

Jessie looks daggers at him. "Nobody asked you."

Lightning flashes behind the clouds, and thunder growls even closer than before. In the distance, a chorus of howls climbs skyward. Lupine falls to her knees, throws back her head, and looses a high warble of a howl.

"Shit," Randall says. "We need to get out of here."

"Why?" Cyn says. She's gripping one of my arms between both hands, so hard that I doubt she realizes she's doing it.

"Before the rival pack gets here, of course," I cut in.

"And how would you—"

Before Cyn can finish her sentence, the unmistakable sound of pounding paws advances on us. White, gray, black—wolves hurtle through the field, tall grass hissing past their pelts as they run. Within seconds, we're surrounded by wolves. Their eyes glow with a strange, feverish heat, what I'd describe only as pure feral.

A big white wolf steps forward, his fur bristling. Lupine wraps her arms around his neck.

"Can I speak to your Alpha?" Randall says.

The white wolf bares impressive fangs.

Lupine points a claw at Cyn. "She hit me."

Cyn's eyes flare. "But she—"

A snarl rips from the white wolf's throat, and he launches himself at Cyn. She goes down with a startled scream.

Heat rushes through my blood. "Cynthia!"

She lies flat on her back, her arms splayed against the dirt, barely breathing. Her wide eyes stare past the white wolf and straight at the sky. The wolf jabs his muzzle in the crook of her neck and inhales slowly, then huffs at her scent.

Cyn meets my gaze. "I'm okay, Br—"

The wolf cuts her off with a growl.

I step toward them, my muscles taut and trembling, but Randall grabs my arm. "Don't."

"Get him off her," I say through clenched teeth, "before I rip his fucking head off."

The white wolf's fur melts away to bare skin, and he shudders into the naked body of a man with tattoos running down his back. He has the same white-blond hair as Lupine, and a scraggly beard that tickles Cyn's collarbone. He pins her wrists with his hands. Sourness rises in my throat at the sight of his body against hers.

"Human," the man growls, his pale eyes fixed on Cyn's face.

"Leave her alone," Randall says. "She's with us."

The man glances sidelong at the rest of us. "Who?"

"Randall of the Bitterroot Pack. And you need to back down. Now."

"I am Frost," the man says, "and you are on Paradise Pack territory."

Isabella slides one high heel forward. "Sir, excuse our mistake," she says in her sweetest, candy-coated voice. "We didn't mean to intrude on your territory. We were just headed down to Wyoming, but there's road construct—"

Frost leaps from Cyn and lunges at Isabella, but stops just inches from touching her. Face-to-face, he whispers, "Do you know Luna?"

His breath stinks with this weird, sweet sagebrush smell. I can't figure out what it is.

I help Cyn to her feet before he can touch her again. "Are you okay?" I whisper.

She nods, but her hands shake as she tugs her clothes straight.

"Luna?" Isabella manages to look amazingly calm, despite her sharp teeth. "Who is she?"

"The Goddess of the Moon," Frost hisses, his eyes wide.

Great. This guy's bat-shit crazy, isn't he?

Isabella clears her throat and doesn't back down. "I'm afraid not."

Jessie slides her cell phone from her purse and hits a button. At the first beep, Frost spins toward the noise and snarls.

Jessie freezes, her green eyes staring straight into his. "I'm calling our Alpha," she says.

"Your machines disgust us," he says. "Luna forbids them."

"Oh?" Jessie hits another button. "Well, we don't believe in Luna, honey."

"Jessie," Randall says in a low, warning voice.

"I've got this," Jessie says. "He's got another thing coming if he thinks his little Paradise Pack should pick a fight with us Bitterroots."

Cyn squeezes my hand and gives me a smile that's supposed to be brave.

Oh, God. Frost has left Jessie in that twitchy, random way of his, and now his hungry gaze slides up and down Cyn's curves. He nuzzles the nape of her neck and she stiffens, her nails biting my skin, as he slides a hand into her hair and brings it to his nose. He breathes in deeply, his eyes glazing over.

"Don't touch her." I try to stare him down. My heart's thudding about a billion miles an hour and I'm praying Cyn won't get hurt.

He's not even looking at me, his fingers tangled in her hair. "She smells delicious."

Isabella and Jessie share a disgusted glance.

Lupine, who was watching us with this smug little smile, pouts and says, "Daddy. Let's go now. I don't like them."

"Listen to Lupine," Cyn says, her voice tight.

"You don't belong here, human." Frost leans in close. "But I like dark meat."

Cyn glowers at him. "And I hate white trash."

He laughs as he slides his claws down her neck, then squeezes one of her breasts.

A snarl rips from my throat and I pound my fist into the side of Frost's head. The bastard goes down hard, dragging Cyn with him, and she cries out. Knocked on his back, he tugs Cyn by her hair, trying to reel her in, but she grabs a fistful of dirt and hurls it into his eyes, jumps to her feet, then kicks him right in the balls.

Yes! I want to howl with savage triumph.

Frost whine-growls, scrabbling at his eyes and squirming on the ground. A clump of Cyn's hair drifts to the grass. Before Frost can react, Randall grabs him under one shoulder and hauls him to his feet. The rest of the Paradise Pack darts at Randall, their muzzles twisted in snarls, and snaps at the air inches from his flesh.

Randall freezes. "I'm betting you're their Alpha." He lets Frost drop onto the dirt again.

Blinking, the Paradise Alpha climbs to his feet. His eyes look red with rage—but that might just be the grit. He still isn't standing up straight.

"Fuck off," I spit at him, choked by my own anger.

Cyn's hand closes around mine. "Brock, no." But it sounds halfhearted.

"Luna demands punishment," Frost says.

Jessie sneers at him. "I texted Winema," she says to Randall.

Sure enough, a car honks on the highway. The wolves' ears swivel toward the sound. Winema climbs out and marches through the grass with Charles at her heels. She scans the scene, then zeroes in on Frost and stops a foot away from him.

"You're the Alpha of this pack?" Winema says.

"Yes," he says, squaring his shoulders, "I am Frost of the Paradise Pack, and—"

"Where are the Zlatroviks?"

"Zlatroviks?" Frost ducks a little, as if they're spying on him. "I don't know."

Winema arches an eyebrow. "You reek of faerie wine. Every werewolf within a ten-mile radius can smell you, so unless you're stupid enough to steal from Cliff Sterling, you have a supplier. Tell us where they are."

I wrinkle my nose at his smell. Of course. He's a drunk, an addict.

Frost bares his teeth. "I have no reason to, trespassers."

"We outnumber you at least two to one. If you won't give us the information we want, we will take it from you."

Frost stops snarling. "Zlatroviks don't run in the wilderness. Look to a city. Denver."

"Fair enough." Winema waves him away. "I would suggest hightailing it out of here before the rest of my wolves arrive."

Frost licks his lips, his eyes glancing back and forth, then nods at his pack.

The Paradise werewolves slink away and disappear into the grass. All except Lupine, who stares first at Cyn, then Winema, then back again.

"Daddy?" Lupine says.

Winema looks at Lupine with pity in her eyes. "You need to go."

Frost grabs his daughter by the wrist and yanks her onward. She yelps and twists free, then runs ahead of him, crying, "I hate you!"

With a backwards glance at Winema, Frost stoops down into wolf form and trots after Lupine, his head and tail drooping.

When he's out of sight, Cyn doubles over and retches.

"Are you all right?" Still shaking from the adrenaline rush, I crouch beside her.

Cyn straightens and rakes her hair out of her face. Her fingers graze over her chest, and she winces. "He bruised me. But I'm okay."

"Are you sure?" I rest my hand on her shoulder.

"Yes." Cyn backs away from me and rubs the insides of her arms. "I will be."

"Come on, honey." Isabella swoops down and bundles Cyn under her arm. "We'll find you some water and get you washed up."

Jessie follows them as they walk toward the convertible. "He's never coming back."

I realize my hand is still outstretched. I let it drop, and stand there.

"Move out," Winema says. "The police aren't far behind."

As the tall grass closes behind Cyn, she glances back at me. The look on her face feels like a kick in the ribs. God, I feel so useless. I should be able to protect her.

thirteen

By the time we make it out of Paradise Valley, thanks to the rival pack and the road construction, the sky is the black-purple of a rotting plum. My nose stays wrinkled at the stink of fresh asphalt. Alongside the new road, twelve-foot-tall rock giants shuck their orange safety vests, their granite muscles rippling. Human road workers scurry around them, looking tiny and useless next to the tons of sheer giant-power.

"Wow," I say. "Those are some huge-ass gic—giants."

"Disgusting," Randall says.

I stare at him. "And you're calling me prejudiced?"

He gives me a death glare. "It's disgusting how those rock giants are being duped. They're working for antifreeze."

"Huh?"

"Antifreeze, not money. So their joints don't crack when it freezes up in the mountains."

"Well, I guess that's a fair trade."

Randall shakes his head. "If they actually got paychecks, they could afford all the antifreeze they wanted, and maybe a house to go with it. But there are no laws saying you have to pay them minimum wage. Legally speaking, they're barely even Others. Some people think they should be treated like animals."

The way he says "some people" makes me think he'd love to rip their heads off.

A rock giant crosses the road in front of us, placing his feet with careful thuds on the soft asphalt. His head swings toward our truck, and his eyes meet mine, just for a second. They smolder red like lava, and I can't pretend like I don't see a slow-moving intelligence within them. I shiver and rub the goose bumps on my arms.

We drive onward and leave the rock giants behind.

Thunder grumbles in the mountains, and wind shakes rain from the sky. I can't stop thinking about Cyn and hoping she's okay.

She's doesn't belong here. How could I forget that? I need to get her out.

Winema gives the order to stop in the Absaroka-Beartooth Wilderness, at the northern edge of the Montana-Wyoming border. Yellowstone lies to the south, but it's too crowded for us to spend the night in the park itself without blowing our cover. Even here, there are still some people camping off the road, but we're going to use them as camouflage to explain away why we're here. That's the plan, anyway.

After we make camp and eat a shitty dinner of canned stew and stale bread, most of the pack slips into the foothills, one by one. Left behind, I stand in the windy dark and look at the campers' flickering lights. They drink their cheap beer and laugh over burnt marshmallows. Hollowness gnaws inside my chest.

"Hey," Randall says, appearing out of thin air behind me.

I try not to look startled. "Hey. Where's everybody going?"

"Out for a run. The pack's been on the road for too long. Want to come with?"

I stare at him. "I'm guessing they're not running around in human form."

Randall touches his finger to his lips and glances at the rowdy campers not too far away. "Yeah. You feel up to it tonight?"

I glance at the sky. Retreating rainclouds whisk across the face of the moon. She looks dimmer by the light of campfires.

I shrug. "Where's Cyn?"

"With Isabella and Jessie, of course."

"Is she okay?"

"Yes." Randall's breath fogs the chilly air. "Are you coming or not?"

I grit my teeth. I mean, what can I say? I'm bitten; I'm a walking time bomb.

"Winema talked with you," he says.

"Yeah. Said you guys would have to kill me if I lost control." It's hard to keep the bitterness out of my voice. "Sounds like fun."

"Brock." Randall's eyes glimmer gold. "We have to do this."

"You think I don't know that already?"

"Then you're a coward." He says it softly, like he's disappointed, even.

My hands clench into fists. "If you're trying to get me angry enough to change, it isn't going to work. I'm not that stupid."

A corner of his mouth twists. "Oh? Then what's stopping you?"

Everything. And nothing at all. Everyone knows who—what—I am. I stand there, deaf and dumb, and try to pretend like my eyes aren't stinging.

"Just leave me the hell alone," I whisper.

"I can't." Randall says, his voice rough. "You know that already, too."

I want to hit him, to rage at him, but right now I just feel so damn tired.

Instead, I decide to stall for time. "What's it like, being a wolf?"

"Jesus," Randall says. "I'm not even going to try explaining."

"Oh, come on."

"It's like trying to describe sex to a virgin."

Heat rushes into my face. "Hey, it can be done."

"But it's not the same. Sooner or later, you're just going to have to do it."

I nod, my jaw set. "Bite the bullet."

"Hey, there's a fair chance your first time won't be too bad. You seem to be made of tougher stuff than most people."

I think of Chris then, and swallow hard.

Randall grabs my wrist and tugs me in the direction of the darkness. "Let's go."

My knees lock, and I have to force myself to walk. I don't know why I'm doing this, or even if I want to. But what else can I do? It's a wild night. I can smell it, with the scent of lingering rain and sweat and excitement. The farther from the road we go, the brighter the moon becomes. Cold shivers trickle over my skin.

"Rule number one," Randall murmurs. "When you change, do it in secret."

We're high in the foothills now. I feel a sharp ache inside my chest, an emptiness that needs to be filled by something I don't want. Up here, the cold, clear air tingles in my nose and invites the wolf inside me to uncurl.

Randall begins to unbutton his shirt. "Come on, Brock."

I'm standing in the shadow of a tree, but he steps boldly into the direct moonlight, his skin gleaming. I side-step after him, and a shudder ripples through me from my neck to my toes. I gasp and take what's supposed to be a steadying breath, but the moon isn't helping—she's driving me crazy. I need to get out of these clothes.

I mutter at the moon, "Don't think you can mess with me, bitch."

"Hey," Randall says, staring sideways at me. "What was that?"

"Nothing."

"Did you call the moon a bitch?"

I grimace, the roots of my teeth itching on the way to fangs. "Maybe I did."

Randall grabs my shoulder. "You can't do that. You have to respect the moon like you would your own mother. Okay?"

I glare at him. "That's bull. You sound like that Frost guy, talking about Luna."

"Why do you have such shitty relationships with women?"

I fold my arms tight. "That's *really* bull."

"You can't deny it. You can't say—"

"The moon isn't a woman, okay? She's—it's—just a lump of rock out in space."

Randall stares at me sideways. "Yeah, and we're just lumps of meat who happen to have the power to become wolves. Listen to me, bloodborn. You're Other now. The moon has a lot of power over our kind, and you have to respect that."

"Fine."

My skin itches something fierce and I want to scratch it away in tatters. I'm shaking uncontrollably. Randall still looks calm, though his eyes burn like embers and the beginning of a silver pelt trickles down his chest.

"How do I do this?" I say hoarsely.

"You've got to let it happen. You can't try too hard."

"I don't even know what I'm supposed to be trying."

Randall flexes his hands, his knuckles popping as they shift. "Focus on the wolf inside you, on how it feels. Then let it loose."

I close my eyes and turn my attention to the tingles building up pressure inside, until all my sensations merge into a sweet, sharp ache. Is that the wolf? Should I feel claws inside my fingertips, a hidden tail at the bottom of my spine? If I imagine hard enough, will it happen? On the full moon, it was all I could do not to change.

"This is ridiculous," I say. "And why aren't you changing?"

Randall cocks his head at me. "You first."

"Show me how."

He shrugs off his shirt, tosses it into the trees. "You don't want to watch. I can tell."

I shake my head. "I do."

Randall stands on his toes. Hooked claws gleam on his hands. His hair fades to silver and flows down his skin, thickening into a ruff around his neck and shoulders. His nose, eyelids, and lips darken to black. He unzips his jeans.

I'm staring now; I can't blink. His pelt glistens in the moonlight. So silver.

"Brock." His voice has become a gravelly growl. "What are you waiting for?"

Clammy-skinned, I unbutton my shirt. My vision wavers, my head feels light.

Let's do this. Let's find out what it means to be a wolf.

But that's the last thing I want to do. I have no idea what I will become, or where my mind will go. What will I do when I'm not human? Will I even remember? Hell, I might not even survive the transformation. Chris didn't.

Randall groans and falls to his hands and knees. He clutches the grass in his claws.

"I don't know," I say. "I don't know if I can."

Randall looks up at me with golden eyes. "You have to." He slurs his words, already more wolf than man. Soon he won't be able to speak.

Another shudder washes over me as I bathe in moonlight. Not as insistent as the full moon's pull, but still a harsh craving, digging at my insides like I swallowed barbed wire. Slowly, I reach for my fly, but my fingers are too clumsy for the zipper.

"Brock." Randall's mouth bulges outward into a muzzle.

I watch as he yanks off his jeans, as his limbs ripple into lean wolf legs. His tail arcs from his spine, already plumed. He shuts his eyes for the last convulsion of transformation, then opens them, staring at me as a silver wolf.

I am only half naked. I am wholly human.

See, I know it already. An ember of hate has been sitting inside me, smoldering, lodged somewhere near my rib cage. Because I know this silver wolf is the one who bit me, turned me, and the one who killed my brother.

It's easier to forget when he has a human face. But I still know who he is.

Randall pads to me, his head held low as if he's going to nudge my hand with his nose. I yank back. Bile rises in my throat as I remember the blood on his muzzle. He tore into my flesh with those teeth. I grab the scar on my biceps.

Get away from me, gick.

Randall whines softly, urgently, his eyes locked on mine.

"No." I force out the words. "I can't."

Before he can try to touch me again, I whirl from him and run. I know he can run faster than me—I don't care—I'm getting out of here, just try to stop me. My breath comes ragged from my burning throat. My legs feel liquid. I stumble and fall and roll, spitting dirt from my mouth, then scramble to my feet and keep running. He's going to chase me—bite me—and this seizes me with a new terror.

Even though I'm already bitten. Already bloodborn.

The burning in my throat infects my eyes, and I blink hard so I can see. Still, I'm as good as blind. I can't see in the night. Not like him.

Behind me, I hear a long, low howl that sends lightning down my spine.

Come back. Run with me.

"No!" I shout.

"Brock?"

I skid to a stop. Cyn perches on a boulder, staring at me with moon-glossy eyes.

Panting, I crouch beside her. "What're you doing alone?"

"Oh, Jessie's around here somewhere, acting pissed off

because she doesn't get to run with the pack." Cyn's voice sounds falsely bright. "Guess it's not too entertaining to play human babysitter all the time."

I lower myself onto the boulder. My heartbeat seems to be slowing from its gallop.

"Who howled back there?" she says.

"Randall."

She nods. Her face looks unmoving but brittle, like a glass doll.

"Cyn." I weave my fingers together to stop their shaking. "Are you okay?"

"I should be asking you that question." She touches the back of my hand. "What happened?"

"Randall."

"You already said that."

"He tried to get me to change. I couldn't." I swallow hard. "Cyn, I know you're not okay, either. I should have kept that bastard Frost from hurting you."

"Well, you did punch him in the head." She smiles thinly. "I don't think you could have stopped him. We were in his territory."

"God, I hate werewolves."

"But you *are* one."

"I know."

Cyn won't look at me now, her gaze fixed on the dirt. "So you hate yourself?"

That sets my teeth on edge. "It's not that simple."

"When you told me you were bitten, I had this crazy,

stupid hope that maybe being a werewolf would change you for the better."

My face tightens. "You *want* me to be a werewolf?"

"No." She meets my eyes, her own fierce. "I want you back the way you were, the Brock I loved, but I know that's impossible."

Loved. Before, not now that I'm a beast.

"Cyn," I say. My voice sounds rough. "I'm sorry."

She tucks her hair behind her ears, her hands trembling slightly. "I don't need your apologies. I can forgive you for what you've done, but I could never forgive you if you threw away your second chance."

"Second chance?"

"You were bitten, but you survived." A tear slides down her nose. "You can't die now."

My ribs feel like steel claws tightening around my lungs and heart. "I don't want to die. But I don't know how to live like this."

She wipes her tears away with the back of her hand, and stares at me with glittering eyes. "I know you have it in you to fight through this and come out even stronger. You need to move forward. You need to change, Brock."

I close my eyes and nod. "I could do that for you."

Cyn touches my cheek, lightly, her fingertips skimming the days-old stubble. I open my eyes to see her looking up at me, her cheeks smudged with tear-streaked mascara, her eyes shining in the moonlight.

"Let me help you," she says.

"I have to do this myself," I say.

She shakes her head. "You don't have to be alone."

"But I—"

"Brock?" she says. "Stop talking."

And then she kisses me. My heart stops beating, I swear. Her lips are so soft. I inhale her bittersweet almond-vanilla scent and slide my hands behind her neck, gently, but she slinks her fingers into my hair and grips tight with a moan. My skin flushes, feverish hot, and I feel the wolf inside me uncurl.

I pull back. "Cyn," I say, my lips against hers. "Cynthia, stop."

She withdraws to look into my eyes, her own full of stars. "Do you not want—?"

"No, I do." I run my tongue along my teeth, feeling their sharp points. "Let's take it slow though, okay?"

"Okay," she says. "Brock, I've missed you."

I bend to kiss her again, this time on the forehead. She sighs and leans against my chest.

"We should go now," I whisper. "Together."

Cyn looks up at me. "Now? You mean, really try to escape?"

I can barely hear her quiet voice, but I nod. "If we don't go now, we might never make it back to Washington. And after that Paradise Pack…"

She shudders and presses closer against me. "I don't want to think about that right now."

"Then come with me. Most of the pack is out running in the hills now."

"Jessie and Randall aren't."

I glance around. "Do you see them anywhere? Jessie's bored and tired. She probably just wants you to think she's watching."

"Go without me." She says it in such a flat way that all the warmth I felt from kissing her fades away. "You can move faster than me, and they won't miss you as quickly."

"There has to be a better—"

She looks me straight in the eye. "Go."

"I'll get help," I say. "I promise."

I'm already backing away from her, distancing myself from the temptation to stay.

Cyn makes no move to stop me, says nothing, just stands there and watches me go. At least, that's what I think happens, since I don't look back. Not even once. Because I know that if I stay with her, we might never escape.

And God, it hurts, but I don't know what else to do.

fourteen

Outskirts. That's where I belong. Here, it's quiet, a damp wind blowing the perfume of sagebrush over the tall blond grass. The spicy-minty smell floods my nose and overflows to the back of my throat. I hike out into the wilderness, away from the warmth and light of the camp, away to where there's no one but me and the stars.

Randall doesn't follow me. No one does. Do they even care?

I laugh when I realize there's no one here to hear me. That was so fucking easy. Just walked away from the whole mess.

Maybe Randall is watching me right now, waiting for me to run.

A prickling grows on the back of my neck until itchy fear spreads through me, and I break into a run. My muscles tighten and release as I plunge down slopes and charge up hills. Sagebrush claws at my legs, but hell, I'm not stopping. I run until my breath is ragged in my aching throat, then stop to pant for air.

I spin around, scanning the horizon, but see nothing but mountains and the moon.

I'm alone.

Now all I have to do is find my way back to the nearest town, call the cops, and tell them where to bust the Bitterroot Pack. Where's the road? I squint into the darkness. The cloudy moon shines weak light on the land, like watered-down milk over asphalt. There are boulders, and some scrubby bushes. That's all I can see.

Okay. Think for a second.

Yellowstone is the most populated place for miles around. That means I should cross into Wyoming and head south. At the very least I'll run into some campers with a cell phone. With a deep breath, I glance at the sky—like that might possibly help me—and start walking in the direction I think is south.

I pass boulders and scrubby bushes. Then some more boulders and bushes.

You know, I kind of wish I didn't skip out on my chance to be a Boy Scout when I was kid. That might have helped me figure out some navigation skills or stuff like that. Right now, all I'm seeing are mountains and trees in the distance, and of course at night, everything looks different than it does in the daytime.

I plod onward through the darkness, time trickling away.

Clouds float past the face of the moon like leaves in a river. The moonlight gnaws at me, whispering to the wolf inside, but I keep my mind empty, my emotions flat. There's nothing else to do but soldier on, and on, and on.

Soon enough, the moon swings low, and dawn glows behind the gray clouds.

I'm stumbling at this point, my feet sore, my throat as dry as dirt. As soon as I get to Yellowstone, I'm going to find one of those campground spigots, stick my head under the cold water, and drink until my stomach feels tight. Maybe that will stop it from growling. I've barely eaten anything in the past twenty-four hours.

Why didn't I bring a canteen? And some beef jerky?

My mouth waters at the thought, and I swallow. Can't waste any water through drooling.

When the sun rises properly, and ragged clouds fall away, the warm light melts dewdrops and stirs bugs from their hiding spots. And then the sun starts to get really hot. I thought my mouth was dry before, but now my tongue sticks to the roof of my mouth. My head throbs with every heartbeat, like my skull is shrinking.

Why does it have to be hotter than hell? I thought winter was on its way.

Maybe it's just the werewolf disease in my bloodstream, simmering to a boil. A fever that's going to cook me from the inside out. My vision's getting kind of ripply, like I'm seeing a heat wave, but I can't tell if it's real.

A white animal stands stark against the shadowy pines. A wolf.

I stare at it, my muscles taut. "Are you a Bitterroot?" I rasp.

At the sound of my voice, the wolf flinches.

"What pack are you from?" I say, louder.

The white wolf lopes into the trees, sparing one backward glance for me, and disappears. What the fuck? I stand there, blinking stupidly. Oh, wait. A laugh breaks free from my mouth. That was a real wolf, not a werewolf. Must have been so damned confused. Is it bad that I was hoping it was a werewolf?

I still have no fucking clue where I am. This doesn't look like Yellowstone, not from what I've seen on the postcards. There are no geysers, for one. I can't even smell them, and I know they're supposed to smell like rotten eggs. But this doesn't look like Paradise Valley, either, so maybe I got completely turned around.

Bristly pine trees stuck between scattered boulders. That's all I see, wherever I look.

God, I'm so thirsty. Maybe I can find a river. There was a river back in Paradise Valley. I'd even fight that psycho werewolf Frost for a drink.

I walk faster, lured by the promise of a cold swallow of water, then slow when my feet complain. I'm not even paying attention to my stomach anymore. It's growling so loud I'm sure anybody within miles can hear it—

A deer. It's standing at the bottom of a hill, one hoof raised, its ears swiveled toward me.

Oh my God, venison.

I'm afraid to blink, just in case the deer is a mirage, or I'm finally crazy, but my eyes sting and I do blink and the deer is still there. Haunches quivering, ready to run. Hot meat on four hooves. My mouth aches. My teeth sweep downward into fangs, full fangs, like they never have before. I taste blood as they prick my lip.

Don't run away. Don't you dare.

That's what I'm saying to the deer in my head, but in my gut I want it—I'm craving it—to bolt into the pines so I can tear after it and take it down. But the logical part of me knows that I'm not fast enough to catch it, as a human.

As a human…

A bird screeches, and the deer flinches. I lunge forward before I can stop myself—claws thrusting through my fingernails—legs twisting. The deer bounds away, white tail held high, and I fall to my knees, too shaky to give chase.

I stare at the claws, black and curved, on my fingertips. More than a little wicked-looking. I'll bet I could take down that deer with one swipe from these. If I got close enough. I grimace, and the claws shrink into human nails. My fangs retreat into dull teeth, and although my bitten lip heals fast, coppery blood still haunts my tongue.

I'd love for it to be the taste of deer's blood. Delicious…

I shake my head hard, ignoring how it makes me dizzy, and keep on walking. South, I hope. I don't even know anymore. Ravens croak hoarsely in the trees, watching me pass. I find no water for the rest of the day, except for a little swampy patch in the shadows of a cliff. I kneel in the mud and strain the muddy water through my teeth, too thirsty to care. By the time I've drained the patch dry, it's already sunset.

How long have I been walking?

A fierce hunger gnaws at my insides. I want to whine at the sharpness of it, to howl for the rest of my pack. No. I'm alone now. Lone wolf.

I can't seem to think straight anymore.

Am I even human? Am I even me? The boundary between Brock and Beast wavers like the sun sinking beneath the earth. The wolf claws at my insides, and I crumple on the ground, clutching my ribs, panting for sanity. I keep my eyes on the gorgeous salmon pink of sunset. Smoked salmon. Jesus Christ, I'm starving.

And the wolf inside me whispers, *Let me out.*

Bile rises in my throat. No. I'm not that desperate.

You? The wolf circles, his jaws open in sarcastic laughter. *You're weak. You're hungry.*

I'd rather kill myself.

Would you? You're so afraid of yourself?

No. You're not me. You're a parasite. You're a tumor waiting to be cut out.

The wolf gnaws my guts, and I groan, pain erasing my eyesight. When I can see again, the wolf is sitting, watching me from the inside out.

You know why you're such a failure?

Shut up.

Because you're a coward. And a liar.

Shut the fuck up!

Nobody believes you. The wolf advances on me. *Nobody believes you're not a monster.*

I struggle not to cry out. Cyn doesn't think I'm a monster. She cares about me.

She pities you. She knows you're killing yourself slowly.

I bare my teeth at the wolf. This isn't my fault. You're the one tearing my body apart. I'm not the one who decided to die this way. I—

You have a choice.

I don't have a choice! I can't go backwards in time and—

Curl up and die, then. Nobody's here to see you now.

Then why does it matter?

A twisted sense of calm settles over me. Nobody gives a shit. Myself included.

I watch the sun slide away. The moon pivots to her place in the heavens. I figure that if I don't make it, at least I will die looking at the sky.

I wonder how long it will take people to find my body.

I shove that thought from my mind and start to undress. There goes the shirt Mom bought me, the hand-me-down jeans from Dad, the boxer shorts Chris teased me about. When I'm done peeling away layers of myself, my heart feels empty, and big. I wonder why I'm not afraid, wonder if I will be. This is it. There's no other reason to keep standing here, naked and alone. I poke the wolf sleeping inside myself and try to stir it to life.

Come on, Beast. I'm going to let you out.

But I just feel a sharp ache inside, as if the butterflies in my stomach have razor wings. I know I should be able to do this. I have to. All those earlier times, I almost couldn't stop. I flex the muscles in my thighs, tighten my abs, clench and unclench my jaw. How does this work? Is there a secret button to press? Stupid.

Wolf. I don't want to say it out loud, but I make myself. "Wolf."

My back aches, my spine cramped. I stretch skyward, trying to work out the pain, then get on my hands and knees.

"Wolf. I want to be a wolf."

I clench handfuls of grass, curl my toes into the dusty dirt. My back still hurts, and so does my chest, my throat, my eyes. How painful will this be? I draw a shaky breath and stare at the moon, feeling her silver light on my face.

"I want—to—be—a wolf."

But I know I'm lying. And she knows it, too.

Did I want any of this? No. Do I want to be myself? No. What am I going to do?

A fat tear rolls down my cheek and slides over to my nose. I shake my head to fling it away, but another follows, and another. I stay on my hands and knees, buck naked, because I don't know what else to do.

The moon swims, blurry, in a soup of clouds.

I tell her, "I don't want to change. But I've got to. And you've got to help me."

I bend double and hug myself against the pain. A shudder, a sob, ripples through me. I fall onto my side and lie limp, not fighting anymore. I let out all the hurt I buried inside myself so nobody else could see. My breathing steadies.

"I'm a bloodborn," I say quietly, to no one in particular. "I'm a werewolf."

A tingling shiver washes over me. I rub my arms, feeling the hairs bristling. My skin feels exquisitely tender, feverish, but worse than any fever I've had before. My stomach muscles tighten against the hollow ache building inside.

Oh. Is this…?

I crouch on my hands and knees again as the ache builds inside me. I focus on it, imagining it pooling, overflowing, spreading throughout my veins. My limbs wobble beneath me. I watch as the bones in my hands swim beneath the surface of my skin, fascinatingly disgusting. Gray fur sprouts on my knuckles, sweeping over my skin, submerging it beneath a rough pelt. Claws poke from my fingernails. I hear a grinding, gristly sound, followed by a sharp throbbing in my knees as they reform.

Oh, man, I don't think I'm ready—

Pain scythes through me, shredding my body, and I black out.

Blinking hard, I clear away the dark. I'm lying flat on my stomach, a sprig of sagebrush poking my nose. The sweet-green scent overwhelms me, and I sneeze. It's not evening anymore, but grayish overcast day. Above me, the moon hangs in the same spot in the sky. I wrinkle my nose. How much time has passed?

I climb to my feet—start to—but my limbs feel wrong. I stumble face-first, getting a mouthful of dirt, then I spit and look down.

Paws. Huge gray paws. Mine? Of course—nothing else can be true—and yet…

I shuffle one paw forward, then the other. Slowly, muscles shaking as if I'm sick, I haul myself to my feet. I glance down at my rangy long legs and silver fur flecked with cinnamon, then back at my haunches and plumed tail.

Wolf.

I skitter back, almost tripping over my paws, new to walking on all fours. A muffled yip of excitement escapes my throat. I wag my tail, and watch myself doing it—man, is it weird to have a different body. It feels like fitting into a hand puppet you've never tried before, but you kind of know what to do with it.

And it's not day after all. No, it's the beginning of night, but hot damn, my eyesight is *great*. Like night vision goggles, only sharper, and silver instead of green. And that sagebrush scent—it's not the only thing I smell. I lift my muzzle to the wind, my nose quivering, and close my eyes against the rush of aromas: sagebrush, juniper, pine, dry grass soaked with trails of rodent urine, rabbits slumbering in their burrows.

Drool seeps into my mouth.

I start to walk, my legs stiff at first, then limber and strong and fast—I'm running now, devouring distance, barely touching the ground. My heart thumps strong in my chest. My thick pelt shelters me from the chilly wind.

Rabbit. Where are you? I shake my head and huff to clear my nose.

The tempting furry scent of my prey floats out from beneath a bush. I creep closer, almost quivering with hunger. A rabbit, sleeping. I paw at the dusty earth, the mouth of the rabbit burrow crumbling away. Fear spikes the air. The prey is awake, ready to run. I dig faster, my tongue lolling, my stomach aching so fiercely I whimper.

Not much farther now. The rabbit can't be—

A flash of movement. Right between my paws! Instinct shocks my muscles into motion, and my jaws snap shut around the rabbit's neck. Tiny bones crunch beneath my teeth. It doesn't even have time to cry out. Blood seeps into my mouth, and I toss the rabbit to the ground to devour the hot meat. I'm in seventh heaven.

I lick the last bits of meat from my muzzle and exhale. Thank God.

I raise my head to the sky. The moon hovers overhead, watching me. I fill my lungs and loose my wordless emotion in a howl. When the last breath fades from my lungs, I barrel down and charge up the hills. I paw at the ground, kick up clumps of grass, and snap a dead branch between my jaws, just to prove I can.

Of all things, guess what I smell on the breeze: chicken soup.

The tantalizing scent of simmering broth, meat, carrots, and peas is comforting in the cold wild night. Back home, we used to butcher some hens and Mom would cook a huge pot of soup from scratch. The house smelled great for days.

I point my nose like a divining rod, then trot upwind.

Then, like a miracle, I see the lights of a town ahead. Jesus, I must have been walking in circles, only a few miles from salvation.

I lope toward the town, my paws grazing over the ground, a floating feeling inside.

Beyond a picket fence, sprinklers click and hiss over falsely green grass. Buttery light pours from a little white ranch house with pinwheels stuck in the lawn and hummingbird feeders on the porch. The scent of soup trickles outside. I pace at the picket fence, then crouch, the muscles in my haunches bunching, and leap. Paws tucked beneath me, I soar over the fence and land in a flower bed, crunching pansies underfoot.

Whoops. I bare my teeth in a wolfish grin.

Through a crack in the kitchen window, I can hear the scrape of a chair, the clink of silverware on dishes, the soft murmuring of dinnertime conversation. Crouching low to the ground, I creep closer to the window. A woman walks to the kitchen sink, right beside me, her eyes downcast. I flatten myself to the ground, trying to melt into the shadows. She sighs, a tired smile on her face, and starts washing her plate. She has strawberry-blond hair that she keeps tucking away from her face, and blue-gray eyes.

I watch her in a daze, as if I've never seen anything so calm and homey before. Maybe it's because I'm daydreaming about walking in there and having some of her soup. Maybe it's because she reminds me of Mom.

Then, the scrabbling of nails on glass, and yapping.

I swing my head toward the noise. A ridiculously fluffy pair of rat-sized dogs—one black, one peanut-colored—stand against a sliding door, barking furiously at me. Their buggy eyes roll back as they fight to get at me.

Jesus. This is too funny.

I wag my tail at the fluffy little dogs, but they aren't any friendlier. I bare my teeth and growl, a low, exciting rumble. The little dogs go crazy, tripping over each other and hurling their bodies against the door. I huff with amusement. The woman frowns, glancing out the kitchen window, and then moves to the other window—

I lunge to my feet and bolt into the night, the lights flicking on behind me and flooding the lawn with light. I don't know how much of it illuminates me, but I'm already over the fence by the time I hear a man speak from the porch.

"I don't see anything, Sadie. You sure you saw something?"

"Yes. The dogs saw it."

"Those dogs see all sorts of imaginary burglars."

As I keep running, their voices fade.

"It wasn't a burglar…it was a dog, a huge dog…"

A sick feeling curdles inside me. Stupid, stupid, stupid. They could have a gun. Dad certainly didn't wait at the chance to blow off Randall's head.

But this is different. How do they know who I am? I'm just some random wolf…though I guess that's the point. I'm a werewolf, nothing more. All they have to do is look at me to know they should fear and hate me.

You're Other, now, Brock. You aren't normal anymore.

As I trot through this little town, my gaze sliding from window to everyday window, I realize I will always be on the outside from now on. Even if I pretend to be human, I belong in the night, in the wilderness, in the loneliness.

My jaw tight, I stalk away. A startled bird bursts from the sagebrush and whirs into the air. I sprint after it, paws thudding, breath steaming the air. The bird peeps and zigzags, then crashes into a low tree and tumbles to the ground.

I stare as it flaps like a broken windup toy. A quail.

My mouth waters, and I lean closer to the bird. It stinks of fear. I can hear its tiny heart, beating so fast the sound blurs.

No. I'm not hungry anymore.

The bird twists onto its feet and flees into the sage-brush. I close my eyes and inhale deeply. Scents unwind on a ribbon of breeze…sweet rain-heavy air, the ozone tang of lightning building in the clouds above, the musk of a man's sweat—

"Really, sir?" says a familiar man. "The little ones?"

"Absolutely," says another man I know all too well.

Sheriff Royle.

fifteen

Deputy Collins and Sheriff Royle stroll along the edge of a gravel road downwind from me, their cruiser parked and silent. Shit, how did I blunder right into them? So much for super-sharp wolfish senses. I flatten myself against the ground and creep behind a sagebrush bush. What are they going to do if they see me like this?

"They're pups, sir," Collins says. "It's easy to see how someone might call them cute."

"Cute?" Royle spits on the dirt. "The littlest ones are the most infectious ones. Just like baby rattlesnakes have the most venom."

They must be talking about werepuppies. No idea if that's a bullshit theory or not.

"Yes, sir," Collins says, not looking his boss in the eye.

"If you see a little one, don't be fooled. Shoot it on sight."

A shudder of disgust bristles the fur along my spine. I can just imagine a dumb little werepuppy skipping up to Royle and trying to lick his hand, only to get a bullet right between its eyes. What kind of asshole kills an innocent pup?

Collins's radio crackles, and he holds it to his ear.

Royle keeps walking and talking. "Don't let that tiny cur anywhere near—"

"Sir?" Collins says. "We're getting a call I think you should hear."

"Is that right?" Royle stops and looks back. "What did they say?"

"Some lady just called the 911 dispatch from Pray, Montana." The deputy's eyes light up. "She saw a huge wild animal, like a dog."

"Like a wolf," Royle murmurs. "I knew the pack was here."

No, you idiot. They're way far ahead, and you're after the wrong wolf.

"Looks like we know who to question first, Deputy."

"Yes, sir."

Royle strides on ahead, his legs kind of bowed like he just rode up on a Wild West stallion instead of sitting on his ass in his cruiser.

Why do the police have to be so useless?

I'm going to have to change back, and explain every-thing. As soon as they're far enough away, I squeeze my eyes shut and concentrate. *Human.* I wait for the shivers, the feverish skin, but all I feel is stupid. Why isn't this working? I grit my teeth and strain all of my muscles, trying to shove them back into human shape. Nothing.

Oh, fuck almighty. I'm stuck, aren't I?

Ahead, Royle and Collins near the little white ranch house. I creep after them, keeping low to the ground. I can still hear the rat-dogs yapping. When I'm as close as I dare, I lie in the shadows and swivel my ears toward the house.

Royle rings the doorbell. That woman—Sadie—answers the door, rifle in hand.

"Oh!" she says, lowering her weapon. "I'm so sorry, I thought you were something else."

Yeah, like wolves can ring doorbells.

I try one more time to squeeze myself back into my human body, but only a whine escapes me from the strain of it. The peanut-colored dog appears at Sadie's ankles, its head cocked, followed by the black dog.

"Ma'am." Royle flashes his badge. "We just happened to be in the area when you called."

Sadie frowns. "911? That wasn't more than two minutes ago."

"A fortuitous coincidence," Collins says.

Man, somebody's been studying really hard for the SAT.

Royle lowers his voice. "Ma'am, we've been on a special assignment for quite some time now, tracking the whereabouts of a pack from Washington."

"What sort of pack?" Sadie says.

Collins steps forward, his hat in his hands. "A were-wolf pack."

Sadie gasps. "Barnes?" she hollers back into the house. "Come here a minute!"

Her husband shuffles up in ratty old slippers. "Police here already?"

"That's what I said," Sadie says, "and then they said they've been tracking a pack of *werewolves* all the way from Washington."

"Yes, ma'am," Royle says. "That is the unfortunate truth of the matter."

All this time, the two rat-dogs are sneaking closer to the door. The black one thrusts its muzzle into the wind, then barks and sprints outside. The peanut-colored dog races after the other one, yapping like Armageddon is upon us.

"Daffy, Trixie, no!" screams Sadie.

Before I can really think about what retarded names those are, both rat-dogs discover me hiding in the shrubbery. The peanut one snarls like an angry bee, but the black one wags its tail frantically and sticks its nose in my face.

"*Daffy!*" Sadie claps her hands, and the black dog flinches. "Don't touch that cur!"

I'm a wolf. And I'm being attacked by fluffy, kind-of-cute dogs. Shit? What's definitely shit, though, is Royle marching up with his gun out.

"Come out, werewolf," he says. "You can run, but you can't hide."

Seriously? This guy wins the award for dumbest sheriff ever.

I sigh, and Daffy licks my muzzle. When I lumber to my feet, she flattens herself against the ground in submission, her tail wagging hard. Trixie keeps growling and yipping at me, never mind that I'm a hundred times her size.

"No sudden moves," Collins says, his gun also pointed at me.

Okay. I'm screwed. There's no way I can explain myself, because there's no way I can get myself back into human form.

When I walk into the light, Sadie gasps. The barrel of her rifle swings up. "It *is* a wolf!"

Barnes whistles low under his breath.

"I said so," Sadie says to her husband. "Didn't I say so? And you said it was imaginary."

Royle shushes her. "Ma'am, step back and let us do our job." He points his pistol right between my eyes. "Change back to human form. Then we talk."

I shake my head and woof to say that I can't.

Royle's forehead wrinkles. "Change back, now."

That's not happening any time soon. I lie down and lower my head to my paws.

"Sir," Collins says, "do you think it might be a real wolf?"

Royle snorts. "Of course not. A real wolf wouldn't understand us."

I nod, then wag my tail like a dog to prove that I'm not dangerous. Daffy dives into a playful bow, wriggling with excitement.

"Oh, Lord." Sadie marches up to us and scoops her dogs into her arms.

"Stand back, ma'am," Royle says. "This werewolf is dangerous."

Sadie purses her lips. "To be honest, sir, I don't think this one is. It acts kind of tame."

"Collins," Royle says, "get the catchpole."

"Yes, sir." Collins jogs in the direction of the cruiser.

Jesus, I wish I could tell them what's going on. Every minute we waste here, the Bitterroot Pack is taking Cyn farther away from safety.

Wait a second...maybe I can tell them.

I climb to my feet and start to scratch in the gravel driveway with my paw. Clumsy, but not impossible. *H...E...*

Collins returns with one of those snares on a pole for catching feral dogs.

You've got to be kidding me.

L... Now Sadie is squinting at what I'm writing. The last letter is the hardest, because it's not all straight lines, but I manage. *P.*

"Give it here, son," Royle says.

Collins tosses Royle the catchpole, and the sheriff advances on me, his boots scuffing my word. *HELP* disappears. I growl in frustration and the sheriff lunges at me, the snare of the catchpole aimed for my neck. I snap at the thick wire, but miss.

"Wait!" Sadie says. "That wolf…help…"

"I could use a little help," Royle shouts.

Collins draws his gun and levels it between my eyes. I bare my teeth at the idiot and let a terrifying snarl ripple my muzzle. He knows I mean business, because he takes a step back, his eyes huge, and—Royle swoops with the catchpole. Wire loops around my neck, digging past my thick pelt and biting into my skin.

I scrabble back, yanking Royle with me. He topples to his knees.

"Don't move!" Collins says. "Or I'll shoot!"

I crouch, my ears flat against my skull, my tail between my legs, and cough at the tightness around my windpipe. If they're going to kill me, why don't they just put a bullet in my brain? Why choke me to death?

Royle struggles to his feet, both hands on the catchpole, and turns toward my flank. The wire twists tighter still, and my growl comes out as a whining wheeze. He swings one leg over my back, like he's going to ride me, and my legs buckle under the weight of him and the fact that I'm just whistling for a bit of air…

Sadie stands watching, clutching her two silent dogs. "What are you going to do?"

"Shut him down," Royle says.

Panic surges through me, and I lunge to my feet, try-ing to buck Royle, but he grips fistfuls of my fur. Blood drains from my head and I black out for a second. Then, a needle-sharp pain stabs me in the scruff of my neck.

I yelp and shake hard like I can fling away the hurt, the needle, the poison.

Both Daffy and Trixie stare at me from Sadie's arms, their bug-eyes huge. Fucking ridiculous. My vision swirls like ink going down a drain. I slump onto the gravel. Royle climbs off me and kicks my muzzle with his boot.

His voice sounds echoing and faraway, like we're all underwater. "We're finished here, ma'am."

I'm finished, too, because…everything…is…black.

Rumbling. Dirty old smell in my nose. I snort, then blink. A car, a man at the wheel.

I fade out again.

When I fade back, it's cold. My legs feel numb. I shudder, and sharpness bites into my skin. With a groan, I pry open my eyelids and discover I've been trussed up with barbed wire, my legs tied together in one big knot.

Still a wolf.

Sheriff Royle stands watching me, his eyes dark and unreadable. "Collins!" he yells.

"Yes, sir?" Collins jogs up with a flashlight.

"This cur's ready for questioning." Royle pulls on thick leather gloves. "Shine the light."

And then I see he's carrying a cattle prod.

A whine escapes my muzzled mouth. Oh, God, they don't know who I am. They don't know that I'm one of the people they're supposed to be saving. And how the fuck do they plan on questioning me when I can't talk?

Royle stares down at me. "You run with the Bitterroot Pack." It isn't a question.

I shake my head, ignoring how the barbed wire cuts into me.

Royle's eyes narrow. "That's a lie." He touches the cattle prod to my ribs.

Electricity jolts through me, stiffening all my muscles, singing my fur. I'm growling, but no sound comes out. Royle removes the cattle prod, and I collapse against the barbed wire. Pain blooms inside me like a widening stain.

"Where is the rest of your pack?" Royle says.

I clench my teeth and struggle not to whimper like a kicked puppy. Please, God, let the next electric shock change me back into a human so I can explain all of this to them—the cattle prod touches my nose. My muscles strain, blazing with pain, then go limp. A high whine leaves my throat. I smell burning flesh.

"Change back now," Royle says, "and tell us what we want to know."

I stare at him, trying to plead with my eyes, to show him that I'm human inside.

"I'm about to tell you something important." Royle's voice drops to a low murmur, like water rising in a river about to overflow its banks. "I don't give a shit what anybody else thinks about you. There might be some high-and-mighty lawyers out there who think we should treat gicks nice, but they wouldn't know a gick if it bit them." He doesn't even laugh at his own joke. "That's a terrible, dangerous kind of ignorance. Those people have never seen a little boy watch his blue-ribbon calf get eaten before his eyes, never seen a dead man with his face gnawed off, all in the name of *gick rights.*" He hisses the words.

My stomach twists at how awfully familiar his words sound.

"This"—Royle raises the cattle prod—"is my kind of gick rights."

I shut my eyes.

"Sir," Collins says. "I—" A muffled thud.

My eyes spring open in time to see Randall standing over Collins's crumpled body with my dad's shotgun in his hands. The flashlight that Collins dropped lies on the ground, shining crazy, crooked light on the scene.

"Get your hands off my bloodborn."

Royle springs to his feet, the cattle prod held aloft. "Don't move!"

Randall shoulders the shotgun. "I don't think you're in a position to give orders, you fucked-up piece of worthless shit."

"Collins?" Royle calls to his deputy, who doesn't move. He reaches for his radio.

"Drop it," Randall says, his eyes smoldering. "Or you'll get a pretty obvious obituary."

The radio falls from Royle's hand and clunks on the ground.

"And the cattle prod." Randall jerks his head. "Throw it away."

Royle looks like he'd rather eat a pile of shit with a spoon, but he tosses the cattle prod into the trees. "You're all going to be brought to justice."

"You call this justice?" Randall's eyes burn hotter. He nods at me. "Cut that wire."

Royle reaches for his back pocket, and Randall lunges about three feet forward, pressing the double-barreled shotgun right between the sheriff's eyes. A growl rumbles from Randall's chest, and he trembles with barely restrained rage.

"I'd love an excuse to be trigger happy," Randall whispers.

A croak comes out of Royle's mouth. He swallows and tries again. "Wire cutters."

"Slowly."

I'm amazed Royle's fingers don't tremble as he fishes a pair of wire cutters out of his pocket. He falls to his knees beside me and starts snipping the barbed wire, yanking it loose. Blood trickles from slashes in my skin.

As soon as he's finished, I stagger to my feet. My legs feel wobbly.

"You all right, Brock?" Randall says.

I lower my head in a nod, then wonder how he knows it's me, as a wolf.

"How far away is the rest of your pack?" Royle says, a dumb, sly look on his face.

"Nowhere where you'll ever find them." Randall looks down the barrel of the shotgun. "Now get."

Royle licks his dry lips, his face pale. "You're a wanted man, Randall Lowell."

"And I never want to cross paths with you again."

Randall fires the shotgun not two inches from Royle's head. Amazingly, no shot peppers his face. When Randall racks the shotgun, Royle rises from his cringing crouch and scrabbles away. I wouldn't be surprised if he pissed himself.

"Brock," Randall says, watching the sheriff flee into the night. "Let's go."

I trot over to him, my head held low, trembling all over. I must look like a dog who just came back from surgery at the vet.

"Can you change back yet?" Randall says.

I shake my head.

He sighs, then kills Collins's flashlight and beckons for me to follow.

Sure enough, the blue pickup idles on the road. Randall opens the door for me and I jump inside, feeling way too big and clumsy. My paws scrabble on the seat and I almost fall onto the pavement, but he helps me in.

Questions swirl in my head, dulled by the throb of pain, but I still can't speak.

Randall releases the brake and rumbles out of Pray, Montana, at more than sixty miles an hour. The truck bumps and creaks over the gravel road. I wince at my aching muscles and curl as best as I can on the bench seat.

Randall says nothing as he drives south in the thick of the night.

I want to change back; I'm tired of this. A small whine rises from my chest.

"You hurt bad?" Randall sounds gruff.

I shake my head. Despite the pain, the barbed-wire scratches have already closed up, already healing. *One of the perks.* The thought of Cyn makes me want to howl. No. I don't want her to see me like this. A wolf.

"You actually did it." Randall says more softly.

Does that mean he doesn't have to kill me, maybe?

"I guessed you would be a silver wolf. Jessie owes me fifty bucks."

I squint at him. Seriously?

"I'll help you to change back," he says, "in a minute."

With a sigh, I rest my muzzle on the dashboard.

Standing in the darkness, staring down at my huge wolf paws, I feel like a fool.

"All you have to do is let go," Randall says, for maybe the tenth time.

All I really want to do is keel over. I shut my eyes and blow out my breath. *Human.* I'm hoping and praying for it to work.

"Brock, no. You're trying too hard again."

I open my eyes to see Randall pacing. He keeps glancing back to the road, like the police could be here any minute. I have to do this fast.

Maybe I'm broken. Am I hopeless? Am I doomed to fail?

Get your shit together. If you fail at this, you're dead meat.

I suck in air, then blow it out slowly. I'm stronger than this. If the old Brock is beyond repair, then I need to be a new Brock now. Even if it means throwing away everything I used to believe just to survive in this fucked-up world.

Why? Because I won't let the nightmares win.

With a shuddering sigh, I unclench my muscles and feel the fever overtake me. Transformation ripples through my body, a wave through water, and my wolfskin disappears. I crouch, naked, trembling…and human.

That was it.

As soon as I stopped cringing, waiting for the pain to hit me, it happened. Painless. Easy.

Chris, convulsing on the bed. Fur bristling from his skin. A tail wriggling from his spine, claws curving from his fingertips, teeth erupting into fangs, yellow eyes rolling back. His body tearing apart from the inside out. Blood. Silence.

Was that really how it ended for Chris? Maybe he didn't die that way. Or didn't have to.

"So, bloodborn," Randall says, trying far too hard to sound happy. "You good?"

"Shut up."

I don't want him to see the tears on my face. How weak I am.

Randall's voice hardens. "What?"

You bit us. You changed everything. Left Chris in a hospital that stank of sickness and death, withering on a bed while the werewolf disease ate him from the inside out. Left me afraid I would kill myself.

"Why couldn't he do it?" I say to the moon. Why did he break instead of bend?

"Who?"

I shake my head, staring at the dark. "It shouldn't have happened. He shouldn't be dead."

Now Randall knows who I mean; I can see it on his face. He crouches before me, but says nothing. What can he possibly say?

"Why did you have to bite him? Why did we have to be so stupid?" My throat constricts.

He lowers his head. "A lot of things shouldn't have happened."

I keep crying. There isn't anything I can do about it. I can't stop people from being stupid, can't stop them from dying. All I can do is give my life everything I've got, because I could be nothing in an instant.

And then I'm quiet, and there is nothing else to do.

I stare at the ground, at myself sitting in the sagebrush. Dirt streaks my skin. It's very dark out here, for a human.

"I feel fucking stupid," I mutter.

Randall touches my shoulder, gingerly, as if afraid I might bite. "You okay now?"

"Besides feeling fucking stupid? Yeah."

"Come on." Randall holds out his hand. "Let's find you some clothes."

I meet the eyes of the one who bit me, then climb to my feet.

sixteen

There's no time to sleep, but exhaustion drags me down anyway. When I wake, the sun has already risen while Randall drives on.

We pass pines with branches like gap-toothed combs, the road following the curves of a boulder-dotted jade river. My legs itch to move. I wish I were outside the truck, running alongside. No, I would run away from the road, into the trees, where the air is sweetly cold and plump rabbits and fat deer wait for my teeth...

I shake my head. Leftover wolfishness.

"How did you find me?" My voice sounds thick with sleep.

"Tracked you down. You left a clear trail." Randall sounds matter-of-fact about it, but he might be too tired for anything else.

"Well." I clear my throat. "Thanks."

"Yeah."

We both carefully avoid looking at each other.

"Where are we going, anyway?" I say.

"South," he says.

Farther away from home. I think back to my bedroom, the cows, Dad. Mom's rose garden, wilting, but still hanging on.

What's left for me there?

The red rose...Cyn. A weight settles on my ribs. I failed her. But how was I supposed to know the police are psycho?

"Why did you run?" Randall says, still not looking at me.

"To get help for Cyn."

He presses his lips into a thin line. "That was a damn stupid thing to do." His voice softens. "But I know why you did it."

I glance at him, a question in my eyes.

"Remember the murders in Klikamuks?"

My stomach tightens. "How could I forget?"

"One of the victims...a dryad...her name was Chloe." His face remains perfectly still. "I wish I could have known her longer. But I loved her."

Killed by Benjamin Arrington, the man I helped. An image of him strangling Cyn blinks into my head, and I blink it away, but a bitter taste lingers on my tongue. I'm beginning to understand how little I knew, back in Klikamuks, when all I thought I was doing was helping a guy run some gicks out of town.

Gicks like Randall. Like me.

My jaw clenched, I stare out the side window. I won't look at him.

Randall hits the brakes. "Traffic jam." He growls under his breath. "We're definitely in Yellowstone now."

"Yellowstone?" A flicker of excitement revives me. "Where are the…?"

But I don't see geysers ahead, just a long line of cars, and tourists swaggering around with two-foot-lens cameras. They must be taking pictures of something. Through the spindly pines, there's a meadow dotted with dark shapes.

"We're going to be here for a while." Randall sighs and kills the engine.

We both hop out to see what's going on in the meadow. Peering through the tourists, I realize the dark shapes are distant elk. They clump in a tight herd, their heads high, their antlers thrown back. Scared. But why?

Randall passes me a pair of binoculars. "Look."

A big white wolf slinks through the grass. To its right, a black wolf circles around. They're sneaking up on an elk with a limp.

"Normal wolves?" I say.

Randall gives me a look. "You think?" The glint in his eyes says it all.

"Damn!" I whistle under my breath. "They're hunting right in front of all these tourists?"

"Shhh," he says.

Right next to me, a family whispers in what sounds like German, their camera shutters snapping. They have these looks on their faces that say they can't believe what amazing Nature we have here in America. If they only knew.

The limping elk's head swings up, and it stamps its hoof. All the nearby elk freeze.

Then, the black wolf charges. I track it through my binoculars, watching its paws pound across the ground while all the elk burst into a run at once. No wait, I know that wolf—Jessie. Damn, she's fast. She doesn't even waver as the enormous prey animals hurtle around her; she keeps her gaze glued to the limping elk.

The muscles in my thighs tighten and every instinct in me is hissing, *Hunt.*

The limping elk gallops through the grass, struggling to keep up with its herd, but it's already flagging. Jessie leaps at the elk's flank and latches on, tearing into its flesh. The elk bucks and kicks, but Jessie jumps away, and the white wolf surges out of the grass and latches onto the elk's nose. The elk stumbles but doesn't fall, flinging the white wolf away. Another black wolf—Isabella?—runs and bites the elk's rump. Blood streams down the elk's flanks and drips as it runs. It's going to bleed to death.

Along the road, the tourists gasp and chatter like this is some sort of fireworks show.

Jessie catches up to the elk again, and, in an impossible leap, soars onto the elk's back and latches onto its neck. Her weight drives the elk to a halt, and the other two wolves attack, pinning their prey. Within minutes the elk's legs fold. As soon as it hits the ground, maybe a dozen other wolves appear from the trees.

Steaming red blood, everywhere. Delicious and disgusting.

I can't even tell if the elk is totally dead before the wolves start feasting. And the scary part is, the wolf in me aches to join them.

"Shit," Randall says softly.

I glance at him, then see what he's staring at: park rangers exiting their jeep. A guy and a lady park ranger. Pretty soon their binoculars are on the wolf hunt, too. When the lady lowers her binoculars, she frowns and says something I can't hear.

Randall grips my arm. "We've got to warn Winema."

"Isn't she out there with the rest of them?"

"Of course not. She can't."

"Can't? But…"

He's not even listening, just jogging toward the truck. We hop back in and start crawling past the clot of tourists. Randall revs the engine impatiently and a few slow-moving, slug-fat women glare at him as they cross the road.

Then I see her: Cyn, running headlong toward the

rangers. There's a hard look on her face. She grabs the lady park ranger's arm, and I can tell by the burning in her eyes that Cyn is seconds away from doing something reckless.

"God dammit," I say. "Stop the truck!"

"What? Why?"

"Cynthia." I jab my finger in her direction.

Before Randall has even hit the brakes, I open my door and jump out. We're going so slow that I hit the ground walking.

What the hell is Cyn thinking, running past were-wolves with bloody muzzles? Jessie's going to kill her when she sees. I already know in the pit of my stomach that Cyn's about to spill the truth to the nearest sympathetic ranger.

Sure enough, the lady park ranger says, "What's the matter?"

And Cyn says, "My name is Cynthia Lopez."

My heartbeat stutters. They have to be blaring her name on the radio.

"Cynthia!" I skid to a stop beside her.

"Brock?" She looks thrown off balance. "Why are you here? I thought you went to—"

"No. Not now." I shake my head, praying she'll get the message. "We need to leave."

"What's going on here?" says the lady park ranger—*Wendelin*, her nametag says. She tilts her head to one side. "What did you say your name was again?"

Has she seen Cyn's face on a missing persons poster? Or mine?

"Cynthia Lopez," Cyn says, her cheeks flushed. "And I escaped the pack."

"Pack?" says the guy park ranger. His nametag reads *Pratt*. "You mean the wolves?"

Randall walks up behind Cyn and his hands descend on her shoulders—she looks tiny next to him. "Let's go. We're going to be late."

"No." Cyn twists, but can't free herself. "Those aren't ordinary wolves."

I can tell by the fear in Randall's eyes that we're losing control of the situation. Cyn's going to blow our cover, if she hasn't already.

Is that a good thing? Is this going to work?

Considering what just happened with Sheriff Royle, I don't even know anymore.

Pratt stoops to Cyn's height, like she's a little girl. "We very carefully regulate the wolves who travel between Yellowstone's borders. Each animal is microchipped, and park rangers like us regularly patrol the area. There's no need to be afraid of werewolves on our land." He grins, flashing too-bright teeth. "There are none."

Cyn's face twists like she wants to spit on his shiny boots. "Well, there are *now*."

Wendelin, staring at me, tells Pratt, "Those wolves do look unfamiliar. Maybe we should call the paranormal unit."

Randall lets go of Cyn and grabs my wrist instead, hard enough that my bones ache.

I frown at him and twist free, then wipe the sweat

from my forehead with the back of my hand. My nails slide sharply across my skin, and my hand slows, my fingers trailing...claws. Adrenaline jolts my muscles; fangs slide from my teeth.

Cyn's face pales. "Shit," she whispers.

"Paranormal unit," Pratt says, still grinning, only this time it looks more like the grimace of a taxidermied animal. "Good idea. I'll call them."

"We'd better go now," I babble, "so we don't get in you guys' way."

Randall sidesteps out of the conversation, and I see Winema approaching, her hand cradling her belly. With one look at the park rangers, her expression transforms from curiosity to fear. "Paranormal? What's going on?"

Wendelin looks at Winema. "Ma'am, we have to ask you to leave. For traffic purposes."

"But my husband's out there!" Winema's eyes widen. "He wanted to get a few photos of the wolves, and I lost sight of him in the trees..."

Yeah, right. If anything, I'd bet her husband Charles is that big white wolf eating elk guts right now. Same blue eyes.

Wendelin shares a scared look with Pratt. "We need to get these tourists out of here."

Randall grabs my wrist and yanks like he's going to wrench my arm out. I grab Cyn, and the three of us snake away through the crowd of tourists while Winema keeps the park rangers busy with her worried pregnant-lady story. I can tell that Wendelin still has her suspicions, though, because she keeps staring at me.

When we reach the truck, I say to Cyn, "Get in."

"But Brock," she says, her eyes boring into mine, even though Randall's literally breathing down her neck.

I shake my head. "Later."

She makes a frustrated noise, but hops into the truck; me and Randall climb in on either side. Pratt shouts something at the tourists and waves his arms, trying to get them to move. Randall honks the horn and starts driving.

"Look." Cyn leans forward to stare out the windshield. "The wolves."

The pack has scattered into the grass; only the white wolf remains, his legs stiff, staring at Winema with pale eyes. Knew it was Charles.

"Cynthia," Randall growls, his voice raw. "Next time you try to escape, don't blow our cover like that. It could get us all killed."

"You think the rangers wouldn't have put two and two together on their own?" she says. "Besides, it's not like they even had guns."

"The paranormal unit of Yellowstone," Randall says matter-of-factly, "is equipped to deal with Others ranging from rogue werewolves to frost giants who don't appreciate cars in their territory. That means a lot more firepower than anybody would ever need to blast a bloodborn off the face of the earth."

Cyn stares at the dashboard like she can burn holes in it with her eyes. "Sorry."

"'Sorry' won't cut it," Randall says. "Especially not when you explain this to Jessie."

"I can handle it," she says.

We're silent as Randall navigates out of the tourists and finally hits open road.

Cyn twists to stare me in the eye. "Brock, what happened to you...after...?"

It's incredibly hard to sit so close to her, her hip scalding against mine, with my fingers still armed with claws. I keep my head bowed, my lips pressed together to hide my fangs. I don't even know what my eyes look like.

"The damn fool bloodborn decided last night was a great night to escape," Randall says. "He wandered around the mountains of Montana for a bit, then had the amazing luck to blunder right into Sheriff Royle. Not sure what happened in between, but I ended up saving his ass when I found the sheriff employing a little bit of torture."

"Torture?" Cyn's eyes darken.

My nostrils flare and I suck in a slow breath. "Yeah. Royle isn't one of the good guys."

"But—what happened?"

I twist my head toward hers and our faces are only inches away, close enough to kiss, or maybe bite. Her breath breezes across my lips.

"I changed, Cynthia." My voice rasps in my throat. "That's what happened."

The muscles in her face tighten, then relax. She takes my

hand in hers and gives it a little squeeze. The tips of my claws press into her palm, but she doesn't let go. I fight the urge to turn away in shame. She smiles, though her eyes look sad.

"I knew you could," she whispers.

"He had to," Randall says.

Nobody says anything after that.

Wyoming whizzes past in a blur of trees and gray hills. Or maybe that's just what it looks like to me, since I'm too distracted by Cyn's bittersweet scent. Maybe it's because I'm sitting so close, or maybe it's because I finally changed into a wolf, but now I'm smelling all sorts of little pieces to the scent: the fading vanilla of her shampoo, the warm-fur aroma of her hair, and an almond sweetness that might be her skin itself.

God, I wish we were alone.

Randall's cell phone buzzes, and he drives one-handed while he fishes it out of his pocket. He flips it open and reads a text. "Really."

"What?" I say.

He flips it shut again and says nothing.

It's got to be past noon now, and my stomach is definitely letting me know it. Randall and Cyn both seem to be ignoring its louder and louder growls. We pass a billboard with a giant, juicy burger on it, and it's all I can do not to drool. And on another billboard, a reclining, half-naked lady. No, more like three-quarters-naked. Her curly blond hair tumbles around her face, and she bites her finger between red lips. Her boobs strain against her almost-see-through-but-still-PG13 button-down shirt, like gravity doesn't exist.

I read the fiery red letters on the sign. "*Demon Dan's*. Wow."

"Wow?" Cyn says. "I can't believe you're drooling over *that*."

"I'm not! It was that burger billboard, I swear."

"That's disgusting," she says, but she rolls her eyes.

Randall laughs. "That's our next stop."

seventeen

Demon Dan's turns out to be a windowless strip club just off the highway, right next to one of those huge gas stations with long parking spaces for truckers. On the walls of Demon Dan's, painted silhouettes of curvy women with devil's tails and horns strike sexy poses with pitchforks and beckoning fingers.

I've never been to a strip club before. Can't pretend like I'm not at least curious.

"Oh, damn," Cyn sighs.

"What?" I say, hoping my thoughts aren't plain on my face.

"This is going to be interesting," Randall says softly.

The cherry-red convertible cruises into the parking lot with Isabella behind the wheel. Before her sister even kills the engine, Jessie hops out in sunglasses and spiky sandals and clicks her way over to Cyn. The way Jessie's crimson lips form a deadly sneer, I step in front of Cyn like I might be some sort of shield.

"Honey," Jessie says straight past me, "I am so very disappointed in you."

Cyn sidesteps from my shadow and meets the werewolf's gaze. "What did you expect?"

"A little bit more loyalty from someone who's been given so much freedom."

"You're asking me for Stockholm Syndrome?" Cyn laughs. "Not going to happen."

Jessie advances, her sneer curling into a snarl that bares her long white fangs. "We treated you like you were one of us."

"Sweetie." Isabella strides from the convertible and takes her sister by the arm. "That's exactly the problem. You've been treating this poor human girl as if she's a werewolf. As if she's your very own bloodborn."

Jessie's snarl melts into a pout. "I've never had a bloodborn of my own."

"Whoa," Randall says, stepping forward. "Jessie, don't even go there. We can't have you turning hostages into more trouble."

I can't tell if Cyn looks flattered or creeped out.

Jessie sighs. "I apologize." But then her face hardens again. "Don't you try running off again, human, you hear?"

Cyn nods, though of course I know she's lying.

"Done?" Randall says. "We've got to get moving."

And so we all enter Demon Dan's. The sagebrush-sweet perfume of faerie wine soaks the air and tingles in my nose. The shadowy room in the front thumps with the beat of techno coming from beyond a curtain. The lady at the desk has death-white skin and bobbed black hair so sleek it looks plastic. Not to mention huge boobs.

She wrinkles her nose at our smell. "Werewolves?"

Isabella gives her a chilled glance. "Yes. Our Alpha wishes to speak with Dan."

"He's busy," says the death-white lady.

"If you're lying, leech…" Isabella lets it hang in the air.

Leech? Christ, this lady must be a vampire. And maybe Isabella doesn't like being one-upped in the seduction department.

The vampire sighs, then says, "He's in the back. Have your Alpha meet him there."

Isabella nods, then slips her cell phone from her tiny purse and dials. "Winema? Yes. Yes, the back room. We'll meet you there."

Jessie strides straight toward the velvet curtain. She pinches it between two nails and pulls it aside as if it's dirty, and Isabella slips through. Randall hovers behind me and Cyn, so I have no choice but to follow them.

My brain shuts off when my eyes overload.

Rainbow lights crisscross the darkness, shining on exotic dancers crouching in cages, clinging to poles, strutting by the bar. A bikinied woman with stoplight-red skin wraps her tail around a pole and slides down; another poses onstage, her platinum-blond hair the exact color of her feathery wings; a third ripples against the bars of her cage, her body sort of see-through. Not like a ghost, but like a woman made of glass.

"They're all Others!" Cyn says over the thudding music.

I look closer at the see-through woman. She has liquid skin and swirling white hair like waterfall foam. When she twists my way, my breath snags in my throat. She's totally naked, with sleek, sexy curves and generous breasts.

Cyn clutches my sleeve. "An undine!" she shouts in my ear, as if I'm not already deaf.

Randall grabs us both by the shoulders and hauls us through the strip club and into the back room, where it's whole a lot darker and less exciting.

On a pink velvet couch, a man sits with crossed legs. Goat horns peek out of his dark curly hair. He's got this weird smell to him, like burnt sugar. He slides a glance from Jessie, to Isabella, to Cyn, where his gaze lingers until her face reddens. He says something in Spanish that sounds an awful lot like a nasty pickup line.

Cyn's face goes from a normal blush to volcanic. "Pretending like I didn't understand," she mutters to me.

The man laughs, flashing a smile I'm sure girls think is hot. "Charmed."

"Demon Dan," Randall says. "Our Alpha."

Winema stands in the doorway, Charles at her heels. The fact that she's having a baby soon looks totally out of place here, but she looks almost bored. "Demon Dan. That's a fairly new name for you, isn't it, Danathiel?"

Demon Dan flinches, his smile dimming. "I'd appreciate it if you didn't call me that."

Is this guy really a demon? Why isn't he red like that pole dancer?

"We need to find Cliff Sterling," Winema says.

Dan's smile shuts off. "Now why would you do a thing like that?"

Winema paces closer to him. "We need his help."

"Oh, you must be fucked." Dan laughs humorlessly and twists a curl around his finger. "Are you in trouble with the law again?"

"Some people aren't as adept at bending the rules."

"You flatter me," Dan says coldly.

"You owe me a favor. Where's Cliff?"

"Have you met him? This is the man who grills mermaids when he feels like seafood."

"An urban legend," Winema says. "And yes, we've met before. Unfortunately for us, we've lost touch, and I don't know where he calls home. But I'm sure you do, considering how much faerie wine you sell here." Her voice roughens. "Does your queen know about your dealings in the black market? I doubt it."

Queen? So he's got to be a faerie. Not a very powerful one, though, if he's working for werewolves and not the other way around.

Dan arches his eyebrows. "She doesn't."

"Danathiel, I don't have very much time, which means I have even less patience."

He grimaces at her use of his true name. "Well, Cliff Sterling isn't here." When Winema growls, he adds quickly, "Try the Moonshine, down in Denver. You won't be able to find it on the map. It's beneath Rex's Steakhouse, through the back door. Tell him that I sent you, if you enjoy keeping your hides intact."

"I will," Winema says. "Anything else we should know?"

Dan shrugs. "If you don't mind me asking, why do you have a human with your pack?"

Winema glances at Cyn. "Hostage."

Cyn keeps her face perfectly cool.

Dan raises his eyebrows. "You *are* in trouble with the police. You'd best be on your way." He pauses. "Is the favor returned?"

Winema shares a glance with Charles, who nods. "Yes."

Everybody follows her back out, with me and Cyn at the rear.

"What," Dan calls after us, "no goodbye kiss?"

Cyn gives him an acidic glare over her shoulder.

His laugh sounds like icicles snapping. "Good luck with the Zlatroviks," he says, like we're really going to need it.

Cyn returns to the red convertible, so it's just me and Randall in the pickup. I'm sad to see her go, but glad I'm not constantly distracted anymore. We gnaw on strips of beef jerky and chug soda without stopping, just drive and drive.

I'd love a Bigfoot Burger right about now, but this doesn't seem like the time to stop.

Fatigue creases Randall's face. His eyelids lower as he nods in time with the radio.

"What's this music?" I say, to keep him awake.

"Vivaldi. The Four Seasons, Concerto Number Two in G Minor. This one is Summer." Randall turns up the volume. "Listen."

On the strings, flurries of falling notes, hard and fast. When I close my eyes, I see pelting rain and lightning ripping the sky.

"Reminds me of a storm," I say.

"Me, too."

We listen to the music whirl and quiet. Evening soaks through the sky like purple ink. Sunset takes forever to die above the prairie. The lights of scattered towns blink on, firefly-bright, in the long stretch of dusty darkness.

Randall's eyelids droop lower.

"I can drive," I say.

He glances at me, his eyebrows raised.

"Just tell me where we're going, and I can drive. You look beat."

Randall looks back out the windshield, then pulls off the road. "All right."

He slides out of his seat. As we cross paths in front of the hood, he gives me a glance. Not wary, exactly, but still calculating.

I buckle myself in. "Denver?"

He sits in the passenger's seat and stares straight ahead, his eyes distant. "Denver."

I release the parking brake and give the truck some gas.

We slide into a monotony of tires humming on pavement, the rumbling engine, and the fading sound of Vivaldi. At last, the radio disintegrates to static. I lean over and switch if off. Randall's head slumps against the back of the seat.

I let him sleep, and keep driving.

The hollowness inside me gnaws harder. I'm a werewolf now. One of the pack. I'm living with them, running with them.

What do you want to be when you grow up, Brock? A career fugitive?

I grip the steering wheel tighter. Klikamuks is looking less and less possible. Maybe I can find a new town, not too far away, where they wouldn't care too much if a new werewolf slipped into their forest on full moons. I wouldn't hurt anybody. I wouldn't even scare the neighborhood dogs. Of course, that would be like asking somebody to let black widows build webs in their basement. Even if the spiders promised not to bite.

I'm beginning to realize just how fucked I am.

In a side mirror, I see a green SUV tailgating us. As we round a curve, I read the gold letters painted on its side: *SHERIFF*.

Wow. I just got that much more fucked.

I give the truck more gas. The needle on the speedometer slides up to seventy-five. The sheriff's SUV keeps pace.

"Randall?" I realize I'm whispering, as if the sheriff can hear. "Randall!"

His head snaps upright, and he blinks at me. "How long was I out?"

"Don't know," I say. "Look behind us."

He twists in his seat, then swears.

We're going eighty now, and the sheriff's SUV turns on its siren. I clamp my hands on the steering wheel and glance at Randall.

"Pull over," he says.

"What the hell! Why? We can't just turn our—"

"We're not as fast as them."

"Oh."

I grit my teeth and ease up on the acceleration. We coast down to seventy.

"Brock. Pull over."

"Shit fuck fire."

I stomp on the brake, and the truck fishtails. Randall yanks on the steering wheel, and we skid to a halt on the side of the highway. The SUV stops behind us, its red and blue lights whirling, blinding in the rearview mirror. A police officer shuffles through papers on a clipboard, slowly, taking his goddamn time.

"Oh, Jesus," I say. "He's not Royle."

Randall looks like he'd enjoy skinning me. "What the hell did you think?"

Just some random sheriff who saw me speeding. And I could have gotten away.

"What are we going to do?" I say.

He looks at me, his eyes black, and shrugs. He's given up, hasn't he?

The police officer exits the SUV and strides up to my window. He shines a flashlight straight into my eyes, and it's all I can do not to bare my teeth. He taps on the window. Squinting, I roll it down.

"Is there a problem, officer?" I say.

It's so dumb that he squints right back at me. "Excuse me?"

I say nothing.

"Can I see a driver's license and vehicle registration?"

Of course, I don't have a license on me. I stare blankly at the officer.

"Sir," Randall says, "he hasn't got one."

The officer moves the flashlight beam onto his face. "Explain."

"He doesn't have his license yet," Randall says.

"Yeah." I force a laugh. "Keep failing that test."

"Let's see a learner's permit, then," the officer says.

My face heats. "See, I kind of left that at home, and—"

"Step out of the car," the officer says. "Both of you."

I clench the steering wheel even tighter, claws breaking from my fingernails. My heart thuds hard against my ribs.

Slowly, Randall unbuckles his seat belt. He meets my eyes, and nods.

"What?" I hiss.

He just nods again. What the fucking hell is that supposed to mean? Shit, I'm going to have to take matters into my own hands.

The police officer's radio crackles on, and he glances down.

I slam my foot onto the gas. The truck's engine roars, but we aren't going anywhere. Randall slams down the parking brake—I must have set it out of habit—and the truck leaps onto the road as if kicked severely in the rear.

Behind us, the police officer scrambles toward his SUV, trips, and climbs to his feet.

"Car!" Randall yanks the steering wheel to the right.

We swerve back into our lane, narrowly avoiding a head-on collision with a little blue sedan. I press the gas pedal to the floor and grip the wheel, the muscles in my arms cording. My teeth itch as they lengthen into fangs.

Okay. Calm down. Now is *not* the time to turn into a wolf.

Sirens pursue us, growing louder and louder. The SUV looks way too big in the rearview mirror. A green sign promises an exit ahead. I yank the wheel and we whip onto the off-ramp, roaring along the curve at full speed. Thank God it's empty. The SUV skids after us, scraping the guardrail with a shower of sparks.

"Asshole!" I shout. "Get off our tail!"

Randall stares at me, his eyebrows sky-high. "Brock. What the fuck are you doing?"

"Getting us the fuck out of here."

At the end of the off-ramp, a sign forbids U-turns. Good idea. I twist the wheel and spin the truck 180 degrees. The tires skid and bounce across the asphalt. Behind us, I hear the screech of the SUV's brakes. Nose in the right direction, I gun the engine again, run a red light, and swerve right onto a side road, then left onto another. I'm sweating hard, terrified I'll hear sirens again, but we drive deeper into silence.

I blow out my breath and slow to the speed limit. "Okay. We're cool."

"We are not cool," Randall growls. "You shouldn't have done that."

"Why not?" I'm grinning now, turbocharged on adrenaline. "It's not like we made anything worse than it already was."

"Speak for yourself. And we're running on empty."

I groan. Then, a tiny old gas station appears like a miracle on the horizon. I don't want to stop, but of course we can't keep going without gas. I glance at Randall, who nods, then pull into the station and kill the engine.

"I've got to make a phone call." Randall hands me a wad of cash. "You pay."

"Right."

Still buzzed and jumpy, I walk into the store, feeling like a movie guy on an important mission. A skinny guy stands behind the counter, leaning over some trashy magazine and chewing on a wad of minty gum.

"Hey," I say, "I need some gas."

"Sure." The guy doesn't glance up.

Maybe it's the gum, or his laziness, or the fact that we're running from the cops, but I instantly hate him. I slap the cash on the counter, loud enough that there's no way he can't hear. He grabs it and starts riffling through the bills.

"How much?" he says, cracking his gum.

I flex my fingers and try not to growl. "Put it all on pump number two."

"Sure…" The guy squints at a twenty dollar bill as if not believing it's real. "Hey, is this one of those new ones?"

I glance out the window and see Randall across the street, pacing beneath the red-and-white sign of a Grocery Mart. He's still talking on the cell phone, probably to Winema. I wonder how pissed she is right now.

"Okay…" says the guy behind the counter. "That's sixty-two dollars."

"Sure," I say. "Go for it."

I glance back again. This time, I see a police cruiser driving nearer.

I sprint out the store, past the pickup truck, and across the street. "Randall!"

He frowns at me. "What?"

"They're coming."

eighteen

I grab Randall's arm and drag him into Grocery Mart to hide. Too-bright fluorescent lights hurt my eyes, and the cheery blue-red-and-yellow bunting decorating the store doesn't look real. We jog past two women talking across their shopping carts, then disappear into an aisle with shelves stocked to the ceiling with pet food.

"There's got to be a back exit," I say.

"Brock." Randall shakes free from my grip. "We're maybe ten minutes away from the rest of the pack. We shouldn't split up."

"Yeah, but if we lead Royle to the werepuppies, he's going to shoot them on sight." My voice shakes with rage. "I'd rather kill the bastard first."

His eyes shine with a mix of sadness and pride. "Let's get these police off our tail."

Together, we stride to the end of the aisle and lope

along the back wall, trying not to move fast enough to be suspicious. I look down the aisles as we pass, meeting the eyes of a clerk, a baby in a shopping cart, a man in uniform—

I freeze, a classic deer-in-the-headlights, while Randall strides onward.

Deputy Collins. He freezes, too. I'm bigger than him, for sure. He must recognize us, because he looks scared shitless. I raise one hand as high as my head, slowly, to show him I'm not some mindless beast.

He frowns and reaches for his belt—the gun at his belt.

"Brock!"

Randall tackles me and slams me to the floor behind a pyramid of oranges. A gunshot cracks, deafeningly close—then screaming—then something sticky rains down on me. I look up at a burst orange, leaking juice and pulp.

"Everybody out of the store!" Collins shouts.

I'm shaking with fear and rage, my spine bending on the verge of wolf. Randall pins me to the floor and stares me in the eye.

"Do not fight him," he growls. "Do you understand?"

I stare at him, my skin clammy, my head foggy. He wrenches me to my feet and half-drags, half-hauls me out of there.

"Stop, or I'll shoot!" Collins shouts, like he didn't already.

Of course, me and Randall keep running. We dodge behind a display of toilet paper, and the deputy's boots rap closer on the tiles. Randall shoves the display, and individually wrapped rolls avalanche onto Collins.

It would be funny, if I weren't so pissed.

My muscles burn with the effort of holding back the beast. I pant against the pain and let Randall lead me onward, away from the deputy and the desire to tear out the asshole's throat for even daring to shoot at me.

"There's nowhere to run," Collins says. "You're surrounded."

Fuck that shit. Randall must be thinking the same thing, because he lunges down an aisle at a dead sprint. Collins darts after him, stops, and raises his gun between two hands. In my head, I see Randall falling, bleeding.

I lumber after Collins like a hunchback, my skeleton reshaping, my hair thickening into a gray pelt. A snarl rumbles from my throat. Collins whirls on me, his eyes glassy and wide. I must look like a monster.

"Don't move!" His voice quavers, but he holds his gun steady.

"Get out of our way," I rasp.

Collins wrinkles his forehead. "Put down your weapons—don't turn into a wolf!"

I laugh a barking laugh. "You have no fucking clue what you're doing."

Behind him, Randall creeps nearer, claws curving from his fingertips. I try not to stare and give him away. I teeter on the brink of wolf.

"Turn back," Collins tells me. "Turn back to human, and lie down on the floor. Do it!"

Randall steals close enough to touch Collins. He raises his glinting claws above his head, then slices the air and hits Collins, who crumples under the blow. The gun skitters onto the floor, and Randall kicks it under a shelf.

"Let's go," he tells me. "But not like that."

I nod, then look at myself. I'm still half-beast, the seams of my clothing strained, my skin shaggy with silver fur. I try to breathe deeper, but it sounds raspy and shallow inside my misshapen rib cage. Fear weakens my legs.

"Can't." I cough. "Can't change."

"You have to," Randall says. "You have to choose, wolf or human."

But what if I can't change back?

I swallow hard and shut my eyes, willing myself to relax into a body. The change ripples through me, and I stagger forward. My eyes snap open; I'm now entirely wolf. I glance around at the shreds of my clothing on the floor. Great.

Randall winces. "Okay, I kind of hoped it would be human. But whatever. Let's move!"

He jogs toward the doors and I follow him, my claws clicking on the tiles. The smells of the grocery store overwhelm me: onions moldering pungently in a heap, plasticky baby diapers, a pickle jar leaking sharp vinegar on the shelf beside me, the warm bitterness of coffee, cold cuts mellowing in the freezer. Scattered throughout the store, a few customers stand unmoving, shocked and gawking.

A drooly little toddler in a shopping cart seat reaches for me. "Doggy!"

"No," murmurs the toddler's mom. "Werewolf."

This is completely and utterly bat-shit insane. I don't belong in this mundane place, in this piece of everydayness. I hold my head low and tuck my tail between my legs, as if I can skulk beneath the bright fluorescent and not be seen. The automatic doors swish open and I trot through into the night, feeling all the more ridiculous. Outside, cops scuttle around the gas station and the baby-blue pickup like hornets on jam.

"This way," Randall whispers.

We slide alongside the windows of the Grocery Mart and hurry down an alley, across the street, and into a park full of whispering cottonwoods. The spicy-sweet perfume of their sap tingles in my nose and snags a memory of the trees beside the river in Klikamuks. For a fragment of a minute, it fills me with wistfulness. I wish I were running for the light-footed joy of it, not fleeing heavy with dread.

A low whistle, like someone calling a dog. I swivel my ears toward the sound.

Grady walks out from behind a tree, dressed entirely in camouflage. He looks like a solider who got lost in the jungle for a few months.

"Over here!" he whispers.

Randall jogs to him. "The cops are on our tail. I tried to warn the rest of the—"

"We know," Grady says. "Winema sent me after you guys."

What, to rescue us? I snort, and Grady glances at me.

"Hot damn! Is this the bloodborn? For a sec I thought you were—"

"Grady," Randall says, "where is Winema?"

He shrugs. "Around here, somewhere."

"She shouldn't be. There are a shit-ton more cops than there were originally. We've got to get out of here before they follow us."

I turn around and point my nose the way we came. I don't smell any strangers.

"Understood." Grady crouches. "Let's move."

Quickly, Randall shucks off his clothes, silver fur already hiding his skin. He changes fast, the wolf breaking free in one convulsion. Grady sheds his ratty camouflage and transforms into a rangy gray wolf.

We zigzag through the park, hiding behind bushes and benches. Why aren't we just sprinting straight into the hills? Hunched behind a statue of a guy on a horse, I growl softly and nip at Grady's heels. Move faster! He glances at Randall, who nods. Grady bolts across the field. A gunshot cracks the night and I hunker low, my ears flattened against my skull. Grady swerves, and another gunshot flings dust into the air where he was standing a moment before. He lunges to the left, toward some shrubbery, and—

A third gunshot.

Grady yelps and thuds on the ground. Blood spurts from the wound in his neck, soaking his fur. He struggles to stand, then falls into a puddle of his own blood. He twists his head to look at us. Within seconds his eyes dull, unseeing.

I hear a high whine. I realize it's coming from me.

I've never seen anyone die before. Not Chris, not even Mom.

Sirens grow louder. Through the trees lining the lane, cop-car lights flash brokenly. Randall woofs, then points his muzzle ahead. There's only one way to go. He leaps out from behind the statue at a dead run.

Gunshots rattle from the darkness, but Randall's too fast for that—he's already streaking through the night like a comet. I don't know if I can keep up, though I have to. Heart hammering, I sprint after him through a fresh hail of bullets. They don't touch me—I'm going too damn fast—but shit, they got Grady.

Randall skitters down an alley, and I follow him. At the end of the alley, past the weedy outskirts of town, the wild night calls to us. Randall bolts for the chance; I'm only a hair behind him. We're almost out of the alley and into the clear when a car screeches to stop right in front of our noses, tires smoking on the asphalt.

Not just any car. The red convertible.

"Get in," Jessie says, "but try not to get any blood on the seats, if you're bleeding."

Isabella holds a back door open. Me and Randall lunge inside. Cyn, sitting shotgun, twists back to stare at us with huge, dark eyes.

"Where's Grady?" Jessie says. "Is he—?"

Randall nods.

"Jessie," Isabella says, her voice tight. "Go!"

A cop stands in the alley, his legs braced in a firing stance, and raises a gun.

"Hold on," Jessie says, and then she guns it.

Wind whistles through my fur and I flatten my ears. Another gunshot, but it sounds miles away. Jessie peels out of there, zooming past the outskirts of town, leaving the cops literally in our dust. She doesn't hit the highway straightaway, but takes a crazy twisting path on a network of roads through the fields. We hit a gravel road, the wheels spitting pebbles, dirt rising in a choking cloud that makes us all cough. Finally, we see the highway again. Our speed levels out to a cruise, the wind whipping past, my eyes watering.

Cyn twists back again, her eyes looking straight into mine. "Who…?"

I shrink down in the seat, trying really hard not to look so huge and bristly and wolfish, but yeah, that's impossible.

"Randall, honey." Isabella eyes us both. "And his bloodborn."

With a woof, Randall nods.

Cyn's eyebrows go so high they disappear beneath her bangs. We're running from the cops at about ninety miles an hour, I almost got shot, and now just happens to be when she first sees me as a wolf.

Could things get any more ridiculous?

"Brock." A smile creeps across Cyn's face. "This is so…strange."

I snort. Exactly what I was thinking.

"Can you change back?" she says.

I nod, then shake my head, because then of course I'd be buck naked.

"Not in my car!" Jessie says.

Randall makes a soft growl and rests his nose against Jessie's headrest.

"All right, all right," she says. "Stop breathing down my neck."

The tires squeal as Jessie hits the brakes and swerves off onto the shoulder of the road. The low rumble of the engine undercuts the rustling of wind in a nearby corn-field. Isabella opens the door and hops out to let me and Randall past. He trots away from the road, shakes as if flinging water from his fur, then starts to transform.

I look away and prowl deeper into the cornfield. I don't want Cyn to see me change.

"Don't go too far," Randall calls after me, his voice still hoarse and growly.

But once I start walking, I don't want to stop. Out here, my nose full of the grassy sweetness of ripening corn, I can imagine I'm back in Klikamuks, just going on a night-time walk. *Down in the valley, fog overflows from the river and spills over the sleeping fields. The thick wet air tickles my throat, scented with river mud, wet grass, ripening corn, and the roast beef of a recent dinner trickling from a window.*

I can't ever go back to that, can I? I'm Other now.

Cyn walks through the rows of corn, a bundle in her arms. Great. Now I have an audience. "There you are," she says.

I give her a look, but she isn't going away.

"They're waiting," she says. "Unless…"

Unless what? Does she think I can run away with her like this? I can't pretend like I was never bitten. Cyn's just going to have to graduate high school and move away to college and keep on living a normal life without me. Anger chokes my throat. I close my eyes, as if that gives me more control over the dark.

"Brock, are you going to change back or not?"

Well, shit. There's no point in pretending anymore. She's already seen Brock the Beast.

With a sigh, I flip myself inside-out, my fur shrinking to bare skin, my paws reshaping into toes and fingers digging into soft earth. Human again, I open my eyes, climb to my feet, and dust off my hands.

I'm not looking at Cyn. She's got to be totally disgusted right now.

"Brock?" she says.

I can hear a million questions in the way her voice rises at the end. "Yeah," I say, "I'm okay. I got shot at, I almost got us arrested, and I keep changing into a wolf whenever I get angry. But other than all that, really, I'm okay."

I'm still not looking at Cyn, but she marches up to me. "You're not."

I shrug, my eyes on what she's carrying. "Hope those are clothes for me."

"Yes." She shoves them into my arms. "Brock, look at me."

I do what she says, not hiding how pissed I am.

"Your eyes!" She takes a step back, the expression on her face resetting itself. "Sorry, I was just surprised...they're *yellow*."

"Yeah?" I laugh. "What did you expect?"

A smile crooks the corner of her mouth. "You don't look bad with yellow eyes. Kind of sexy." She cups my face in her hands.

A heat other than anger spreads through me. I'm more than aware that I'm naked, and she's standing so close to me with this burning curiosity in her eyes. We lean together, slowly, and I kiss her. When she kisses me back, twisting her fingers in my hair, a moan escapes me. I wish we didn't have to be out here in the middle of a cornfield with cops on our tail, and a pack of werewolves waiting...if only the muddy ground were a soft bed, then I'd let her devour me the way I know she wants to.

But no. That's never going to happen now. I'm infected.

"Cyn." I withdraw from her. "I can't."

Her eyes flare, and I can see the hurt on her face. "What's wrong?"

"I'm trying to move forward, like you said, but—" My voice breaks. "But I know this is impossible. I can't be with you."

"Why?"

"Because I'm not the guy you want!" The words explode from me. "I'm a gick, okay?"

"Don't—"

"You wanted me to change, and I have. This is who I

am now. I'm a werewolf. I'm never going to be able to go home with you, Cyn."

She stares at me with bright eyes. "You don't know that."

"How can I go back to Klikamuks? When they all know what I am, they'll hate me."

"Not everybody hates werewolves, Brock."

"The ones who do are enough." I dump the clothes onto the ground, grab a pair of jeans and start pulling them on. "Don't ask me how we're supposed to escape the cops and clear our names and live happily ever after."

"Happily ever after?" Randall strides closer. "For starters, get your asses moving."

"Sorry," Cyn says, her jaw clenched. "We're moving."

She stalks back to the road, and I have no choice but to follow.

nineteen

We see the lights of Denver, staining the sky purple, before the city itself. Skyscrapers jut on the horizon, their glittering windows outshining the stars. Driving straight down the highway into canyons of steel gives me this tight, jittery feeling—how the hell can this be a good idea, going toward the crowds and the cops?

"Almost there, almost there," Jessie chants under her breath.

I want to hold my breath until we're there, until I know we're safe.

Finally, we find an old brick building without any windows, the curly red neon letters spelling *Rex's Steakhouse*. After Jessie bitches about scraping the paint on the convertible, we park in an alley, then skulk around behind the steakhouse. Winema is already there with Charles, watching a rat scuffle under a dumpster.

"Classy," Cyn mutters.

"Jessie, Isabella," Winema says. "You're with me."

The sisters flank their Alpha, their eyes flashing in the darkness.

"And us?" Randall asks.

"Bring the bloodborn, and the girl. To explain things."

Randall plants his hand between my shoulder blades, and my back stiffens. He shoves me forward, and we march up to the door marked *Employees Only*. Winema raps on the door, her knuckles making a dull metallic ping. After a minute, the door opens and there's a huge guy in a tight black T-shirt, his face all scarred up.

"Yes?" he says.

"Danathiel sent us. We would like to speak with Cliff Sterling."

The huge guy arches a battered eyebrow, but says nothing.

Winema's about a foot shorter than this guy, but she stares straight into his eyes. "I'm the Alpha of the Bitterroot Pack. I'd like to ask him a favor."

The huge guy's gaze slides away, and he steps aside. "Come inside."

We follow him through a dark stockroom that smells a lot like cardboard and a little like blood, then down a dusty staircase with a single light bulb swaying above our heads. Claws itch in my fingernails. This looks like the perfect place to murder somebody and chop their body up into tiny pieces—maybe serve it in the steakhouse later.

We reach a single door at the bottom of the staircase.

Another guy, even huger, nods at the first guy, then opens the door for us.

Down here, the sweet sagebrush perfume of faerie wine is so thick it makes me dizzy just to breathe. This must be the Moonshine, all slick black leather and glass mixed with scarred wooden tables and roughhewn granite. Jazz music smoothes over the clink of knives carving meat. Backlit bottles glow green, blue, and amber along a wall at the bar. Men in tuxes and women in evening gowns sip leaf-green faerie wine from champagne glasses, their eyes predatory as they scan the room. I feel like a dirty five-year-old in my borrowed jeans and T-shirt, and I'm very aware this isn't our territory.

"Cliff must be in the VIP lounge," Winema says.

She leans on Charles's arm as she navigates through the crowd. Ahead, there's a doorway with red curtains tied back by gold ropes, trying a little too hard to look swank. The room beyond is dark and denlike; wall-to-wall leather couches circle a low table. A man sits alone. A black cowboy hat shadows his face as he bends over his plate, sawing into a bloody, raw chunk of steak. At least, I hope it's steak.

"Excuse me," Winema says. "I wondered if I—"

"Haven't seen you in years," the man says in a soft voice. "Please, have a seat."

He brings a piece of steak to his mouth and I glimpse a flash of fangs. When Winema sits opposite him, he looks up at last.

So this is Cliff Sterling. Blond hair, a reddish beard, a weatherworn face zigzagged by scars. He looks about as old as my dad. Pinned to his lapel, there's a mysterious gold-dusted lily the color of sky. From the Faerie Queen.

"Welcome to the Moonshine," Cliff says. "Are you hungry?"

"Yes," Winema says, "but we don't have much time."

He dabs his mouth with a napkin and shakes his head. "You're safe here. The law wouldn't dare set foot in my den."

"Thank you," Winema says. "How much do you know?"

"The gist." Cliff sips some faerie wine—guess he samples what he sells. "You've been outlaws for quite some time, but it appears a particular sheriff is hell-bent on taking you down. I'm impressed you lasted this long."

Winema raises her eyebrows. "An advantage of keeping your pack small. Mobility."

"Would you like a drink?" Cliff slides a crystal bottle across the table. "This is one of the finest vintages, by the Faerie Queen's personal distiller."

"I can't." Winema's hand rests on her pregnant belly.

"Ah, forgive me. I wasn't thinking." Cliff frowns. "When are you due?"

"Soon. Too soon. I don't want my baby to be born in these circumstances."

Charles rests his hand on Winema's shoulder. Cyn glances at me, her eyes gleaming darkly in the shadows.

Cliff tilts his head and closes his eyes for a moment. "You need my help."

"Are you willing to offer it?"

He gives her the thinnest of smiles. "Always. But you

will no longer be an Alpha. The Bitterroot pack will simply…" He sips his wine. "Vanish."

My stomach tightens. "Vanish?"

Cliff's pale gray eyes latch on mine, and I look away to show submission. I'm probably out of line even opening my mouth.

"A bloodborn?" says the Zlatrovik Alpha.

"He's mine, sir," Randall says. "He's new."

"I could tell." Cliff's gaze slides to Cyn. I hate how he's looking at her like she's a heifer for sale. "And the human girl?"

"A hostage." Winema's face hardens. "She won't be staying with us much longer. I trust you can help us in that regard?"

Cliff nods. "Once you become Zlatroviks, your past lives will cease to exist."

My past life will cease to exist. Like me and Cyn never met. Like there never was a Brock before.

"Provided," Cliff adds, "that each of your wolves proves their loyalty."

"There are children in the Bitterroot Pack," Winema says.

Cliff smiles. "You would be surprised what a child can do."

Winema stares at the empty wine glass on the table. Her eyes look like she's trying to stare years ahead. Charles squeezes her shoulder, his face tight, but his eyes glitter with the kind of hope some people call desperation.

"That's what I can offer you," Cliff says. A waitress

refills his glass of faerie wine, and he sips it slowly. "Nothing more."

"Winema," Charles says, "this is why we came here."

"I know," she says. "But—I know."

Jessie and Isabella share a glance. I wonder if they're worried about their Alpha showing weakness. Our Alpha. I'm a part of this.

"I would suggest that you sleep on it," Cliff says, "but I doubt you have much time."

"Yes." Winema looks him in the eye. "We will join you."

Cliff smiles. "Welcome to the family." Despite the sweet way he says his words, there's a hint of bitterness in his voice.

Winema keeps Charles, Isabella, and Jessie with her and Cliff in the VIP lounge. They all order dinner, on the house, so there must be a lot of negotiating ahead. Me and Cyn follow Randall back to the main room of the Moonshine, where we sit at the bar. Nobody looks at us, their faces shadowy and impossible to read.

Cyn nudges me with her elbow. "What's going on?"

"Hell if I know." I look at Randall. "Do you know what you're doing next?"

His eyes look like embers in the darkness. "What *we're* doing next," he corrects. "You're going to have to prove to Cliff that he should make you one of his own, a Zlatrovik, just like everybody else will. Or…well, there isn't an or.

Unless you're happy with the idea of facing a really fucked-up justice system."

I feel like I swallowed ice. "Me?"

He claps his hand on my shoulder and gives me a crooked smile. "I told Winema what happened, blood-born. You're part of the pack."

Cyn finds my hand beneath the bar and grips it tight. "What if he doesn't want that?"

Randall doesn't even look at her. "He doesn't belong with you." His phone buzzes, and he digs it out of his pocket to read a text.

I stare blankly at the reflections in the polished wood of the bar. She doesn't belong here, either. She can't be part of this plan. I don't know what's going to happen to her, but they won't let her get away and tell the police.

"What about Cyn?" I say.

Randall shuts his phone and slips it into his pocket. "I don't know."

Something in his voice tells me he's lying, that he knows what the Zlatroviks do to humans who know too much.

Cyn leans across me to stare at Randall. "I can't be your hostage forever. Right?"

He looks at her with dark, dark eyes. "We don't need you anymore."

What did that text say? Did Winema order him to hand Cyn over to the Zlatroviks? Take her to an alley and kill her himself?

"I can find my own way out." Cyn stares boldly into his eyes. "If you let me go."

"It's not going to work like that," Randall says.

I squeeze her hand tight. Don't do anything reckless, Cyn.

"Brock," she says, half-standing. "Let's go."

I can feel Cyn's hand sweating in mine. She glances at me, a bright shard of hope in her eyes, full of maybes for me and her.

"Go?" Randall shakes his head and laughs, but it sounds fake. "Don't try to play hero. You're both going to get yourselves killed the moment you set foot in the street. Either by the police or, more likely, Cliff's men."

"But we joined their pack," I say. "They wouldn't kill us, they—"

"We haven't earned their loyalty yet." Randall glances at the time on his cell phone and growls. "Jesus, what's taking so long?"

"What is?" I say, but he ignores me.

Cyn hesitates. "Brock, have you heard about these tests of loyalty?" Without waiting for my reply, she keeps talking. "The Zlatroviks are infamous. They're going to make you murder one of their enemies. At the very least."

I clench my jaw. "Yeah, I figured."

"Finally," Randall mutters.

A tall man in a black shirt sits on the barstool next to Cyn. He smiles for her eyes only, and his goatee makes him look devilish. He reeks with a sickly sweet aroma, like faerie wine mixed with something burnt.

"Can I buy you a drink?" he says to her, like I'm not even there.

I press my fingernails into Cyn's palm in warning.

"Sure," she says.

My eyes snap to Cyn, and I see a slow smile bloom on her face. The wrongness of it twists my guts. She watches, smiling, as the stranger buys a bottle of faerie wine and pours her a glass of the green liquor himself.

"Cyn!" I say. "What do—"

"Please," says the stranger.

He glances at me, and his eyes glitter like black glass. A drunken feeling clouds my head. My hand goes limp, and Cyn's sweaty fingers slide past my skin.

Who is this stranger? He doesn't smell like a wolf… more like Demon Dan. A faerie.

I swing my head toward Randall, my pulse throbbing in my temples. "Randall."

He's staring at Cyn with a carefully empty expression, but I can see pain sharpening his eyes. He was waiting for this.

Cyn lifts a glass of faerie wine to her lips. She drains it dry.

"Cynthia." The word escapes me as a growl, cutting through the clouds in my head.

Randall catches my arm. "Brock," he says in a low, intense voice. "Leave her alone. You have to let her go."

"No," I say, my own voice too loud in my ears. "Cynthia, stop."

She glances at me, her eyes glossy and unfocused. "Try some, Brock! This stuff is…really good." Her forehead hits the bar, and she giggles, her shoulders shaking. "Some more, please," she slurs, her voice muffled.

She's shitfaced already? Christ, faerie wine must be toxic.

"Brock." Randall drags me away from the bar. "They're helping her forget."

"Forget what?"

"All of this. And then she can go home."

My eyes burn. "What's all of this?"

The words rattle from Randall's mouth like bullets. "The kidnapping, the police, the pack, the faeries, everything. You have to let her go."

I shake my head and try to step past him, but he blocks my way.

"Do it for her," he whispers. "Not for yourself."

"No!"

The faerie guy glances at us. "Would you like me to give him some wine, as well?"

To forget it all. To know nothing about the teeth that scarred me, the disease that took my brother away, the hate that fills my family's eyes.

To start over. As a bloodborn. Alone. No, as a member of the Zlatrovik pack.

Without Cyn. Without Dad.

I wouldn't be Brock anymore.

"I'm going to have to say no." My voice shakes, but I'm looking Randall straight in the eye. "And you can't take away Cynthia's memories without asking her. You can't force her to change, like you did to me."

Randall looks at me as if he's been betrayed by his own son. "Brock."

"Sorry." I shake my head. "Definitely fuck that shit."

He tries to grab my shoulder, but I twist away and make it to the bar. I grab the bottle of faerie wine and hurl it against the wall. The crash attracts the attention of everybody in the Moonshine. Dozens of glowing eyes fix on me.

Randall snarls and sticks his face into mine. "Bloodborn! You're out of line."

I'm not even going to bother with his werewolf dominance games. I'm not even going to pretend I'm a part of his pack anymore.

"Get the fuck out of my way."

Fangs unsheathe from Randall's teeth. His hair pales to silver. "Brock, don't do this."

"It's too late."

I feint a lunge, then sidestep and barrel past him. Off-balance, Randall stumbles against a barstool and falls. I don't look back, just get the hell out of that place with its stink of faerie wine and betrayal. Randall's snarl echoes after me.

He's going to hunt me down as the silver wolf. I've failed him as a bloodborn. Spurred on by adrenaline, I charge up the stairs, into the stock room, and out the back door. I slow only to unbuckle my belt and kick off my shoes. Then I'm running again, peeling off my shirt, stoking the anger inside me to speed the change. I stumble on twisting legs, then dive into the shape of a wolf, my paws hitting pavement.

Stronger, faster, I hurtle through the dark streets of Denver.

A howl splits the night. Rage, fear, and sadness twist together as the sound rises above the city. My ribs tighten, and I choke back an answering howl.

I have to find help for Cyn, before it's too late and she's forgotten me forever. She might remember the old Brock, the guy she dated and dumped, but not the new Brock, the one she might love again.

Do it for her. Not for yourself.

Would it be a kindness to let her forget? To let her go?

Blindly, I run through the darkness. I don't belong here anymore. I don't belong anywhere, but I can't stop moving, even though the people on the street gasp and shout and catcall as I sprint past them.

A woman screams, "Don't let it bite me!" with no way of knowing that I won't.

I'm the silver wolf now. Randall has made me in his image, and God, I hate it.

Then, as I run, I hear a girl's trembling voice. Cyn? I veer down a street, paws thundering on the sidewalk, and spot a cop car pulled over beside a familiar sedan. Inside the car, a girl with long, dark hair cries as she speaks. I know her—I saw her in the meadow, that first day I saw the Bitterroot Pack all together.

From the back seat, a baby wails and a puppy howls. A werepuppy.

I slow to a trot and hide in the shadows.

Royle. The sight of him loosens a growl inside me, but I swallow it back.

"I won't ask you again," he says. "Step out of the car."

"I can't," the girl says, her teeth bared, her voice ragged. Her fear sharpens into anger, and she sounds so much like Cyn it hurts. "I can't leave them."

Royle levels his gun at her face. "Open the door or I'll end things now."

The girl wipes her eyes and unlocks the door. Royle wrenches it open, hauls her out of the car, and forces her to the pavement. In the back seat, the werepuppy starts yipping and snarling. The baby cries so loud it goes hoarse.

"Let me go," the girl cries. "I haven't done anything!"

"It's what you are, gick, not what you've done."

I can't fucking believe this. I'm going to rip a hole in this bastard. Police brutality won't even come close to what I'm about to do.

Fangs bared, fur bristling, I step from the shadows.

twenty

"Stop!" A voice rings out over the sound of approaching sirens.

A woman in a white dress appears from the night like a ghost. She solidifies into the shape of Winema, her shoulders squared, her face steeled for battle. Her hand lingers on her belly, though, and her eyes betray pain.

Royle crouches over the girl, keeping her down, but looks up.

"Let her go," Winema says, her voice commanding. "She's done nothing wrong."

Royle springs to his feet, reaching for his holster. "You, on the other hand…"

Shaking with a barely restrained snarl, I creep toward Royle, the fur along my spine bristling, my teeth itching to bite.

"Let her go," Winema repeats.

"I should put a bullet in your brain right now and spare myself the paperwork."

The girl crawls away and grabs the car door to lift herself. A werepuppy scrambles into the front seat and runs to her, licking her tears.

"I can tell you," Winema says, "that this girl, and these babies, are innocent."

"Innocent." Royle shakes his head. "How can a gick be innocent?"

And I would have said the same thing, before.

Winema's eyes glow yellow. "We are not gicks."

"It doesn't matter," Royle says, his face almost calm with triumph. "You gave us quite the chase, but once we knew you were heading for Denver, we surrounded the area. You and your pack have nowhere to run."

Winema's face reveals nothing. "We're done running."

Royle laughs, shaking his head. "There's no hope of talking your way out of this one. No matter how sympathetic the judge is to gick rights."

"What makes you think we're going to *talk* our way out?"

I'm almost into the light now, and Winema sees me, but Royle still doesn't.

"What did you do with the human girl?" The Sheriff cocks his head. "And her infected boyfriend? They better not be rotting in the woods, because their parents aren't too far—" His gaze swings to me. "Shit!"

Yeah, shit. I hoped you wouldn't notice me until I had my teeth in your throat.

Winema curls her lip, her teeth lengthening into fangs. "You aren't making this easy."

I growl, a low rumble that shakes my bones.

The werepuppy jumps from the car and sinks its needle-teeth into Royle's ankle. Royle staggers back, bellowing like a bull. He kicks the werepuppy away, ignoring its yelping, and aims his gun between its eyes.

He's going to shoot it. Shoot a baby as if it's nothing more than vermin.

"No!" It tears from Winema's throat, more snarl than word.

She throws herself at Royle, her face mutating into a wolf's muzzle. He barely has time to shout before she clamps her jaws on his neck and rips his flesh, silencing him. Royle thuds on the road with a last gurgling breath.

She killed him.

Winema's wolfish face retreats into that of a woman. She wipes the blood from her mouth with the back of her hand, then gasps.

"Winema?" the girl says, touching her elbow.

Our Alpha holds her belly in both hands. "I shouldn't have changed." Her face twists with pain. "Ah. The baby."

Oh. This is why I've never seen her as a wolf. Oh, no.

A bloodstain spreads on Winema's skirt. She grits her teeth. "Get Charles."

"I'll call him." The girl snatches a cell phone from her pocket and dials. As the phone rings, she pets the whimpering werepuppy.

Winema leans against the side of the car, straightens,

and opens the door. "Shhh." She scoops up the bawling baby and pats it on the back. "It's okay. It's all right." Slowly, Winema lowers herself onto the car seat.

I don't know what to do. I am supremely useless.

As if reading my mind, Winema looks at me and says, "Where's Randall?"

I left him behind. We betrayed each other.

Maybe she can read my mind, because she closes her eyes and tilts her head back. A moan escapes her clenched teeth. Blood—so much blood—soaks her dress, until it looks more red than white.

I run away from death, into the night. I try to remember the musky, mossy smell of Randall, but my mind won't stop whirling like a broken merry-go-round. We, the whole pack, are nothing more than monsters to them. None of them would look at a werewolf as a person—a *person*, for crying out loud, not a beast.

Not even the innocent among us are safe.

In the distance, I hear police sirens and a chorus of howls. I wonder if the pack is mourning their dead. I wonder how many are dead. Where are the Zlatroviks, come to save us all from our own destruction?

Ahead, I hear the unmistakable snarls and yips of a dogfight. Though I can see now that they're not all dogs. A trio of German shepherds are attacking a silver wolf from all sides. Blood drips down his pale fur. Randall. I stand rigid with fury as the dogs gnaw on him, tear him up—I've got to figure out how to save him—

Paws thump the pavement behind me. I whirl. Barreling down on me, a brindled pit bull.

Blackjack?

Before I can think, Blackjack slams into the knot of German shepherds and latches onto Randall's neck. No. This is all wrong. This happened before—it shouldn't happen again—this is wrong. Randall isn't supposed to die.

I fling myself into the fight.

I'm at least twice as big as the dogs, and definitely twice as pissed off. A German shepherd turns on me, jaws snapping. I sink my teeth into its shoulder and toss it away, then tear into the hindquarters of another before it has time to react. The third German shepherd gnaws on Randall's leg while Blackjack holds him down. Randall twists and tears at Blackjack, but the pit bull's loose skin protects him.

The pair of injured German shepherds gang up on me, then, and bite my legs, my flanks. I'm too pumped full of adrenaline to feel pain, and I shake them off like mosquitoes. The dogs come back for more, panting hard, their muzzles bloodstained. I dodge one dog, bluff an attack, then bite the other in the neck. It yelps and staggers back. Blood dribbles down my chin, and I swallow the bitter-iron taste.

Randall's growls rise into whines. His legs buckle beneath him.

I snarl ferociously at the second German shepherd, and it skitters away with its wounded companion. The last German shepherd still chews on Randall's leg, its teeth scraping his bone. Blackjack's jaws squeeze his windpipe. I look into the silver wolf's golden eyes. Inside them, I see his beastly rage and his human fear.

They terrify me.

I launch myself onto the last German shepherd. Jaws wide, I put all my weight behind my teeth in the dog's neck. Bones crunch, and it slides to the ground, limp. Now, there is only Blackjack. My dog, who I trained to be a monster.

He's closer to my size, and I know he's vicious. I know he remembers fighting wolves.

Randall tries to struggle to his feet, but his paws keep slipping in the puddle of his own blood. I have to get Blackjack off him.

The pit bull eyes me as I stalk closer, but he won't stop strangling Randall. He keeps his jaws locked and shakes his head from side-to-side, his teeth sawing deeper into flesh. Randall moans, low in his throat.

My muscles tremble with tight rage. I won't let him die.

I fly off the ground and hurl myself at Blackjack. My teeth clamp into his shoulder and slice his skin. Blood ribbons down his leg. I leap and scrabble onto the pit bull's back, driving him to the ground beneath my weight.

Blackjack growls and twists his head to look at me. In his eyes, I don't see a trace of the dog me and Chris raised from puppyhood. I see only bloodlust.

I can't let you live.

While Randall wheezes for breath and Blackjack's

jaws keep crushing, I bite the pit bull's neck and clamp down. He still won't let go, even when I drive my fangs deeper and feel hot blood pouring into my mouth. He keeps growling, even when I jerk my head savagely, tearing his neck apart. Then, finally, he lets go, and his growling fades. I retreat from Blackjack and watch his eyes cloud and become unseeing.

I'm sorry, boy. I'm so sorry I did this to you.

On the ground beside me, Randall staggers to his feet. He's bleeding hard, his fur matted and soaked. His head sways, held low.

I nudge him with my nose. *Are you okay?*

Randall swings his head toward me, the fire in his eyes going out.

Come on. You've got to heal yourself.

"No!"

A man's voice—I know him—but it can't be…

A dark figure runs toward us, his face so white and twisted I almost don't recognize him at first, but I don't want to recognize him, don't want him to see me like this.

He stops on the edge of the sidewalk. He carries a rifle, with the barrel pointed at me.

Dad, no. It's me, Brock.

I step closer to him and wag my tail, a whine escaping. Dad looks between my bloody face and Blackjack's ruined body.

"You killed my dog." His voice sounds hoarse. "You gick bastards."

But I had to, Dad. I try to tell him with my eyes. Randall growls softly behind me.

Dad's shoulders stiffen. "Oh, Jesus...I know you..."

Why did I think he would have forgotten the silver wolf? I was the one who told him who that wolf was.

Randall starts to run, but he's limping badly. And Dad's already aiming. He sights down the barrel of the rifle and fires.

No!

The one who bit me, the one who made me—Randall—collapses on the pavement like a marionette with its strings cut.

Dad turns to me now, his rifle ready. I'm going to die, aren't I?

I whimper again, pleading with my eyes, trying to show him that Brock the Human still lives inside Brock the Beast.

Dad hesitates.

And I wrench myself from wolf to human form. My skeleton reshapes in a red-hot agony, my fur melts away from me and bares my skin. I kneel before him, naked and defenseless, then raise my head to meet his eyes.

"Oh, God." Dad recoils, lowering his rifle. "No."

"Dad." I stagger to my feet as if unused to human legs. "Dad, it's me."

"What did they do to you?"

"I...I changed. I'm a werewolf."

"Oh, God, no." Dad's voice quavers now. "I didn't think...what did they *do* to you?"

"Nothing. They treated me all right. They—" I glance back.

But Randall is gone. A bloody trail of footprints disappears into the alley. He's dragged himself away to die.

I'm never going to see him again.

"Jesus." I'm shaking now. "Dad, you shouldn't have done that. He was good to me."

"He *bit* you."

"He had to! It had to happen that way!" I realize I'm screaming and struggle to control myself. "Dad. You didn't have to kill him."

Dad looks horrified. "He killed Chris."

"I know, but—"

"There is no *but*. Have they warped your mind? Made you think that they're not so bad?"

"Dad, no—"

"A gick is a gick."

I swallow hard. "Are you going to shoot me now?"

His face hardens. "I followed the police here to rescue you, or put you out of your misery. Whichever I had to do. And now…"

"You think I'm a beast," I say. "You think I'm not the same Brock at all."

But I know that to be the truth, when I look down at my bloody hands and Blackjack lying dead at my feet. And it breaks my heart.

I speak barely above a whisper. "Do it."

Dad raises the rifle. His eyes glitter. "Are you asking me to?"

"You don't want a gick for a son. You would rather see both of your sons dead and buried than see them become werewolves."

Dad says nothing.

"If you're going to do it," I say, amazed how level my voice sounds, "you can't touch the werepuppies. Okay? They still have a chance."

"Werepuppies?" Dad squints at me. "You mean these curs have pups?"

And I know he will never see Others as anything more than gicks.

"Yes." I stare him down the way I never could before. "And I won't let you hurt them."

Dad lowers his gaze, and it wavers over the bloodstains on the road. He doesn't seem to know what to say or do after his hate has weakened.

"If you're going to kill me," I say, "do it now."

He won't look at me.

"Do it!" I advance on him until the metal of the rifle barrel presses into my chest. My voice cracks. "For Christ's sake, do it."

"Brock, no." Dad's face crumples. "Brock."

He withdraws from me, but I keep walking. Fear sharpens his eyes, and my throat constricts. Does he think I would kill him? I stop following him. Finally, he lowers the rifle. We stand so close I can feel his breath.

"Dad?"

I wonder if he will hug me now, and admit he's crying. But he still won't touch me.

"The past five days," he says, "we thought you were dead."

It took less than a week to change everything.

I speak, barely above a whisper. "Did you hope I was?"

"Brock, no." Dad's voice sounds gravelly. "First Chris, then you—" He looks away from me and runs his hands over his face.

I swallow hard. "I missed his funeral, right?"

Dad shakes his head. "Not yet. We had him cremated."

"Can I come?"

Then I will know it's real. The realness will beat my nightmares.

Dad nods, his chin trembling, and he looks so old and weak it tears me up inside.

"Before we go," I say, "we need to tell the police about Cyn. They drugged her with faerie wine, to wipe her memory, and—"

"The police already know where the pack is," Dad says. "Cyn should be safe soon."

"We need to make sure. I can't abandon her."

"Brock, you talking to the police right now isn't a smart move."

I clench my jaw. "Then let's go back and get her ourselves."

Dad sighs, but nods.

I follow him to a pickup in an abandoned parking lot. For a heartbeat I think it's Randall's, but no, of course it isn't baby blue. It's Dad's pickup from the dairy. He opens the door, tosses me a pair of jeans, then climbs into the driver's seat. I pull on the jeans, grateful to not be naked any longer, and climb in after him.

We drive to Rex's Steakhouse. Outside, the lights of an ambulance and cop cars swirl in the blackness of the night. I jump out of the truck and run to the back door, but Cliff Sterling is already there, talking to a cop.

"One of my patrons discovered her in the alley," Cliff says, casually smoking a cigarette.

Oh, God. Discovered her dead?

"What did you see?" the cop asks Cliff.

The Zlatrovik Alpha shrugs. "Nothing. I suspect she had too much to drink, that's all."

"Okay." The cop scribbles something down.

"I can only hope she has a better day tomorrow." Cliff flicks his cigarette into the street. "I have business to attend to, if you don't mind."

"Sorry for the inconvenience, sir."

"Not a problem."

Cliff's gaze meets mine, and he stares longer than someone would with a stranger. I look away—he might be my future Alpha.

"Brock?" Dad calls. "Come here."

He's standing by the ambulance. I run to him, and then I see her. Cyn, lying on a gurney, her face pale and sweaty. She's wearing an oxygen mask. Relief floods through me—she's breathing, she's alive. The ambulance's doors close before I can talk to the paramedics, but I know this glimpse will have to be enough.

"We can go now," I tell Dad.

We drive back to Blackjack's body. Together, we lift him into the back of the pickup. It, not him. It's hard to think of my dog as an unmoving thing.

We're done with Denver. We hit the highway and drive for I don't know how long, then turn onto a gravel road that heads through the slumbering prairie. Dad refuses to look at me. He pulls over beside a ditch, beneath a wrinkled old cottonwood.

He grabs a shovel from the back. I shiver. Did he bring it to bury me?

"Help me carry him," Dad says.

We move Blackjack beneath the cottonwood and take turns digging his grave. Finally, we lower the dog into the earth. I toss a handful of dirt onto Blackjack's body. Before we leave, I crouch in the ditch and wash the blood from my hands and mouth. I can't help but think he could have been a good dog.

I can't help but think I could have been a good guy.

twenty-one

Nine days. Nine days without Chris, but it feels like forever.

Everyone clusters around his grave like a flock of gloomy crows in the rain. When they bury his ashes in the dirt, and when Grandma June gives me a tight hug, amazingly, I don't shatter and reveal how weak I am. She still smells like oatmeal soap, but when I shut my eyes, I don't feel like a kid anymore.

"We missed you, Brock," Grandma June whispers.

I nod, since I have nothing to say to that.

"Your father did, very much. He just doesn't know how to show it."

I look at Dad, stone-faced and statuesque, bending over the grave.

"Yeah," I say.

"You're coming to my house this evening." Grandma

June straightens my collar. "We're having a dinner for you and Chris."

I try to smile past the burning in my throat. She's so sweet, even if she's wrong.

Nobody but Dad knows that I'm not staying. Even with Sheriff Royle dead and Cliff Sterling's promise to wipe our records, going to this funeral is all that I dare. Besides, it's easier to walk around wearing my best black suit, to use it to explain away my stiff face and scanty conversation. People murmur with sympathetic looks when I pass; maybe it's because of my brother, maybe it's because of me.

Then, across the field, I see her.

Cynthia.

She crosses the lawn in ridiculously pointy heels, her ankles wobbling. She's wearing a black dress that manages to be both sad and pretty. The pink streak in her hair has faded. I swallow hard. Of course she would be here.

What did the faerie wine do to her?

I walk up behind her, hoping she'll hear, but she doesn't. I reach for her shoulder, then pull back and clear my throat. "Cyn."

Her head snaps toward my voice, and she takes a step back. "Brock."

I stand there, barely breathing, hoping so hard I ache.

"I'm so sorry about your brother," she says.

I nod. Please, Cyn. Remember.

She leans forward and wraps her arms around my waist. I let out my breath in a shuddering sigh. I slip my hands behind her shoulders, but she stiffens under my touch. My throat tightens, trapping the words I wanted to say.

I missed you. I still love you.

"Brock, please." Cyn pulls away from me, gently, but she could be shoving me away and it would hurt the same.

My voice sounds hollow. "Do you remember our last conversation?"

"When we broke up?"

Jesus. The faerie wine erased everything. She doesn't even know I'm a werewolf.

I can't stand to look at her anymore. "That whole week we spent together…it's…gone."

Cyn's face goes white. "What are you talking about?"

I shake my head and stride away, too pissed to talk. "Fuck!" I kick an iron fence, like that might jar her memories loose.

"Brock!" she hisses. "This is a funeral. Don't swear."

I could hate her for not knowing, but I can't.

"They told me I might not remember," she whispers.

My head snaps toward her. "Who? When?"

"Brock, were we kidnapped by a pack of werewolves? I know it sounds insane, but that's what the police told me. They said I had amnesia, and weeks are just gone from my memory." Cyn presses her fingers to her temples. "The last thing I remember, I was on a flight to Mexico. I don't remember being in Mexico, and I don't remember coming back. After that, I woke up in a hospital and my family took me home."

I touch the back of her hand. "It's true. You went to Mexico to visit your grandma. When you came back…"

How am I going to tell her? To make her understand?

She sucks in her breath. "Brock, tell me what happened next."

"Not here." I shake my head. "It's a long story, and not everyone should hear it."

Cyn opens her purse and pulls out a handkerchief. When she opens it, a tiny red rose falls into the palm of her hand. Maybe its scent is more powerful than the faerie wine clouding her mind. Maybe it will unlock her memories.

"I dreamed that you gave this to me." Her forehead furrows. "Was that a memory?"

"Yes." I try not to hold my breath, try not to hope.

"You told me I could have the rose, because you wouldn't need it where you were going… and I was afraid for you, and wished you would stay…" She looks away, her gaze trailing over the tombstones. "And is it true? About you?"

I have to tell her again. I wish it didn't have to be like this.

"Yes. I'm a werewolf."

Her eyes widen, sharp with fear, and she says nothing.

I sidestep around her and stride into the evening. I've done this before—standing at the edge of a lawn, yearning to run into the woods. But this time I do it. I kick off my shoes and jog into the trees, needles beneath my bare feet.

"Brock?" She follows me. "Where are you going?"

"Away," I say.

"But there's so much you haven't told me."

I stare at her as I unbutton my shirt. "I can tell you I used to hate Others. Thought they were all just gicks and weren't people at all." I clench my thighs against a shudder of transformation. "And I used to hate myself."

"Brock…" Emotions tangle on Cyn's face. "I don't know you anymore."

I look up through the needle-sharp trees, at the dying sun. A cutting wind raises goose bumps on my arms, and my pelt begins to grow. She watches me with saucer eyes. I can't tell whether she's horrified or amazed.

"This is who I am now," I say.

I'm a werewolf. I'm never going to be able to go home with you, Cyn.

Already halfway on the way to wolf, I strip away my jeans and the last remnants of my humanity. The change sweeps through me from nose to tail. I stretch my long legs and yawn, feeling Cyn's stare on my fangs.

I trot to her and lower my head to her hand. She yanks it away with a sharp gasp. I look up at her, trying to tell her not to be afraid. Slowly, I touch my muzzle to her fingers. Trembling, she strokes the fur between my eyes. I lick her fingertips. Not the way I wanted to kiss her, but it will have to work for now.

She smiles, only the shadow of a smile. "You're scary big, you know?"

I whine and wag my tail. *Don't look at me like that.* She falls to her knees, hugging me the best she can. I rest my chin on her shoulder and breathe in deep, holding her bittersweet smell inside me until I have to exhale.

But I know that this is impossible. I can't be with you.

Cyn withdraws, tears streaking her face. "You need to go, don't you." It isn't a question.

I wag my tail again, then glance at the wilderness, where I belong.

She climbs to her feet and dabs at her smeared mascara with a tissue. "Come back, okay? For me. I want to know what I've lost."

I dip my head in a nod.

"Goodbye, Brock." She smiles through her tears.

In some ways, it's easier being a wolf and not having the words to say goodbye. I want to howl at how this hurts, but I know I can't, not here. So, with a last look at Cyn, I turn from her and lope into the woods alone.

Wind hisses through the pines, masking the sound of my footsteps. The spicy-amber smell of sap twitches my nose. Ahead, I hear rushing water. Trees thin until I see a snowmelt river, swirling down from the mountains, foaming into white rapids, reforming into still, blue-green pools so clear I can look six feet down and count the pebbles.

I change back to human. I'm naked, and I'm shivering, but I don't care.

That water's got to be as cold as hell is hot. I poke the shoreline with my toe, then run into the water until I'm in up to my waist, and yeah, it's testicle-shriveling cold. My breath comes in quick gasps as I wade deeper into the water, then dunk my head.

I surface with a gasp. "C-Christ!"

Teeth chattering, I swim toward a half-sunken cedar log and climb onto it. My skin tingles, almost warm now. I stare at the log's split wood, bright red against the blue water, and run my hands over its silky grain.

Why didn't I come out here earlier? It's beautiful. I wish Chris could have seen it.

A knot tightens in my throat, but I frown at myself. Just because he's gone doesn't mean I shouldn't still be alive. I slip into the numbing water again and float on my back, staring at the sky. Twilight creeps into the clouds, like purple and blue watercolors on white paper. A deep calm settles in the marrow of my bones.

It's over. Chris is gone.

The crescent moon hangs above me like a crooked, sad smile. First frost glitters on the forest, making ordinary firs and pines look crisp and otherworldly. My muscles ache, at first, when I run, but then they warm and I fly through the woods as a wolf. My blood pumps through my veins, and my head feels clearer than it has in days.

Between the bars of the trees, I glimpse a flicker of silver.

I slow to a trot, then stop. My heartbeat thunders inside my chest.

No…I was just seeing things. Hoping things.

I huff to clear my nose, then trot along, sniffing the wind—a tantalizing blend of sweet night rain, grassy ferns and lichen, and sap seeping from the trees. Then, a hint of fur. Again, I stop, my breath snagging in my throat.

Moonbeams slice between the black trees ahead. Among them, like a dream, walks the silver wolf. Wind ruffles his fur, and I can see scars crisscrossing his skin. He limps, also, and that is how I know he is real.

Randall. My tail wags a slow, hopeful rhythm. He comes to me; we touch noses.

Then, Randall withdraws and begins to change. It's slow, halting, and his face twists with pain. It hurts me to watch him. I wait until he is human, then make my own quick transformation. We stand opposite each other and try to speak.

"Hey," I say finally, my voice rusty. "You're alive?"

"Yes." A corner of Randall's mouth curves in a smile. "As you can see."

"What the hell happened back there?"

He rakes his fingers through his thick hair. "I survived. That's one advantage to being a werewolf: you heal fast."

"I know. But Jesus, those dogs chewed you up."

"They did." His voice catches, and he clears his throat. "But I'm alive."

"Jesus," I say again.

Randall just stands and watches me, his face betraying nothing but fatigue.

It's hard to say what I have to say. "I'm sorry. I know I failed you as a bloodborn."

"Brock." He smiles, and it's the saddest smile I've ever seen. "I bit you."

"I don't get it."

"You're always going to be my bloodborn."

"Well, yeah. I just know I've been a total traitor."

He folds his arms. "I saved your ass, you saved mine. We're even now."

"Sure." I clear my throat. "What happened to the rest of the pack?"

"We were outnumbered by the police, and it got pretty bloody until Cliff sent some Zlatroviks to bail us out." He laughs bitterly, then grimaces. "Hope that doesn't mean we're even more in debt to him."

"And Winema?"

Randall's face darkens. "Winema went to an emergency room, for her baby's sake."

"Her baby...?"

"Made it. Barely. He was born almost two months premature, but Cliff pulled some strings to find a hospital with paranormal specialists who deal with babies." His face softens. "I think he'll survive. He's a fighter."

I look away, feeling that this is somehow my fault.

"Are you ready to go?" he says.

"I belong here," I say. "And I don't."

"I know."

Slowly, I inhale and square my shoulders. "Give me a little time here. To say goodbye."

He nods. "Good luck, Brock. I'll see you again soon, I'm sure."

"Yeah." My voice sounds hoarse. "Try not to get yourself killed first."

He laughs, flashing fangs, his pale pelt already cloaking his skin. I don't want him to become a wolf again, because then I know he'll leave me, but then I do, because I know he needs to run. I'll follow him soon enough.

Randall—the silver wolf—stares at me, nods, then disappears into the darkness.

I watch him go. The wolf inside me scrabbles against my ribs, aching to follow him, but the human in me still craves the touch of Cyn. I hate goodbyes, and I hate starting over. But at least I have a second chance to live.

Can't wait too long. Don't have much time.

I start to run, not toward Cyn, not toward Randall, but into the unknown night. I want to savor this moment before I must go, a stillness trapped in moonlight, where there's only me and the endless miles ahead.

I am Brock. And I am bloodborn.